Two in the Churchyard Lie

TWO IN THE CHURCHYARD LIE

KINLEY ROBY

FIVE STAR

An imprint of Thomson Gale, a part of The Thomson Corporation

THOMSON
GALE

Detroit • New York • San Francisco • New Haven, Conn. • Waterville, Maine • London

LIBRARY OF CONGRESS CATALOGING-IN-PUBLICATION DATA

Roby, Kinley E.
  Two in the churchyard lie ; a Harry Brock Mystery / Kinley Roby. — 1st ed.
    p. cm.
  ISBN-13: 978-1-59414-599-5 (hardcover : alk. paper)
  ISBN-10: 1-59414-599-7 (hardcover : alk. paper)
  I. Title.
PS3618.O3385T86 2007
813'.6—dc22
                                                                    2007020698

First Edition. First Printing: October 2007.

Published in 2007 in conjunction with Tekno Books and Ed Gorman.

Printed in the United States of America on permanent paper
10 9 8 7 6 5 4 3 2 1

For Mary

A simple Child,
That lightly draws its breath,
And feels its life in every limb,
What should it know of death?
—"We Are Seven," William Wordsworth

1

"Reel it in!" Rob MacDougal shouted.

The rusted and battered tow truck groaned and creaked and sank another two inches into the soft earth at the top of the bank as the tow cable snapped taut, flinging weeds and water off its greasy length. At the foot of the bank, shin deep in the Luther Faubus Canal, MacDougal, short and solid as a stump, was peering into the murky water and, by way of encouragement, waving his hand at Rooster Hobart, who was operating the winch.

Jefferson Toomey in a john boat, bobbing in a clump of white water lilies, stood leaning on a long pole shoved into the canal's muddy bottom. He was a tall, thin black man in a ragged yellow T-shirt and mud-spattered jeans. Like MacDougal, he was staring hard at the spot where the cable entered the water.

"You see anything, Jefferson?" MacDougal shouted.

"She's rising," Toomey called as a roil of brown water swirled suddenly around the quivering cable.

MacDougal hauled his feet out of the mud with a loud slurping sound and scrambled up the bank, his short, heavy legs pumping, and shouted, "Don't stop, Rooster! Keep it coming!"

Rooster shoved the throttle ahead and gave a crowing rebel yell as the rear end of a badly rusted sedan broke the surface of the water.

"Keep it coming! Keep it coming!" MacDougal shouted, his thick, red beard bristling with excitement.

The muck- and weed-draped car rolled backward up the bank, water streaming from it in gurgling, brown torrents. With a dull crash, the window on the driver's side fell down inside the door.

"Lord Jesus!" Toomey bellowed. "They's somebody in there."

MacDougal ran toward the car and suddenly went back on his heels. He had come face to face with a weed-draped skeleton sitting upright in the seat, wearing the remains of a Miami Dolphins cap, its bony fingers still gripping the steering wheel.

"Hold it, Rooster!" MacDougal shouted, waving both arms as he backed rapidly away from the car. "We've got us a resurrection."

2

On the planked terrace of The Blue Duck Café, Harry Brock sat alone at a table overlooking the Seminole River, watching the last of the sunset fade out of the sky and listening to a girl with a guitar singing "Botany Bay." For a moment her voice, the words of the song, and the evening breeze off the river became everything beautiful he had ever known.

He was about to say, "And lost," but he stopped himself and waved his glass at the waitress for a refill. For a while now, he had been having a lot of refills. He ran his hand over his cropped salt and pepper hair and thought ruefully that his forehead was getting taller every day. Crowding fifty, he was still fit, and since he had taken up running again after a lapse of several years he was beating the spread.

"That's four of them, partner. You thinking about eating something?" Eadie, his increasingly familiar waitress, set the drink down and regarded him with a mixture of concern and disapproval.

She was short, doe-eyed, and fully accessorized.

"Persuade me," Harry answered. He had come to regard youth, however attractive, as a different and only marginally interesting species.

"I'd go for the chowder and a side of the honeydew. Everything else is pretty much SF."

"Science fiction?"

"No, dummy, saturated fat."

"Bring on the chowder and the honeydew."

"Plus coffee," she said, passing judgment, and hurried off.

" 'Oh, how her going taketh me,' " Harry murmured, watching her departure and momentarily forgetting he was now a different species. Too late, he remembered he hadn't asked what was in the chowder. In The Blue Duck it could be anything from sand shark to snake fish.

He lifted the whiskey just as his phone rang. Swearing under his breath, or so he thought, he put the glass down and stood up to extricate it from a front pocket of his age-distressed jeans. The people at the next table looked at him as if they expected him to unzip his fly.

"My name's Martha Roberts." The woman's voice was full of country sprawl. "Bob Arnell over at Arnell Property Management said you're a private investigator."

Harry did not respond right away. The whiskey accounted for some of it, but most of his delay was due to the name Arnell. His wife Katherine had worked for Bob Arnell back in the good old, bad old days when he and she were still a team, which they were no longer and which was his excuse for drinking alone at The Blue Duck at seven in the evening instead of eating his dinner at home on Bartram's Hammock where he belonged.

"What can I do for you, Mrs. Roberts?" he asked, feeling the memory-induced gloom settling on his spirits like a cold fog.

"I'm not married. For starters, you can meet me somewhere in the next day or two so I can tell you a story. After that, maybe I can persuade you to help me do something nobody else seems to want any part of."

Thinking of Katherine had sobered him. Eadie appeared with his order. He pushed the glass back to make room for the dishes.

"Eat all of it and drink the coffee before you even think of leaving," she said, ignoring the phone, "and you're not honor bound to finish the whiskey."

"All right," he said, feeling sorry for her father.

She gave him a backhand on the shoulder and left.

"Are you related to the Roberts who was pulled out of the Luther Faubus Canal last Saturday?" he asked.

"Yes, I am. John is my brother."

"This story you want to tell me . . ."

"Has to do with the discovery," she said. "But I'm a lot more interested in finding out how Bunny got into that canal in the first place. Will you talk to me?"

Bunny. A private name?

"How about tomorrow morning?"

"Is nine okay?"

"Yes. Where do you live?"

After he hung up, Harry ate the chowder and the melon and drank the coffee. The darkness had come on quickly, and the whiskey sat winking in the flickering light of the small oil lamp on his table. Bats were darting over the terrace. Harry tried to think about whether or not to finish his drink, but his mind drifted away to the John Roberts business.

By the time he had paid his bill, he had forgotten the whiskey. Eadie passed him at the cash register, balancing a loaded tray of dirty dishes on her left shoulder. His drink was riding jauntily at the top of the pile. She grinned and gave him a thumbs-up with her free hand. She looked just as good to him coming as going.

Harry woke to the hammering of a pileated woodpecker tearing into the bark of an oak a few yards from his bedroom window, and for one awful moment he thought the noise was inside his head. He eased himself onto his feet and squinted through the screen at the big, red-crested bird, and was surprised to find he felt pretty good.

"Thank you, God," he said aloud, remembering on his way into the bathroom that he had left the fourth drink for the kitchen crew. Looking in the mirror was a disappointment, but despite that setback he realized there was something to be grateful for. He hadn't died in the night from eating The Blue Duck's chowder. A green tongue was a small price to pay for such recklessness.

After breakfast he climbed into the Land Rover and set off for his appointment with Martha Roberts. Old cars are classics, antiques, or wrecks. The Rover was a wreck. The paint had faded to a lusterless brindle. Its canvas, once white and taut as a full-bellied sail, now flapped around the rusted frame in tatters, but the roof still kept out most of the rain. Harry's judgment, moderately reliable, slid into klutz where the Rover was concerned. He tended to lose people but clung to the Rover like a limpet.

As he crossed the short, humpbacked bridge over Puc Puggy Creek, which separated Bartram's Hammock from the rest of the dry land in Tequesta County, he noticed a green and yellow PROPERTY FOR SALE sign nailed to a slash pine across the road from the bridge. Tucker is not going to like that, he thought, irritation gradually growing into anger. As the only people living on Bartram's Hammock, he and his old neighbor put a high value on their privacy. But I'm not getting into it, he told himself and purposefully turned the Rover south toward East Avola.

He drove south to the intersection of County Road 19 and Cottonmouth Road and swung east on Cottonmouth for eight miles straight toward The Everglades. When he finally turned off the highway into the Pecan Grove Trailer Park, he found himself on trash-laden, potholed streets, among trailers with peeled paint, abandoned cars, broken fences, barking dogs, and listless children playing in the dirt. Harry's heart sank. The place was a slum. But he quickly recovered because in contrast to the surrounding squalor, Martha Roberts's double-wide was

14

freshly painted, and its window boxes were bright with red and white wax begonias. A short, white picket fence enclosed a pocket-sized lawn, scrupulously maintained.

"Come in, if you can wade through the mess," she said, reaching out to shake his hand.

She was approaching thirty, Harry guessed. And there was something very familiar about her. He wondered if had met her and then forgotten the encounter. Then he saw it. She reminded him of his daughter Sarah. They would be about the same age, nearing thirty, slim, dark, intense, with the same lustrous brown eyes.

Sarah.

He had not spoken to her in a long time. A guilt trip was getting under way. How long since he had talked to his son Clyde? Too long. Breaking free from the inquisition, he brought his mind back to Martha.

Harry stepped inside and found the place full of light and spotlessly clean. Even the three-colored cat, which trotted forward to greet him, bushy tail erect, looked as if she had just been washed and blow-dried.

"Puts my place to shame," he said in admiration. Harry liked to think he held himself to high standards in housekeeping, but this woman had him beat standing.

"It wouldn't look this good if I had any kids," she said flatly. "Sit down. Can I get you some coffee?"

"Sounds good."

He lowered himself into a rocker, puzzled by what he'd found. The trailer park was a downer, but Martha Roberts certainly was not. The cat was standing on its hind legs, its front paws resting on Harry's knee, looking at him quizzically. He stroked her head, and she began to purr.

"Her name's Calico," Martha said, returning with two cups of coffee. "She's usually standoffish. Do you like animals?"

"Better than I like most people," Harry replied, taking a closer look at Martha.

She was obviously someone who took care of herself, and the cut of her crisply ironed white blouse and narrow black skirt told him she didn't clean other people's houses for a living. What, he asked himself, was she doing out here in Pecan Grove? There must be a dozen low-rent, safe, clean condo associations within a half-hour drive of this hard-times place. Why wasn't she in one of them?

"My mother and father live out on Panther Trace. Do you know it?"

Harry wondered if she'd read his mind. "Yes."

"I like being near them," she said, sounding defensive.

Harry nodded. She had not smiled or tried, so far as he could tell, to make any particular impression on him. He liked her for that and decided she was more interesting than he had expected.

"Panther Trace is pretty much in the woods," he acknowledged cautiously.

"That's right. But I don't apologize for them or me."

Harry raised his hands. "No criticism intended."

"None taken."

"What is it you think I can do to help you?"

"How much do you know about my brother's death?"

Harry settled back in his chair. Calico decided to try his lap. "If I remember correctly, he disappeared about four years ago. No one the police talked to knew where he went or why."

"Anything else?"

Harry shifted a bit uncomfortably. "I recall your brother had some issues with the police." The answer was a conscious evasion. John Roberts had been headed for jail when he disappeared.

She nodded in acknowledgment of the point and moved on. "The police gave Bunny's disappearance about the same attention they would have paid if I'd reported Calico missing."

She clasped her hands tightly in her lap and leaned toward him. "They did nothing!" Her face tightened with anger. "And now Bunny's been found, they're going to do nothing again."

It startled Harry to see that she was close to tears.

"What is it you want them to do?" he asked, trying to give her support.

She caught her breath and dropped her hands. "Find out who killed Bunny."

"How do you know he was murdered?"

"There was a bullet hole in his skull."

That was a surprise. "The newspaper didn't mention that Roberts had been shot."

"No. The medical examiner's report came in after the article was printed."

"Did your brother live in Pecan Grove?" He made a silent bet on the answer.

"Yes. Well, part of the time. Sometimes he was at home, but . . ." She stopped.

"But?" He was careful to ask the question quietly.

She averted her eyes. "He and my father weren't getting along."

She was clutching her hands in her lap. It didn't take much imagination for Harry to see how painful talking about this was for her.

"Fathers and sons," he said. "What else should I know?"

"Bunny would never have committed suicide. Never in this world."

"Is that what the police are calling it?"

"Not yet, but if I push, that's where they'll go. They found a gun in the car. It's the same caliber as the one that killed him."

"What makes you think your brother didn't kill himself?"

"Bunny was a sweet, simple, happy person. He couldn't have

thought of such a thing."

The answer surprised Harry. "Was your brother . . ."

"Retarded," she said in a quiet voice. "Mr. Brock, I probably knew him better than anyone else in the world, even better than my mother knew him. There were years when he was the closest friend I had. If he had candy, he shared it with me. If he found a butterfly, he showed it to me. He was that kind of person all his life, and I loved him for it. I want to hire you to find out who killed him and why."

Harry weighed the chances of finding the answers to her questions. Given the length of time since his death, they were not good. She was sitting with her hands locked so tightly in her lap the knuckles were white. He watched her and admitted it was probably hopeless, but Martha Roberts had touched something in him. Part of that something was her resemblance to Sarah. But that wasn't all of it.

She deserved to have somebody make an effort. He could give it a week. It wouldn't cost her much, and she could say she tried.

"All right," he said, not liking that he felt beaten before he began, "but you have to understand, it's been four years. Everything having to do with your brother's death is history. The trails are all cold. People who might have been able to help have died, moved away, forgotten. But I'll give it a shot. And call me Harry."

"Okay, Harry," she replied, "but you've got some things wrong. My pain isn't history. My love for Bunny isn't dead. And I haven't forgotten anything."

3

When Harry got home, he parked under the big corner oak and walked the half mile of narrow, soft, white sand road winding from his house to Tucker LaBeau's farm. He could usually lose himself in the Hammock's teeming life just by stepping out his door. But today his thoughts kept returning to Martha Roberts and the dead brother she called Bunny with such loving tenderness. She and her story had caught him where he was most vulnerable. Although what he had learned about John Roberts's death was grim, he was able to recall his conversation with Martha with pleasure.

On his left the tangle of oaks, cabbage palms, gumbo limbo, Jamaica dogwood trees, and twisting vines and dense undergrowth crowding up to the road was full of cool shadows and mysterious musical sounds, which provided a pleasant background for his thoughts. On his right the marshes of Puc Puggy Creek shimmered in the April sun. Cardinals and mockingbirds sang and fluttered in the shrubs beside the road, and small flocks of ibis, snowy egrets, and solitary herons waded in the mud and shallows of the creek's ragged shoreline.

All these tugged at his attention, but he went on asking himself what held Martha Roberts so closely bound to her dead brother and why had he agreed to take on the investigation. It made him uneasy to think he might have acted on an impulse, especially an impulse with cropped black hair and beautiful brown eyes. By the time he reached Tucker's farm, he had decided to believe it was her passionate commitment that had snared him.

Harry and Tucker were the only people living on the Hammock. The state had leveled the cabin where Katherine had once lived, and the ground where it had stood was now chest deep in saw palmetto palms. Having taken possession of the Hammock as a buffer for the Stickpen Nature Preserve and its miles of cypress swamp, the state of Florida decided two dwelling places were all it was going to allow on the Hammock.

"Oh, good," Helen Bradley had said when Harry had told her about the Division of Recreation and Parks's decision. "Now we've got a preserve for hermits."

Harry had been offended, but Helen offended him on a regular basis. That didn't stop him from being her best friend and something more whenever they stopped arguing, which didn't happen all that often.

Several years ago, Tucker had deeded his farm to the state in exchange for being allowed to live there until he died, but Harry then found himself under threat of eviction. But to his great relief, the state changed its mind because Harry had once been a Maine game warden and was a deterrence to poaching. His lease was made renewable as long as Tucker lived. When the old farmer died, the Hammock would become a state park and his farm a working museum-farm. But as long as Tucker stayed above ground, the Hammock and his farm would remain as they were. It cheered Harry a little to believe that sometimes the good guys won. He did not think of himself as a good guy, but he knew Tucker certainly was.

Oh, Brother!, Tucker's black mule, was waiting for Harry at the end of the driveway and walked with him to where Tucker was weeding strawberry plants in his vegetable garden. Harry was accustomed to the big mule's wearing a straw hat, but he had never figured out how Oh, Brother! knew he was coming.

"Where's Sanchez?" he asked the mule as he walked along beside him with a hand resting on the tall animal's glossy shoulder.

Sanchez was Tucker's old bluetick hound. Oh, Brother! lifted his head and blew out his breath in a way that Harry had no trouble interpreting as an expression of mild criticism of his friend's behavior, which meant that Sanchez was sleeping. Harry was going to say something more and checked himself. He tried to limit his conversations with the mule. Otherwise, he might begin thinking the mule was answering him. Tucker, on the other hand, talked to the mule without apology, insisting he could understand whatever was said to him. For reasons he hadn't explored, it troubled Harry to think the old farmer might be right.

When Tucker saw Harry and Oh, Brother!, he came out of the garden to meet them. In his bib overalls and straw hat, the skinny old man reminded Harry of an animated scarecrow that had lost most of its stuffing. Not a lot over five feet tall, he looked as if a good wind would blow him away, but so far nothing the world had laid on him in eighty years had even made him step backward. Gripping Harry's hand, Tucker grinned mischievously.

"Where's your transportation?" he demanded. "Has it finally given up the ghost?"

Harry ignored the shot. Tucker usually referred to the Rover as The Flying Dutchman. "I've got some news."

"All right. Let's go into the house. I'll make us some tea."

Just then Sanchez roused himself from where he'd been sleeping under the oleander bush at the corner of the barn and came hurrying up to plunge his head into Harry's midsection, his thick tail swinging wildly in greeting.

Harry grabbed the hound's big head and gave it a good shake. The dog grinned with pleasure. "You're going white as Tucker,"

Harry told him, but Sanchez only woofed and turned to lead the procession toward the house.

"How old is he?" Harry asked Tucker.

"I figure twelve or thirteen. I don't know how long that Mexican family owned him before he came to me. But he spoke only Spanish when I got him." Tucker shook his head. "It was a trial teaching him English, but he finally made the transition. Of course Oh, Brother! was a big help. He kept encouraging him."

Harry had never been sure how much Tucker believed what he said about his animals. But Harry had the feeling that the answer might be all of it. What he believed about Tucker and his animals was a work in progress. As they passed the hen run, Longstreet, the big Plymouth Rock rooster ran out to greet them by crowing and flapping his wings, scattering his hens and pullets in squawking protest. Sanchez went over to press his nose against the fence to commune briefly with the rooster and then went back to his point position.

"We've all been saying that Bonnie and Clyde are overdue for a visit," Tucker said, looking down at the rooster. "There's bound to be cubs by now, and I expect these new pullets are looking more and more attractive."

"This war of yours with those two gray foxes has lasted almost as long as the War of the Spanish Succession."

Tucker laughed, his blue eyes dancing and his fringe of white hair floating around his head like a halo. "Longer. If it is a war, it began with Bonnie and Clyde's grandparents and can't be won. But I prefer to think of it as a cultural disagreement between men and foxes over the role of hens in creation."

Sanchez picked up his pace as they passed Tucker's beeyard, and Oh, Brother! gave Tucker a push with his nose to hurry him up. Both the dog and the mule regarded the bees as dangerous pests. Tucker pulled open the stoop door to usher Harry into the kitchen. Oh, Brother! and Sanchez continued around the corner of the house.

"There's something in the citrus orchard that's got their attention," Tucker said, putting on the kettle. "When it's time, they'll let me know what it is."

Tucker laid a red-and-white checked cloth on the table, set out a plate of gingersnap cookies, and took the singing kettle off the black stove. A breeze was lifting the gingham curtains at the windows and the smell of Indian tea drifted in the room. Tucker's kitchen was very special to Harry. He had come to the Hammock from Maine with his life shattered, having been tried for murder and acquitted and then divorced by his wife who gained custody of their two children. It was in Tucker's kitchen that his healing had begun.

Tucker brought the steaming mugs to the table and said, "I've also got something to tell you, but let's hear your news first."

"Do you know Martha Roberts?"

Tucker paused to think. "Does she belong to the Roberts family that lives on Panther Trace?"

"Yes."

"Then I know who she is."

"I've agreed to help her find out why her brother died. The police think it's a suicide. She says he was murdered. The catch is he's been dead four years."

Tucker sat back in his chair. "Bunny Roberts?"

"That's right," Harry replied, not surprised by Tucker's knowledge. Harry had come to expect it. The old man knew almost all the native Avolan families back at least two generations.

"I'm guessing here, but isn't Martha the youngest in that family?"

"That's right."

"Do you have any ideas about the death?"

"No. I don't really have a feel for the case yet. So far, it's a ladder with most of the rungs missing."

"And you're having second thoughts."

"Maybe." Harry told Tucker about his conversation with Martha and his questions about why she was living in Pecan Grove. "It's got to be the forcible entry capital of the world. I don't know why her trailer isn't sitting on its roof or burned out."

"Fear rules," Tucker replied, reaching for another cookie.

"Who's protecting her?"

"Her brother Matthew. He's the oldest of the children. I think Ruth and James had seven children, all told. Two died—Bunny and Adam, who died on the West Coast. Matthew works for the sheriff's department. The inhabitants in Pecan Grove know that if anything happens to her, the place will be razed and salt spread on the ground. Their savings accounts are all in the form of stolen property. A police raid would be very costly."

"Where was Matthew four years ago?" Harry demanded. "If Martha's telling the truth, the police closed their investigation of John Roberts's disappearance without really opening it."

Tucker nodded. "The police claimed there was no evidence of foul play and nothing to prove young Roberts was dead. They probably figured he just skipped."

"Right into the Luther Faubus Canal with a bullet in his head."

"And the police are saying it's suicide?" Tucker poured himself some more tea.

Harry put a hand over his mug. "According to Martha. What's your news?"

"Before we go to that, I want to tell you that not too long ago the Robertses were living in the mountains of Tennessee. Don't forget it. They're still a tribe. And Martha's probably a lot less sophisticated than she appears."

"Okay," Harry said. Sometimes Tucker's warnings made him

feel about six years old.

"You know I've been taking an interest in some butterflies I found in that slash pine upland west of the county road," Tucker went on.

"You said you thought they were an isolated colony."

"That's right. Here's the news. I sent a couple of specimens to Figuel Miranda—he's Executive Director of The Florida Fish and Wildlife Conservation Commission—along with a description of the area where I collected them. I got a letter yesterday from Fred Casanova, one of the Commission's lepidopterists, saying the specimens I sent may be a previously unrecorded variant of the Florida Atala, *Eumaeus atala florida.* He wants to take a look at the site."

"Are you going to have a butterfly named after you?" Harry asked, delighted with Tucker's success.

"Probably not. The Florida Atala is a subspecies of the *Eumaeus atala.* Before that could happen, it would have to be determined that these butterflies are sufficiently differentiated to warrant a name change."

Harry's memory suddenly kicked in, and his ballooning good feelings fell hissing back to earth. "I've got some bad news, Tucker. This morning I saw a For Sale sign nailed to a tree on that piece of ground where you found the butterflies."

Tucker shot up straight in his chair. "Whose name is on the sign?"

"I don't remember seeing one."

"Is it green with yellow letters?"

"I think so."

"Then it's that carrion-eating auctioneer Lancelot Mayberry. He's got his hands on the estate. And you know what that means."

"No, I don't."

"The only thing it can mean." Tucker's face puckered with

disgust. "Lucy Mott Covington has finally died, and the heirs have put the Covington estate under the hammer. And that means Bevel's Sand, Stone, and Gravel Company will be bidding on the property."

Harry groaned. He did not have to be told what that meant.

4

Harry went home fuming about the possibility of having a sand and gravel company for a neighbor, then decided to stop worrying about something that might never happen and find out as much as he could about John Roberts.

But that decision created a different kind of discomfort because the logical thing to do would be to talk to Jim Snyder, a captain in the Tequesta County Sheriff's Department. He and Katherine and Harry had been friends. After Katherine left, he stopped seeing Jim because seeing him reminded him of Katherine. Seeing him again would, he was afraid, stir up all the old anguish surrounding Katherine's leaving. But perhaps, he reluctantly admitted, it was time to take the step. And there was no way to do this job right without talking to Jim.

Moving quickly before he could change his mind, Harry went to his supply closet and took a notebook out of a box, carried it to his desk and wrote ROBERTS and the date on the top right-hand corner of its red cover, officially opening the case. Mercifully, he was not embarrassed by simplicity or the possibility of being thought cheap.

Wearing a broad grin, the tall, lanky policeman leaned across his desk and put out his hand. "It's been a long time Harry. I'm damned glad to see you."

"It's good to see you, Jim." And to his surprise he was glad, despite the pain that came with it.

Snyder's cropped hair was so blond it was nearly white, and he had the fair skin to match it. He also had big ears which flushed red whenever a strong emotion moved in him. They reddened as he spoke now. "I thought I'd better let you come to see me . . ." he began and stumbled into silence.

"I should have come. It's not your fault."

"You hear anything from Katherine?"

"Not a lot. Minna, Jesse, and the baby are fine." Harry assumed no news was good news.

"That's good. Thornton must be three by now."

"Closer to four really."

"I always wondered if Thornton was a family name."

"Her mother's maiden name was Thornton."

Snyder nodded. Harry watched him and wondered if Snyder still loved her. Before he and Katherine got together, she and Snyder were close. How close, Harry had long ago decided, was none of his business. But he still wondered.

"There's no chance you and Katherine might . . ."

"No."

Snyder nodded, sighed, and appeared to pull himself back from something. "You working on a case?"

Harry was grateful for the query. "Yes. Martha Roberts has asked me to find out what I can about her brother's death."

"Sit down." Snyder dropped back into his chair. "I owe her one for bringing you in here. That's the good news. The bad news is that there isn't anything to find out. The poor soul shot himself. The slug was still in his skull. It fell out on the coroner's examination table."

"You recovered the gun?"

"Yes. The state lab's got it and the slug. It's going to be a match."

"In your view there's no chance somebody else shot him and pushed the car into the canal?"

Snyder frowned. "There's always a chance, but there's no reason to think so."

"Why do you think Roberts shot himself?"

Snyder paused and rubbed his head, something he did, Harry recalled with amusement, when he was unhappy with what he was about to say.

"He was mixed up in a break-in at the Jiffy-Fix Automotive Supplies on the East Trail. According to our records, he was implicated by another suspect. We questioned him a couple of times. The warrant when it came had his name on it, along with three others. But when we went for him, he was gone. We concluded he'd run. Looks like he did, farther than we figured."

"Do you remember talking to him?"

"No. A couple of deputies did the interrogation. Our division never got directly involved. It was pretty small stuff—chrome wheels, mufflers, some tools."

"Martha Roberts says her brother was retarded."

"There's nothing about that in the records, but I don't think he was the only one," Snyder said with a chuckle. "The four of them broke into the Jiffy-Fix through the front door, which faces the main street, and turned the lights on so they could see better."

Harry relaxed enough to grin. "Has Martha Roberts talked with you?"

"Oh yes." Snyder blew out his cheeks. "She's not happy with us. She thinks the department didn't try hard enough to find John when he disappeared. Now she thinks we're trying to cover up his murder because we figure he was a throw-away person." Snyder looked offended. "Now you know I don't regard anybody as trash. I tried to tell her so, but she wasn't listening."

"What do you think of her?"

"Stubborn and opinionated. She's a Roberts all right. But I do admire the way she's trying to defend her brother. Except that maybe she's trying a little too hard and fighting a battle that's already lost."

Harry stood up, agreeing with Jim about Martha's being stubborn but not ready to believe she was wrong about her brother's death. "Thanks for your time, Jim. It was good seeing you."

"Would you be all right with me stopping by if I'm out your way?" Jim asked, walking Harry to the door.

"Better than all right," Harry responded, pleased with the prospect. "We can visit Tucker and have some of his tea."

"Lord," Snyder said, his eyes widening, "the first swallow I took of that witch's brew, I thought I was headed for St. Peter's gate. After the second, I broke into a sweat and feared I was going the other way."

They were shaking hands when Harry remembered to ask if Jim knew Matthew Roberts.

Jim gave a good-natured laugh. "The master of 10-30. Everybody knows Matthew."

"What division is 10-30 in? I never heard of it."

"That's what we call the Evidence Section. But not in Matthew's hearing. Matthew Roberts is a very solid citizen. He's been supervisor of the section for years and years."

"Why 10-30?"

"Matthew 10:30: 'But the very hairs of your head are all numbered.' "

"Sorry, it must be the hour."

Jim was grinning happily. "The Evidence Section is responsible for every piece of evidence we collect or comes our way. Its principal responsibility is to keep that evidence safe and maintain a record of where every piece of it is and who's handled it. Believe me, Matthew keeps the record clear and untarnished. Hence, Matthew 10:30."

"The chain of custody."

Harry wanted to be amused, even delighted, but although his head was amused by the melee, his heart wasn't laughing. It had been three years and nine months since Katherine had left for Georgia. Anger and hopelessness boiled in his chest. But turning quickly, he strode toward the Rover.

"No!" he said loudly. "I'm finished with that." But his expression said otherwise.

The raccoons bolted for the woods.

The Evidence Section was housed in a single-story, buff-colored stucco building behind the sheriff's department headquarters. It huddled in a stand of pin oaks, hung with Spanish moss. When Harry shut off the Rover, the buzz and zing of locusts and cicadas fiddling in the trees were deafening. Usually, Harry liked the energetic racket, but this morning he was too uneasy about his upcoming meeting with Matthew to enjoy it.

The building's air conditioning was set at arctic, and the middle-aged receptionist hunched over her computer wore a heavy orange cardigan. The clicking of the keyboard was the only sound Harry could hear, and its steady rattle echoed hollowly down the narrow, dark corridors at her back. The place had the dusty, mingled smell of an old barn. Now and then a phone rang dimly in the distance.

The receptionist listened to him without looking up from her monitor. "Straight ahead, fourth on left. Don't be surprised if he shouts," she said in a gravelly voice.

Nothing that happened in this place would surprise me, Harry thought.

Matthew Roberts's office décor was early cement block. Without windows, pictures, or plants, it was furnished with an immense oak refectory table covered with neatly spaced objects that might have been set out for a garage sale in a part of town where no birds sang. The tiled floor behind the table was

covered with a piece of abused, green industri[al] enabled Roberts to roll in his chair from one end the other. When Harry stepped into the room, [He was in] transit, holding a sawed-off shotgun aloft in his le[ft hand]

Ignoring Harry, he put the shotgun down in [a box] on the table, filled out a brown tag with two strin[gs at one] end, and tied it to the gun's trigger guard. Then [he took a] Magic Marker out of shirt pocket and wrote a [number] on the back of the tag. Harry glanced at the ha[lf-dozen] plastic bags stuffed with white powder, bunche[s of dried] plants that looked like faded bouquets, taped [rolls of] currency, jack handles, a pile of blue jerseys, an[d other] incongruous objects, all tagged and numbered.

Roberts kicked his way back down the table [to an] open ledger that looked like an old store daybo[ok, made an] entry. Then he jumped to his feet. He was we[ll over six feet,] broad, and gone a little to fat and belly, but H[arry saw he] was still a very formidable man. He had black [hair,] too black to Harry, a low forehead, a square ja[w, and the same] dark, smoking eyes as his sister.

"Murder," he said in the loud, harsh voice Ha[rry recalled] from the phone call and jabbed his finger at [a] hunting knife with a rusted blade. Walking along[, point-] ing at individual objects, he said in the same [voice,] "Arson, rape, suicide, aggravated assault, for[gery." He] made a final jab at a lilac silk scarf. "Impersona[ting an officer] to commit a felony." No smile.

Still without looking at Harry, he checked [his watch. "Ten] o'clock. Let's go."

Harry trailed Roberts out of the room, dow[n the dim] corridor, and into a drab space that looked [as if it had been] decorated in the dark. On their way, Harry [saw shadowy] figures, burdened with files or boxes, walking

"Right. And there are no weak links in Matthew's chain."

"Any reason I shouldn't talk to him?"

"Not that I know of. Just don't mention 10:30." Jim lost his grin. "Oh, yes, he's touchy about his brother. At least he used to be, and he's not a man much given to change. Look before you step." He regained his cheerfulness. "If you can, get him to show you around. Once you see the place, you'll understand the joke."

The next morning Harry called Matthew Roberts.

"Roberts." The voice was deep, gruff, and loud.

"My name's Harry Brock. I'm a—"

"I know who you are. What do you want?"

Harry braced himself. "I'd like to talk with you about your brother John's death."

Roberts breathed into the phone for a while. "Ten o'clock. I'll give you fifteen minutes. That's how long my break lasts."

The line went dead. Harry swore quietly. After Katherine left, he stopped slamming doors and dragging chairs across the floor or banging pots on the stove. It was as if someone had died. Being quiet in the house had gradually become a habit. He glanced at his watch. Nine.

Still feeling irritated with Matthew Roberts, he went out into the yard. Another sunny morning. Stretching, he took a deep breath and crossed the lawn to the southeast corner of the lanai. The big wisteria covering the south end of the roof was in full spring growth, and its purple blossoms smothered the screen at that end of the lanai.

A sudden squalling pulled his attention away from the wisteria to a mother raccoon and four small cubs digging for grubs in the soft ground beside his toolshed. The cubs were brawling over something one of them had found. The mother ignored the uproar and went on digging and eating.

31

Harry wanted to be amused, even delighted, but although his head was amused by the melee, his heart wasn't laughing. It had been three years and nine months since Katherine had left for Georgia. Anger and hopelessness boiled in his chest. But turning quickly, he strode toward the Rover.

"No!" he said loudly. "I'm finished with that." But his expression said otherwise.

The raccoons bolted for the woods.

The Evidence Section was housed in a single-story, buff-colored stucco building behind the sheriff's department headquarters. It huddled in a stand of pin oaks, hung with Spanish moss. When Harry shut off the Rover, the buzz and zing of locusts and cicadas fiddling in the trees were deafening. Usually, Harry liked the energetic racket, but this morning he was too uneasy about his upcoming meeting with Matthew to enjoy it.

The building's air conditioning was set at arctic, and the middle-aged receptionist hunched over her computer wore a heavy orange cardigan. The clicking of the keyboard was the only sound Harry could hear, and its steady rattle echoed hollowly down the narrow, dark corridors at her back. The place had the dusty, mingled smell of an old barn. Now and then a phone rang dimly in the distance.

The receptionist listened to him without looking up from her monitor. "Straight ahead, fourth on left. Don't be surprised if he shouts," she said in a gravelly voice.

Nothing that happened in this place would surprise me, Harry thought.

Matthew Roberts's office décor was early cement block. Without windows, pictures, or plants, it was furnished with an immense oak refectory table covered with neatly spaced objects that might have been set out for a garage sale in a part of town where no birds sang. The tiled floor behind the table was covered with a piece of abused, green industrial carpet that enabled Roberts to roll in his chair from one end of the table to the other. When Harry stepped into the room, Roberts was in transit, holding a sawed-off shotgun aloft in his left hand.

Ignoring Harry, he put the shotgun down in an open space on the table, filled out a brown tag with two strings fixed to one end, and tied it to the gun's trigger guard. Then he pulled a big Magic Marker out of shirt pocket and wrote a large, black 2B on the back of the tag. Harry glanced at the handguns, knives, plastic bags stuffed with white powder, bunches of marijuana plants that looked like faded bouquets, taped stacks of paper currency, jack handles, a pile of blue jerseys, and a dozen more incongruous objects, all tagged and numbered.

Roberts kicked his way back down the table, stopped at an open ledger that looked like an old store daybook, and made an entry. Then he jumped to his feet. He was well over six feet, broad, and gone a little to fat and belly, but Harry guessed he was still a very formidable man. He had black hair that looked too black to Harry, a low forehead, a square jaw, and the same dark, smoking eyes as his sister.

"Murder," he said in the loud, harsh voice Harry remembered from the phone call and jabbed his finger at a bone-handled hunting knife with a rusted blade. Walking along the table, pointing at individual objects, he said in the same driving manner, "Arson, rape, suicide, aggravated assault, forcible entry." He made a final jab at a lilac silk scarf. "Impersonation with intent to commit a felony." No smile.

Still without looking at Harry, he checked his watch. "Ten o'clock. Let's go."

Harry trailed Roberts out of the room, down another deserted corridor, and into a drab space that looked as if it had been decorated in the dark. On their way, Harry glimpsed shadowy figures, burdened with files or boxes, walking swiftly along the corridors. A large coffee maker stood on what had once been a boudoir table, and a faded blue couch, missing legs on one end, sagged against a wall. The smell of disinfectant was stronger here.

"Coffee?"

"No thanks," Harry said.

"Wise decision. Sit down. For the next fifteen minutes, the place is mine. Now, what the fuck do you think you're doing?"

Harry settled himself on what he took for a church pew and tried to figure out what Roberts was asking. Because the man seemed to say everything in the same aggressively loud voice, Harry was not sure whether he was angry or asking for information.

He rolled the dice. "Martha asked me to look into John Roberts's death. I decided to begin by talking to you."

"You deaf or something? I asked you what the fuck you think you're doing?"

Roberts had flung himself down on the couch and sat sprawled in a position that suggested the couch had just collapsed. He glowered at Harry, who waited, aware that big brother was angry, and unless he found a way to deal with it, he was not going to learn anything useful from him.

"Let me ask you a question back," Harry said calmly. "Have I harmed you in some way?"

"Yeah. You've put your fucking nose in where it don't belong." Roberts hunched forward as if considering coming off the couch in a hurry.

Harry put some weight on his feet, just in case. "Your sister came to me and asked for my help, Mr. Roberts. She was upset. I told her John Roberts had been dead a long time, that it was likely all the leads were cold. Further, she said that, pressed, the police would say her brother had killed himself. Her very definite response was that he couldn't have killed himself."

Harry had no idea what was going through the man's mind. He seemed to have been put together with wires and galvanized by lightning.

"Why not?" Matthew demanded loudly.

"She doesn't think he was capable of doing it, but you're his brother. What do you think?"

"My sister is an ignorant kid. John was facing arrest for theft. He was boozing. My father had kicked him out of the house. He was practically living on the street. Anybody who can lift a gun can shoot himself, Brock. So what are you dancing around here?"

Something prodded Harry awake. "I think the real answer probably depends on how severely your brother was retarded."

Roberts was on his feet, fists clenched. "It's a good thing we're on county property, or I'd rip your tongue out of your goddamned throat," he shouted.

"Hold on. Your sister told me he was mentally deficient," Harry said quietly. "I never knew the man."

Roberts glared. Then he unlocked his hands as if he had turned something off and turned toward the door. "I'm going to show you something. Follow me."

Harry followed, wondering if he was being taken off county property. They went down a winding corridor as silent as the others and turned into a room that looked like a small warehouse. Floor to ceiling, open, unpainted wooden shelving ran in rows like library stacks the length of the room. Roberts led Harry to the end of the first row and banged on the end of the stack with his fist.

A young, black woman wearing a dark-blue jumper suit and cradling a clipboard in her left arm was moving slowly along the stack, making check marks on a thick list on her board. She ignored their intrusion and did not even look up at Roberts's pounding.

35

"You see all this stuff? Hundreds of items. Evidence, Brock. No evidence, no trial. No convictions."

Overwhelmed by the number and variety of objects, Harry tramped behind Roberts up and down the rows of shelves, listening to him lecture on the need for order, accountability.

When they came to the end of the rows, he turned to confront Harry. "The chain of custody," he repeated for the eighth or ninth time in a voice that suggested he was quoting Scripture.

Harry's head was full of Roberts's loud voice. There were numbers everywhere. Every row was numbered, every shelf, every compartment on every shelf, and every item in every compartment. And that wasn't the end of it apparently.

"In another room we have numbered files for every item on these shelves, and in those files are numbered and signed lists of every person who has handled these pieces of evidence. Chain of custody, Brock!" he shouted. "Do you get it? A place for everything, everything in its place, and a record of how it got there. Order, Brock. Order. Accountability."

He checked his watch and pushed past Harry and strode away down the aisle as if suddenly summoned to assume command of Mount Rushmore. Harry hurried after him, swearing silently. Roberts reached his office and turned, blocking the door and glaring at Harry.

"It's ten fifteen, Brock. Listen up. John was lost for four years. Now he's found. He shot himself in the head because his life had come to a dead end. I loved my brother and tried to help him, but it didn't do any good. Killing himself might have been the best thing that ever happened to him. When the police are finished with his remains, I'll bury them. And when I've taken care of that, the case will be closed. Do you understand?"

"I'm beginning to," Harry said. He had been dragged around and shouted at enough, and he opened his mouth to ask Roberts if he'd picked out a number for John's gravestone, then

36

changed his mind and tried to speak calmly. "Despite what you've said, until your sister tells me to stop, I'm going to try very hard to find out if your brother really did kill himself. Thanks for the tour, Mr. Roberts. It's been interesting."

5

Driving home, Harry found he couldn't reconcile the conflicting assessments of John Roberts that Martha and Matthew had given him. Was he the sweet, simple, and loving brother Martha remembered or the thick-headed wastrel Matthew had described? He was also puzzled by the harshness with which Matthew had dismissed Martha. It was clear he had a lot more digging to do before he could form a clear idea about John Roberts or the dynamics that shaped the Roberts family.

Half a mile from the turnoff to the Hammock, Harry slowed for a dump truck that was backing a trailer into the ditch on the west side of the county road. Squatting on the low trailer bed was a big, yellow tractor with a heavy steel bulldozer blade anchoring it to the bed of the trailer. Harry stopped beside the fat man in the white plastic cowboy hat directing the truck's driver.

"Y'all live out here?" he asked, continuing to wave the driver toward him.

"Bartram's Hammock. What's going on?"

"We're gonna scrape out a space so the surveyors can get parked and set up their gear without getting run over." He laughed. "You're the first person I seen so far. Say, you know Mr. Tucker LaBeau?"

Harry said he was a neighbor.

"Tell him Hubbard Clampett's boy Wetherell was asking after him. Tell him my daddy's not doing too well. He might want to stop in on him."

"I'm sorry your father's sick. I'll tell Tucker."

"Thank you kindly."

"Who's having this work done?" Harry asked.

The man leaned back, thrust out his belly and surveyed the woods. Then he turned back to Harry and said, "This here land belonged to Miss Lucy Mott Covington until she passed. That woman had more dollars than these pines have needles, but she's not going to need them now." He paused to grin. "Ain't it what the preacher says? You come into the world bare assed and you leave the same way. My only complaint is that so far I ain't laid up nothing to speak of in between."

Harry laughed. "So the land's going to be sold?"

"That's what I hear. I believe Bevel's Sand, Stone, and Gravel has a strong interest." A man's complaining voice shouted, "Wetherell!" Wetherell stepped back, grinning. "Y'all take care," he said and waved Harry on his way.

Harry drove away thinking, There go the butterflies.

Helen Bradley had called while Harry was out. He dialed the Three Rivers Bank and Trust where she was Head of Personnel.

"You'd better have a good reason for calling me at work," she snapped when she heard his voice.

"I'm returning your call."

"Excellent reason. Are you free for lunch?"

"Let me check my calendar."

"Are you trying for a laugh?"

"Okay, I'll pick you up at twelve."

"Park the Rover away from the bank. I don't want to become a laughingstock. It's bad enough being seen with a man of your age."

"I hope you're wearing slacks to hide your skinny legs." Harry hung up quickly and fisted the air over his head.

They had argued about where to eat and compromised on

Ma Fong's, which Helen called The Inn of The Eighth Fried Rice.

"Got time to walk me around the park?" she asked when they came out of the restaurant.

While they ate, she had caught Harry up on the latest bank gossip, and he had told her about Tucker's butterflies and the bulldozer.

"I think the bank's got an interest there," she said. "But that's all I know."

As they walked into Blackfin Park with its ficus-shaded brick walks winding between the Avola art center at one end and the public tennis courts at the other, Helen linked arms with Harry.

"If you don't want to hear this, just tell me. I'll understand. Riga's coming back to Avola. I've had a letter."

She did not look at Harry directly as she gave him the news, but she kept glancing at him out of the corner of her eyes.

"Riga Kraftmeier," he said, failing to keep his voice even. "How will I contain my enthusiasm?"

"Okay, we don't have to discuss this. I just thought . . ."

"You just thought you'd be able to have a civilized conversation with your close friend Harry Brock about the return of probably the most beautiful woman in Southwest Florida, who is also your ex or not so ex-lover without having him shout and make a display of himself."

"Brock, you're such a shit." But she was laughing before she got it all out.

"This is not good news, Bradley."

She squeezed his arm with hers. "I know it. I really don't think it's funny. And I do know it may be unfair to you, but I've got to talk this through with somebody, and you're the only one who knows . . ."

"You're not finishing your sentences."

She walked with him in silence for a few moments then

stopped and turned to face him. "I'm ashamed of myself, but I don't want to be alone tonight. Will you . . ."

Harry looked at her through a rainbow of emotions, most of them in the purple to black range. Jealousy was boiling up in him, and he hated himself for being so weak. He waited until he was sure he would not explode before answering her. "How about dinner?"

"Great," she said with a smile and gave him a quick kiss.

After dinner they went back to Helen's place, as they always did. The good reason for it was that if Harry stayed the night, it would be easier for her to get to work in the morning. The real reason was that Harry didn't want Helen in the same bed he had slept in with Katherine. He occasionally thought of Riga's having shared Helen's bed, but he told himself he didn't care—or if he did, he wouldn't admit it. And because Helen never questioned the arrangement, Harry hadn't gotten around to buying a new bed. At least that's what he told himself.

"You shouldn't be so hard on Riga," Helen said when they had settled down on the sofa with a tray of cheese and crackers and a bottle of Robin's Hill merlot on the table in front of them. "She's brought up Cheryl alone for the past three years. Can you believe it? The child is five now."

And Katherine's Minna is almost ten, he thought. To get his mind away from the subject of children, he asked where Tom Burkhardt was. Helen flinched.

"What?" he asked.

"I still can't hear his name without having guilt grab me by the throat. I know it's foolish, but . . . what did you ask? Oh, yes. After he left Riga, he went back to the Hawkswood Beach & Tennis Club. I think he's Head Pro there now."

"I still can't see why Riga would want to come back to Avola unless it's to be near you. The last I knew, she had a partnership in a major law firm in Tallahassee."

Helen set her wine glass on the coffee table and frowned at Harry. "I don't know any more than what she told me in her letter, and that wasn't much."

"Some things don't change."

"You saved her life, Harry. And sometimes I think you were half in love with her yourself." She took his glass away from him and put her arms around his neck. "It's an old story, Harry. I fell head over heels in love with her. The rest you know. You also know you married Katherine."

And then she unmarried me, Harry thought. "Do you still miss her?"

"Riga? Of course I do."

Fair enough, Harry thought as he kissed her. She was a brave and honest woman, but he scrupulously avoided asking himself if he loved her.

Harry sat on the lanai in the early morning sun studying a list of names. It had taken some sharp skirmishing for him to persuade Martha Roberts to let him talk to the people on it. They were all members of her family, and when he told her he had already talked with Matthew about John, she jumped to her feet and said in a very loud voice, "I know, and I didn't hire you to talk with my relatives."

"Does everybody in your family shout?" he asked.

Her face darkened. Then she clenched her fists and strode into her kitchen and made a lot of racket that sounded to Harry like pans being thrown from one end of a cupboard to another. That was followed by a short silence at the end of which she came back to where Harry was sitting, carrying a small blue tray and two cups with tea bag strings hanging out of them.

"It's not my best feature, but, yes, I do shout." Harry didn't think she sounded very apologetic and probably she wasn't. "I remember a lot of shouting. Mostly about God and what he expected from us. For a long time I thought the Trinity was made up of God, my mother, and my father. They were so much in agreement on so many things I never found the idea of three in one at all confusing. Now it's more complicated."

"The Trinity's always dodgy." Harry regarded her with a straight face.

She laughed and said, "That's not really funny. What do you think you're going to gain talking to my family?"

"Did Matthew tell you about our conversation?"

"He told me."

"What did he tell you?"

"That Bunny shot himself." She sat down opposite Harry and stared at her hands.

"That's it?"

She shook her head and set her tea aside. "He told me to get rid of you."

"Why?"

She hesitated. Harry wondered if she was deciding how much to tell him. Perhaps under her apparent openness she felt family business was not for publication. "He doesn't want anyone outside the family poking around in Bunny's life."

"And getting rid of me would put an end to that?"

"Yes."

"Am I history?"

"Do you want to be?" She looked pained.

"No. The last thing I said to your brother was that until you told me to stop, I intended to go right on trying to find out whether or not your brother killed himself. Does Matthew threaten you often?"

"Threaten me?"

"Martha. Don't pretend you don't know what I mean."

"My father's no longer well, and Matthew's just trying to do what Pa always did. Somebody's got to take charge of the family. You still haven't told me what you expect to gain by talking to the people on that list."

"I need to learn as much as I can about John. You and the others on this list knew him. I didn't."

She sighed. "There's really not that much to know about Bunny." She paused, apparently lost momentarily in her own thoughts. Then she said, "But I loved him."

"So you said."

Harry noted with disappointment that she had avoided his question, and he saw with increased clarity that the relationships in the Roberts family were more complicated than he had assumed. When Harry drove out of Pecan Grove, the few children and dogs he had passed coming into the trailer park had disappeared. An uneasy silence lay over the place. Easing through the potholes, he thought the stillness was more sullen than peaceful. He didn't breathe easily until he gunned the Rover onto the main road.

6

Harry folded the list of names lengthwise and tapped it on his thumb. "How did it all begin?" he asked the mockingbird hopping importantly across the lawn. "With the parents. All right, then I'll begin with the parents.

"Talking to a bird. I'm spending too much time alone," he said aloud as he climbed into the Rover without feeling inclined to do anything about it.

James and Ruth Roberts lived several miles east of Martha on Panther Trace, in a back corner of Tequesta County on a dirt road that was used more by wild pigs than people. Their house was surrounded by a tall ficus fence, reinforced by barbed wire. It enclosed a couple of acres of land divided between a citrus orchard and a big kitchen garden. But its real job was to hold the wilderness at bay.

The house was a two-story rectangular box sheathed in aluminum siding and a tin roof. A wide, screened lanai, furnished with cast-off chairs and sofas, stretched across the front of the structure. "Seven children plus James and Ruth makes nine," Harry marveled as he knocked on the screen door. "All in this shoe box."

The man who answered his knock looked like Matthew thirty hard years on. The frame was still there, stooped and gaunt, as if the flesh had shrunk around the bones, the face was worn, and the eyes staring and sunken.

"Who the hell are you?" he demanded in a voice that Harry

would have recognized in a coal mine. Matthew One.

"James!" a woman's voice said sharply, "Give me that gun."

Someone pulled James around, and Harry was alarmed to see that the old man was holding a double-barreled shotgun, which the sunlight on the screen had obscured.

She was tall, gray haired, dressed in a flowered dress and a blue apron, and stared at him through steel-rimmed glasses. There was no welcoming smile on her sun-darkened face. Harry knew who tended the garden. "You lost?"

"No. Is that gun loaded?"

A very brief smile softened her expression. "Oh, yes. My husband's kept a loaded shotgun under his bed for long as ever I've known him. What do you want?"

Harry explained who he was and waited. She looked at him for a while.

"Come in and set," she said at last. "There's coffee. You had any breakfast?"

She led him into the kitchen, pushing her husband in front of her, holding the shotgun as casually as if it had been a broom.

"I'm of two minds about this," she said when James was seated in a rocker by the window and she had poured Harry and herself the coffee.

"I'm not surprised," Harry said.

"Martha's a good girl, but her judgment's not to be trusted," Ruth said.

The sound of their voices apparently roused James.

"Who the hell are you?" he demanded loudly, staring at Harry angrily.

"He's a friend of Martha's," his wife said without looking at him.

"My children fear the Lord," the man said, his hands jumping on the rocker's arms.

"That's right," Ruth answered, waiting to go on until James

turned back to the window. "How does she think we can help?"

The old man in the rocker and the enduring, worn woman facing him chilled Harry's heart. "I'm sure you're not finding any of this easy, Mrs. Roberts, and I'm sorry to be adding to your pain."

She regarded him in silence, her gray eyes giving Harry no hint of what she was thinking. He swore silently. What had led him to think he had any right to comment on her pain?

"Martha doesn't believe that John committed suicide," he said to her quietly.

She did not flinch away from his words. "The police think otherwise."

"So does your son Matthew. But it would help me to know what you think."

"He was a difficult child. When John was fifteen, Matthew found out he couldn't read or write and took him out of school and found him a job at the quarry."

"Bevel's Sand, Stone, and Gravel?"

"I guess there might be others. He worked there right up to . . ." she faltered then continued, "the end."

"Did he live here with you?"

"Not for the last year." She glanced at her husband. "He lived with some other men from the quarry in Pecan Grove. Mr. Brock, we are a God-fearing family. We are strict observers. James did not like John drinking, and he didn't like his friends. When John refused to change his ways, James told him to leave. He might have been right. There were quarrels. My husband was becoming more and more upset." She paused and then seemed to speak to herself. "He was a sweet, good-natured child, and some of that stayed. We might have given up too soon."

She was explaining, not apologizing. James pushed out of his rocker and, seeing Harry, stopped and said in the same loud voice, "Who the hell are you?"

"He's Martha's friend," Ruth said.

James stood by the table, wavering, glaring at Harry until Ruth got up and led him back to his rocker and eased him into it.

"My children fear the Lord!" he shouted.

"That's right," she said and came back to stand by the table. Harry got to his feet.

"Do you think John killed himself?" he asked.

"No," she said.

The expression in her eyes wrenched Harry's heart.

"Neither do I," he replied.

"Can you prove it?"

"I'm going to try."

Harry got home to find Sanchez lying on the grass under one of the live oaks where it was cool. The dog got up slowly as Harry drove into the yard and trotted around the Rover to greet him and deliver the note pinned to his red bandanna collar.

"Come over if you can. There's someone here I want you to meet."

"Looks like you've got company," Harry said. "Come on, I think I can find you a couple of Milk-Bone biscuits."

While Sanchez cleaned up the crumbs and took a final drink, Harry put away his notebook and pulled on his boots. On the way back to the Rover, he noticed the day had turned still and hot. The change felt good, and he forgot himself and told Sanchez, sitting beside him, he hoped they'd seen the last of the spring winds. He tried to pretend the dog, sitting on the front seat beside him, hadn't really understood what had been said to him, but Sanchez did take his eyes off the road long enough to grin at Harry.

★ ★ ★ ★ ★

"Harry, this is Dr. Fred Casanova from the Florida Fish and Wildlife Conservation Commission," Tucker said. "He's an entomologist and something of a specialist on the Florida Atala butterfly."

Sanchez and Oh, Brother! were standing near the stoop, looking in the kitchen door.

"This is a fascinating find," Casanova said, shaking Harry's hand energetically. "As far as I know, this is just about the farthest point west we've ever located a hairstreak colony. Hairstreak's another name for Atalas, and this colony may have been isolated long enough to be on the brink of evolving into a subspecies."

Harry liked Casanova and envied him his enthusiasm. It had been a long time since he had cared that passionately about anything. He looked at Tucker, who was grinning with pleasure. Harry also glanced at the screen door and saw Sanchez and Oh, Brother! apparently listening. Harry quickly looked away.

"Step over here," Casanova said, grasping Harry's arm and drawing him closer to the table. He moved the box a little to let more light fall on the two butterflies climbing on the green stems, gently waving their wings. The three men bent over the table as Casanova pulled a pen out of his shirt pocket and held it like a pointer. "I think we can assume these are Atalas although the North American Butterfly Association may want to weigh in on the identification.

"In Atalas the front wings of the female are black with a dusting of blue toward the center. The males' front wings are black around the margins with a metallic green intruding on the upper median areas."

Casanova gave his listeners a moment to study the butterflies then plunged on. "As you've seen, these two fit the description. But now things get really interesting. The upper surface of the hind wings in both sexes is black. Check it out."

"They're black all right," Tucker said, "but there's more color out toward the edges."

"Right. Now look carefully. In all the Florida Atalas I've ever seen or seen described, the males have a submarginal row of green spots and the females, blue spots. But look again. Tell me what you see."

"There's an orange diamond in the center of both hind wings in both butterflies," Harry said.

Casanova snapped upright as if Harry's comment had released a spring.

"That's it," Casanova said loudly. "These two Atalas have a pattern of coloration different from that of any other Atala. If they are Atalas, they've evolved this on their own. You may be looking at a subspecies never before described."

Casanova grinned, clicked his pen a couple of times, and even executed a few dance steps as if the stress of his excitement had infected his feet.

"How about taking a look at where I found these two?" Tucker asked.

"That's what I'm here for." Casanova was already pulling on his hat.

Harry experienced a fellow feeling when he saw the hat. It had once been some shade of green and possessed a wide, stiff brim, but now the brim sagged as if in despair, and rain, sun, and using it to pick up things that bit and stung had stripped away all its original color and left it a stained disgrace. Ha, Ha, Harry thought, wait till Oh, Brother! gets a look at that. Then he checked himself.

"I notice your mule wears a hat," Casanova remarked in a neutral voice as the three men headed out the door.

"That's right, and it would be a good idea not to make any derogatory remarks about it either. Harry can vouch for that."

"That so?" Casanova was doing a good job of keeping his face straight.

"Some time ago, I may have said something about it that he mistook for criticism," Harry said uneasily. They were moving toward the road, making a small parade with Sanchez in the lead and Oh, Brother! bringing up the rear. Harry was walking just in front of Oh, Brother! and was taking no chances.

"What happened?"

"He's still taking my hat off every now and then, just to remind me."

Casanova turned and looked at Oh, Brother! "I've been thinking of getting one of those."

Harry laughed and Oh, Brother! took an extra-long step and grasping, the crown of Harry's hat in his teeth, lifted it off his head and passed it back to him over his shoulder. Harry put it back on his head but refused to look at the mule. People in glass houses . . . Harry started to say, then clamped his mouth shut. It was ridiculous.

"What about the animals?" Casanova asked as he and Tucker and Harry climbed into the Rover.

"They'll look after things while we're away," Tucker said.

"Oh," Casanova answered, fastening his safety belt.

"We may as well try out the parking lot," Harry said sourly, turning into the newly bulldozed road.

Twenty yards into the woods, the track opened into a roughly scraped rectangle of black earth. Trees and brush were pushed into a tangled heap at the west end of the opening. The sharp smell of raw dirt and crushed vegetation greeted them as they stepped out of the Rover.

"What's going on here?" Casanova asked in obvious alarm.

"The Covington estate has just gone on the block," Tucker said grimly. He swept his arm in a wide arc. "This whole section of upland pine forest is part of the estate."

"Bevel's Sand, Stone, and Gravel Company is bidding on this piece, about a hundred acres." Harry tried to keep the anger out of his voice.

"Didn't you say Bartram's Hammock is now a state preserve?" Casanova demanded. His long legs and his eagerness were carrying him ahead of Tucker.

"Whoa," Harry said. "We're leaving our guide behind." Keeping up with Casanova was going to be like being taken for a walk by a greyhound.

"The state owns the Hammock," Harry agreed, "but that's not going to protect this place."

"This far out, I'd expect all this to be designated agricultural land."

"That's right," Tucker said, catching up, "but Tequesta County Commissioners have a history of allowing mining in these areas. From what I've heard, there's good quality sand under our feet, along with substantial quantities of limestone. Bevel's a big company. It's done its homework."

"And more to follow by the looks of that road," Casanova remarked, nodding down at them like a worried crane. "But we can't do anything about it today. Take us to the butterflies, Mr. LaBeau."

"So this is a coontie plant," Harry said in surprise. "I don't think I've seen any of these on the Hammock. It looks like a cross between a palm and a fern. And these caterpillars are new to me too."

The three men were sitting on their heels, studying a dark green, three-foot-high plant as wide as it was tall. A couple of dozen bright orange caterpillars were crawling over the plant, feeding voraciously. The coontie was growing in an open space among the tall, bare trunks of big slash pines whose feathery tops swayed and hummed in the high, light wind far above the men's heads. In the open understory beneath the pines, half a dozen butterflies flickered in and out of the shifting bars of yellow sunlight, their wings glittering.

"I believe they were common at one time pretty much all over Florida," Tucker said, referring to the coontie plant.

"That's right, and your description's a good one," Casanova said, glancing at Harry. "The Florida coontie is a cycad. That means it belongs to a family of plants similar to palms. And without the coontie, there would be no Atala. These orange caterpillars are coontie grubs. Except in the coolest weather, Atalas breed year round. I don't see any on this bush, but if we look closely at some others, I'm sure we'll find eggs."

An hour later, Casanova, satisfied with what he had seen and having caught and released several of the butterflies in all parts of the four or five acre area where the coonties were growing, put away his notebook and digital camera and beamed at Harry and Tucker.

"I won't have the last word on this, but it surely looks to me as if we've got a subspecies here or something very close to it. Every Atala I've examined has the orange dot. That means the aposomatic marking is persistent and consistent."

"Aposomatic?" Tucker asked.

"Warning coloration," Casanova said quickly. "It's present at every stage of the Atala's development. This little colony has added an orange spot for extra protection."

"Then they're poisonous," Harry said.

"That's right. Atalas lay their eggs only on coontie plants, all of which contain a toxic cycasin compound. In its larval stage the Atala eats the coontie leaves and the toxin permeates the grub, making it unpalatable to predators. The toxin persists in the butterfly and in its eggs."

As they tramped out of the woods, Casanova revisited Tucker's comment that coonties were once common plants in

Florida. "In the nineteenth century," he said, "there was a major mill economy in Southeast Florida based on harvesting and processing coonties to recover the starch from the stem, almost all of which grows underground like a tuber. The grub stage of the Atala is almost entirely dependent on coontie plants. They'll feed on a few other cycads, but after the destruction of the coontie by overharvesting, the Florida Atala just about vanished. From the 1950s to the 1970s it was thought they were extinct except on the Keys."

"I believe the Calusa and the Timucua Indians found a way to grate and wash the coontie tubers that made them edible," Tucker said.

"So did the Seminoles and the white settlers in Florida," Casanova added. "It was once an important food source in the state, but the plant takes about thirty years to mature, so there wasn't much incentive to cultivate it."

They drove back to Tucker's farm.

"What do we do about the threat to that piece of butterfly breeding ground?" Tucker asked when Casanova had finished storing his gear in his pickup.

"First, let me get some feedback on what we've got here. If it's what I think it is, I'll get the word to the Department of Environmental Protection and the Audubon people. Then I'll talk to our Executive Director Ron Stuart and see if we can get some special protection for the little critters."

"What form would that be likely to take?" Harry asked.

"The director will talk with federal and local agencies, and if the discussion is productive, he might issue an executive order immediately listing the butterfly as endangered."

Casanova shook hands with Harry and Tucker and climbed into his truck. As he turned around, he shouted out his window, "Keep your eye on them. If anyone shows up in there with a bulldozer, you call me."

"I'll do more than that!" Tucker answered.

"Just don't shoot anybody," Casanova replied, driving off grinning merrily.

Tucker watched the truck disappear down the road. He turned to Harry. "Caught in a stampede, my inclination is to run. What about you?"

"Which way?" Harry inquired.

7

Martha Roberts's call woke Harry from a troubling dream. As he answered the phone, shreds of it clung to him like seaweed on a roughly weighed anchor.

"Harry, I'm scared," she said in an unsteady voice.

He swung his legs out of bed and looked at the clock. One-thirty a.m. "Where are you?"

"I'm at home. Somebody just shot out two of my windows."

"Are you hurt?"

"No."

"Have you called the police?"

"Not yet."

"Do it as soon as I hang up. I'm on my way."

Harry found Sergeant Frank Hodges and Corporal Morton Weeks sitting in Martha's trailer talking with her while two Crime Scene officers were working with lights outside the trailer, searching for evidence.

"Brock," Hodges said cheerfully, his mouth half full of chocolate cake, "you making house calls now?"

His red face was beaming, and his uniform fit him like the skin on an oversized sausage. Weeks was younger and bigger and a lot more serious. But despite his promotion to corporal, he still wore a look of puzzled surprise.

"Hello, Frank. Hello, Morton." Harry stepped past the policemen to sit down beside Martha. She was wearing black slacks and a red sweater. Her face was pale and her eyes were still wide with fear. "These are good people," he said to her. "You're safe now. How are you feeling?"

"A little better. I was asleep when suddenly there were two or three loud bangs and crashes. When I got up and put on some lights, I found this." She gestured toward the windows in the area where they were sitting. Harry counted three holes in the window behind him and three more holes in the wall he was facing.

Hodges anticipated the next question. "They went right through. Looks like a 9mm or a .45. I suppose it might have been a rifle. Ms. Roberts says she didn't see anybody or hear anything after she got out here."

"Did you see or hear a car?" Harry asked.

She shook her head. Harry noticed how tightly her hands were clasped and he guessed she was trying to stop them from shaking. He would like to have wrung the neck of whoever had done this to her, and he wondered what, if anything, this had to do with her having hired him to look into John Roberts's death.

"Has Sergeant Hodges asked you if you have any idea who did this?" he asked.

"No," she said quickly.

"Ms. Roberts means she doesn't know who fired the shots," Weeks said. "We did ask the question."

Harry decided the rest of his questions would wait until he and she were alone. He noticed Hodges and Weeks had coffee mugs beside them, but Martha had no cup near her.

"Have you got any tea bags?" he asked her.

"Sure. The water's still hot." She started to get up.

"I'll do it," he said and went into the kitchen before she could stop him. He turned the gas on under the kettle, located the tea bags, and as soon as the kettle sang, he made the tea in a white mug and carried it to her.

"I'm not . . ."

"I know, but drink it anyway. It will help a little." Give you something to think about besides bullets crashing through your house, he thought.

Hodges was studying his notes, and when he finished, he ate the last of his cake and stood up. Crumbs rolled off his belly onto the floor. "We'll write this up, Ms. Roberts. When that's done, we'll ask you to read it over and sign it. You have any questions before we leave?"

"No," she said. "Thank you for coming so quickly."

"No problem. Come on, Weeks. Good to see you, Harry. Stop by the station sometime."

"Take care, Frank."

When the two men were gone, the room seemed to be a lot larger. Martha had drunk some of her tea and looked less frightened.

"Harry," she said, then paused. She looked around the trailer as if she hadn't seen it for a long time. "What's going on?" she blurted, tears welling suddenly.

"I was counting on your telling me," he said, taking her hand. "Of course, given the neighborhood, it might be nothing more than drunken high spirits."

He did not believe it, and she looked at him as if he had insulted her.

"You don't think so?"

"No." She dug in her slacks pocket for a tissue and blew her nose.

Good, he'd made her a little mad. "Then you try."

"How am I supposed to explain anything this crazy?"

"Given where you live, this kind of thing can't be all that unusual. My guess is a percentage of your neighbors get a bullet through their trailers every once in a while."

"Maybe," she snapped, "but I don't."

"What's broken the magic circle? Don't ask me what magic

circle because you know what it is."

"Why are you talking to me like this?" She sounded frightened again.

"Because you're lying about not having any idea what caused this."

They were interrupted by one of the Crime Scene people, a big, gray-haired man wearing rimless glasses. He took off his cap and tucked it under his arm as he stepped into the trailer.

"We've done what we can, ma'am," he said in a loud, earnest voice. "And we've rousted the neighbors to the point they might anytime begin shooting at us." He paused to laugh. "But nobody's seen nothing, and that don't surprise me. We'll be back when it's daylight and give things another look."

Martha thanked him, and he left. Then she turned back to Harry. "You talked with my mother and father."

"I talked with your mother. Your father was there."

"It's sad, isn't it?"

He nodded. She stared at the wall for a moment. Harry waited, not knowing where she was going. "I had no idea Matthew was going to be so upset over my hiring you."

More silence. He could see the struggle she was going through just mentioning Matthew.

"It seems to me all out of proportion," she said finally. "Maybe it has something to do with our father's condition, which Matthew won't discuss or allow anyone to name."

"Has he threatened you again?"

She shrugged. "He's overwrought."

"But when you called me, you thought he might have been trying to scare you."

"Maybe, in my panic, for a minute or two, I might have thought that."

"But not now."

She straightened her back. "No."

Harry admired her courage, but he also remembered Tucker's comment about the Robertses being a tribe. What did happen, he wondered, when someone in the tribe began acting like an individual?

Harry got home about four o'clock and decided to try to sleep for a while. Since Katherine's departure, he made an effort not to be awake in the house at this hour of the morning. For the first year, if he woke, really woke at this time, he would go out and run for an hour. By then the new day would have started.

He lay in bed, thinking about what Martha had said to him about her mother and father and about Bunny and Matthew. What didn't he know about that relationship? Then he thought how complicated it was to be part of such a large family. He had no way of understanding what it was like. He had been an only child. His parents had died years ago. Then he thought of his own five children and two ex-wives, not counting Tucker and Helen, who were almost family. Did they make a tribe?

Startled by the thought, he rolled over and told himself not to be an idiot. Jennifer, his first wife, and Katherine were certainly no longer family. He had seen almost nothing of Sarah and Clive while they were growing up, and it was months since he had seen Minna, Jesse, and Thornton. If he had been hoping the brief family get-together in his head would result in a warm and fuzzy feeling, he was mistaken.

He didn't remember falling asleep, but he woke to what sounded like somebody trying to break down the door. It was Frank Hodges and Jim Snyder.

"These bachelors," Hodges said in a loud voice when Harry appeared on the lanai to let them in.

"You under the weather?" Snyder inquired.

"I'm guessing he's got some underage chick up there. You think we should investigate, Captain?"

"Very funny, Frank," Harry replied, waving them into chairs on the lanai.

The sun was making a run at midmorning, and the last of the mist was burning off the Creek. Despite the abrupt awakening, Harry found the day reassuring. He liked mornings.

"I don't suppose this is a social call."

Snyder leaned forward and propped his elbows on his bony knees. "It's about Martha Roberts. Now, I know the residents of Pecan Grove are born suspicious of the police, but this is ridiculous. Somebody fired a large caliber gun three times at Roberts's trailer."

"And unless the perpetrator has the wings of an angel," Hodges said, overcome with excitement, "he had to walk, run, or drive to wherever he went after the shooting. Nobody heard or saw anything. Why don't I believe it?"

"Did you mistake this place for the temple of Apollo?"

"What?" Hodges demanded.

Snyder grinned. "Ignore him, Frank. We're looking for help here, Harry. Have you turned up anything while you've been working for Roberts that would shed some light on why she was shot at? I'm having trouble believing the renters of Pecan Grove have suddenly lost their minds."

"The shooter was an outsider?"

"What do you think?"

"I don't think it was a drunk."

"Could have been," Hodges said.

"I agree with Harry. The bullets went through the living area window, well away from where she was sleeping. The shots were grouped. My guess is a message was being sent. But why to Martha Roberts?"

"She's pretty uppity, but who would blow out her main window for that?" Hodges asked.

Harry almost said Matthew Roberts, then changed his mind.

61

Would Matthew have shot out his sister's windows? Not too likely. The Matthew Roberts he knew would have gone straight for her or him.

"I'd guess it has to do with finding John Roberts," Harry said. "Somebody doesn't want his case reopened."

After Snyder and Hodges were gone, Harry thought about what he had told them. He had been planning to talk with Mark Roberts next and then, possibly, telephone Luke and Esther, both of whom lived out of state. But now, he decided, it might be more productive to talk first with the people who had found John Roberts. He looked in his clippings file and wrote down a name and an address.

Harry eased the Rover across the pothole-riddled sand and dirt yard and parking lot leading to Rob MacDougal's First Choice Body Shop. He parked in a small swirl of dust and crossed the dusty, sunbaked ground, looking without success for the rusted Malibu among the wrecked and wounded cars snapping and pinging in the growing heat of the sun.

A man built like a refrigerator trundled out of the open front of the garage, peering cheerfully at Harry from under the brim of his cap and scratching his bristling red beard.

"See anything out there you like?" he asked. "The name's Rob MacDougal. What's yours?"

"Harry Brock. You still got that Malibu you pulled out of the Luther Faubus Canal with John Roberts in it?"

"No. The sheriff's people hauled it off to the compound as evidence. Say, you know, if I could have kept that car and charged a buck to everybody wanting to see it, I could of retired a couple of years early. Anything else I can do for you?"

As he talked he wiped his hands on a tattered purple hand towel.

"Maybe. I'm a private investigator, and if you've got the time to spare, I'd like to talk to you about how you came to pull that car out of the canal."

"Let's go inside out of this sun. On the way, you can get out some ID."

MacDougal's office was a scarred desk surrounded by stacks of boxed parts and catalogues. The visible parts of the walls were plastered with old-fashioned girlie calendars.

"Sit down," MacDougal said. He waved at the pictures. "I been collecting these things for years. I've got some from the twenties. This here's only a few of what I got. I spend too much money and too much time messing with them. I swap, buy, and steal when everything else fails." He laughed happily and passed back Harry's ID. "What do you want to know about Bunny Roberts?"

"How well did you know him?" Harry was surprised that MacDougal knew the nickname. He had heard only Martha and Tucker use it.

"I've known him since he was a kid. I liked him. You know, he was pretty funny for someone playing with a short deck. And he noticed things you didn't expect him to. I'll miss him. I'm damned sure his sister will. They were really tight. You know her? Funny thing. She's the only one outside of Matthew not to put some distance between herself and that old bastard of a father. By God he was mean. I hear he blew a head gasket. You know anything about that?"

"Dementia of some kind, I guess."

"That's too bad, but, Christ, he was a pain."

"How did you come to know the Roberts?"

"Hell, I grew up out there on Panther Trace."

"Did you and John go to school together?"

MacDougal laughed and slapped his leg. "You couldn't really say Bunny went to school. He was there some of the time, but it didn't make no difference. He didn't larn anything, except to

63

draw. He could paint you a flower that looked so real you wanted to smell it."

"Matthew took him out of school."

"Yeah, he did." MacDougal shook his head and looked sad. "But it was probably the right thing to do."

Another surprise. "How did you happen to be the one to haul Roberts out of the canal?"

MacDougal kicked his chair back from his desk and clasped his hands behind his head. "Jefferson Toomey started it. A couple of his grandchildren were swimming in the canal, and they saw the car down there on the bottom. That got him thinking. Then he remembered about Bunny disappearing and called me."

"Did the kids see Roberts's skeleton in the front seat?"

MacDougal laughed. "Nope, the glass in the windows was all caked with slime and weeds. Some of it slid off the windshield while we was dragging it up. That's when Toomey shouted. But hell, I never saw it till that side window fell down inside the door."

"The paper said you guessed it was Roberts."

"That's right. That old Malibu looked familiar, and the minute I saw that Dolphins cap, I knew we'd found Bunny."

"Do you think he shot himself?"

MacDougal pulled his arms down and leaned toward Harry, grinning. "Never in a hundred years, Brock. Bunny was in love. His family didn't like it, but Bunny was planning to marry a black woman by the name of Theresa Allgood."

8

"Rob MacDougal said your brother John was getting married."

Her face blank, Martha Roberts stared at Harry for a moment and then turned her head away as if she couldn't bear seeing any more of whatever she was looking at. They were on the deck of the Blue Duck. It was Martha's choice. She had refused to let him pick her up at her office and had driven herself to the restaurant. When he said the food wouldn't be especially good, she said, "You're right, and no one I know will be there."

He had decided to let that ride and focus on MacDougal's news. It was clear Martha wasn't pleased with what she'd just heard, but when she faced him again, he saw that she was making an effort to overcome whatever was troubling her.

"That's vicious gossip," she said in an unsteady voice. "Rob MacDougal hasn't got a straight bone in his body and Bunny wasn't going to marry anyone. If he had been, I'd have known."

Still struggling with some strong emotion, she dropped her spoon into the conch chowder with a splash that she ignored.

"MacDougal seems pretty certain of himself. Do you know Theresa Allgood?"

"No. Look, I've got to go back to work. We can talk about this later."

With that she was on her feet and out of the restaurant. Harry let her go. He was more interested in talking to Theresa Allgood than trying in public to calm down a woman as upset as Martha Roberts. He went back to his chowder. He had been right. It wasn't very good.

Theresa Allgood lived in Perkins House at 10 Trap Street on the west side of Old Avola. People who needed temporary or permanent help living on their own eventually found Perkins House and were seldom turned away. Harry was greeted by the house director, Althea Watson. She was a tall, very dark, imposing woman with glasses that glinted dangerously in her office's slanting light. Harry should have done some homework because things got off to a bad start when he referred to Perkins House as a group home and asked if Theresa Allgood was retarded.

"Perkins House, Mr. Brock, is neither a group home nor a halfway house," Watson said stiffly. "We have no ex-convicts living here. Perkins House is an Integrated Community Living Arrangement. And another thing, we do not refer to Theresa or any of our other residents as retarded or mentally challenged. We refer to them as people. Speaking of their deficits, we say they are developmentally disabled. People first, Mr. Brock, then the disability."

Harry felt his ears burning as he struggled to fill the icy silence that followed her stern lesson in the social service's taxonomy of mental disability. He thought he had probably nailed shut the gate to Perkins House, but when Ms. Watson had heard him out, she said, "I knew John Roberts. If you will agree to my being present when you talk to her, and if Theresa is willing to talk to you, I'll arrange a meeting with her."

"I'd be very glad to have you present," Harry said. "Perhaps you might even be able to help me make the questioning as non-threatening as possible."

When Althea Watson called the next day, she told him they could meet at four-thirty. "That will give Theresa time to get home from the Fitzwaller Beachfront Hotel where she works," Watson told him sternly. "She is a very responsible person.

Among other things, she keeps the inventory of the hotel's linen. In fact, her composure may be a little misleading. Keep your questions short and very specific."

Theresa Allgood opened the door in response to Harry's ring.

"Please come in, Mr. Brock," she said.

She was short, with a smooth oval face and clear brown eyes, and wore her hair in a curly black cap. She closed the door behind him and they shook hands. Her small hand gripped his firmly, and she seemed to be counting silently as she moved her hand up and down three times and then turned away.

"This way, please." She led him down the wide corridor.

The house smelled of bread baking, and the oak floor was polished to a high shine. A young man with very round blue eyes and pale hair came hurrying down the stairs that rose from the corridor. "Hello, Theresa," he said loudly, coming to a stop near the bottom of the stairs. "Who is he?"

"This is Mr. Brock. He is my guest. Mr. Brock, this is Robert Bigby."

"Do you work at Theresa's hotel?"

"No, he doesn't, and don't shout, Robert. We're not deaf. Good-bye."

Althea Watson was waiting for them in what Harry took to be a mix of library and living room. There was no television in the room, but there were games and books in the book cases and magazines on the three tables arranged around the room. And the old-fashioned planters in front of the long windows were bright with petunias. A large green and cream Chinese wool rug covered the center of the large room. Watson led them to a corner still bright with the afternoon sun.

"Please sit down, Mr. Brock. Theresa." Watson gestured toward a chair facing Harry's and took a seat herself slightly out of the circle. "Please go ahead, Mr. Brock."

"Miss Allgood . . ."

"Please call me Theresa."

"And you call me Harry."

"You're older. I should call you Mr. Brock."

"That's fine. Theresa, did you know John Roberts?"

She was sitting very primly, her navy skirt pulled down over her knees, her hands folded in her lap. She had been looking at Harry, but now she dropped her gaze to her hands. "Yes," she said somewhat hesitantly.

"Were you and he close friends?"

Her head came up again, and to Harry's chagrin her eyes were full of tears.

"Bunny and I were going to get married," she said. Despite the tears, her voice was strong.

"Theresa, that may not be quite true." Watson's voice was not sympathetic.

"Yes it is, Ms. Watson. If Bunny hadn't died, we would have been married, even if nobody wanted us to."

"Who didn't want you to get married, Theresa?" Harry asked.

Watson stiffened. "That's none of your business, Mr. Brock."

"Ms. Watson didn't want us to marry. Neither did Bunny's family. They were being very mean to him."

Theresa's eyes brimmed again, but she kept her composure.

"Who is 'they'?"

Watson tried to cut her off and failed.

"His brother Matthew and his sister Martha. I guess his mother didn't want it either." Theresa continued to ignore Watson's protests.

"Are you sure Martha opposed her brother's marrying you?"

"Yes. She told Bunny not to marry me. She said it was wrong."

Harry was disappointed that Martha had opposed the marriage and both puzzled and angry that she had lied to him about John and Theresa.

"Do you know why, Theresa?" he asked.

Watson interrupted again. Her voice was hard. "This line of questioning has nothing to do with what you told me you wanted to discuss with Theresa, Mr. Brock. I'm not going to . . ."

"I'm going to tell him," Theresa countered.

Harry could see the response had surprised Watson and for the moment left her with nowhere to go.

"He's white and I'm black," Theresa said. "Ms. Watson thinks blacks and whites marrying is wrong. So did Martha and Bunny's older brothers, Matthew and Mark. His father was too sick to say. But we talked to Mr. Bosco about it, and he said if we loved each other it was all right."

Harry wondered what Mark Roberts's role was in all this and mentally added him to the list of people still to be seen, but he asked about Bosco. "Who is Mr. Bosco?"

"He's my minister at The Unitarian Universalist Congregation."

"Mr. Brock, it's not true that I opposed Theresa's marrying John Roberts on racial grounds," Watson said firmly. "There were other considerations."

Harry nodded but decided it was time to keep his mouth shut and listen.

"Bunny made a mistake. He didn't do step two," Theresa said, visibly upset by what Watson was saying.

"Step two?"

"It's part of their Check First program," Watson said. "Step One is think carefully and Step Two is ask your counselor. John was involved in a robbery. He did not choose his friends well."

Theresa was very agitated. She was trembling and her eyes had filled with tears again. "Bunny made a mistake," she said in loud voice. "But he didn't kill himself. Mr. Bosco said he didn't. He talked to Bunny just before . . ."

She couldn't go on.

"Thank you, Theresa," Harry said, getting to his feet. "I'm sure you're right about Bunny. I don't think he killed himself either."

"Misleading Theresa won't help her to deal with John Roberts's death," Watson said, jumping up and glaring at Harry.

"I'm not offering Theresa false comfort, Ms. Watson," Harry said firmly, looking at Theresa as he spoke. "Nothing I know about John Roberts has made me think he took his own life."

Harry went from Perkins House to Harvey Bosco's church, where he found Bosco on a ladder at the back of the white building putting white primer on a section of new clapboards.

"You have to have some pioneer blood in you to do this job," Bosco said cheerfully as he climbed down the ladder.

He was thin and quick moving and sported a shock of thick red hair.

"I'm taking a night course in plumbing," he told Harry, setting down his paint bucket and shaking Harry's hand, "mostly in self-defense." Northern Minnesota was all over his speech.

"How did you get way down here?" Harry asked.

"Running from the wolves," Bosco said. "I let the dog out one morning, and the next thing I knew it was playing at the edge of the woods with a young wolf. That did it, along with the winters. What about you?"

"I was just running. Could I talk with you about John Roberts?"

"Do I need to clean my brushes?"

"No. I won't keep you long. I'm looking into John Roberts's death for a client. I just talked with Theresa Allgood. What she told me and what Althea Watson said raised some questions I'm hoping you can answer."

"I'm going to be limited in my responses, Mr. Brock. I'm

Theresa's pastor and her counselor."

Harry nodded. "Were Theresa and John thinking about getting married?"

Bosco answered with a smile. "They had their hearts set on it, and I was all in favor. I think they would have been very good for one another."

"Theresa thinks John's family was opposed to the marriage on racial grounds."

"I'm not breaking any confidences to say his family was split on the issue. His sister Martha, who was pretty much John's gatekeeper, and Matthew, his oldest brother, and Mark, another brother, were strongly opposed to the marriage, but I don't think the issues were entirely racial. Mark's wife was very much in favor of John's marrying Theresa."

"Can you tell me what the issues were in addition to race?"

"Well, the Roberts family background is extremely conservative. Some of the children have moved farther away from their roots than others. But I think they all cling to at least some of their old, internalized values, many of which remain unchallenged."

Harry detected a darkening in Bosco's mood and an increased sharpness in his speech. "Do you think John shot himself?"

"No." The response was immediate and unqualified. "There were problems, but he and Theresa were very happy together. I think John was probably happier than he had ever been before in his adult life. Their loneliness, their sense of inadequacy, their fear of a world that was often confusing and threatening were all mitigated by the love they shared. For Theresa, the loss of Bunny has been terrible."

The minister's words brought the lives of the two people into sudden focus.

"Thank you, I guess," Harry said. "But I feel a little like the

Wedding-Guest."

Bosco grinned. "It's the first time anyone's called me the Ancient Mariner. It's a fraught situation and in some ways still is, but believe me, Mr. Brock. John Roberts did not commit suicide."

"Not even over the prospect of going to jail?"

"Absolutely not. They were prepared to deal with that possibility. In their own way, they were remarkably realistic and brave young people."

"Have you thought about where your conclusions lead?" Harry asked.

Bosco gave him an appraising look.

"Of course I have. He must have been murdered. I don't see how it's possible to come to any other conclusion."

"Neither do I," Harry replied, shaking his hand. "And if I can, I'm going to prove it."

9

Harry had intended to interview Theresa Allgood and return to talk again with Martha Roberts. But talking with Allgood had sent him to Harvey Bosco, and Bosco's comment about Rebecca Roberts's sympathetic support of Theresa and John's marriage plans sent him to her. Without actually facing the possibility, he may have been postponing confronting Martha. Thinking had only made him angrier over her lying to him.

Rebecca and Mark Roberts lived in North Avola in a white stucco house on Leeward Drive. A well-tended lawn of thick Bermuda grass surrounded the single-story house, and a silver Ford Explorer and a red Hyundai sedan filled their roofed parking space.

"Come in," Mark Roberts said. "We're sitting in the living room, enjoying a drink and listening to some old Beach Boys stuff. Either of them interest you?"

"I'd drink about anything cold without a stick in it. I haven't thought about the Beach Boys in a long time."

"Same with us. That's why we dug some out."

Roberts looked a lot like his brother Matthew, but his ready smile and quiet voice made Harry wonder whether it was nature or nurture that had made the difference. A slim woman in a navy skirt and a white blouse got up to meet him. Her cool gaze pleased Harry.

"I'm Rebecca," she said, shaking his hand. "We've wondered why it's taken you so long to find us. In fact, if it had taken you much longer, we were going looking for you."

"Should I be worried?" Harry asked. He liked her voice and her slightly sardonic smile.

"Perhaps. Just why have you taken so long to get here? Please sit down."

"I've just been talking with Reverend Bosco. He gave me a reason to get to you sooner rather than later."

"What reason?"

"Are you being grilled?" Mark said, returning from the kitchen.

"Yes."

"She's a teacher with most of her profession's bad habits. Did I hear you mention Harvey Bosco?"

Rebecca picked up her glass and answered for him. "Bosco's been talking to him."

"Then the cat's out of the bag," Mark said.

"Have you talked with Matthew?" she asked. Harry said he had. "You're going to find out, but I'll tell you so you can be prepared. Mark and I disagreed over John and Theresa's getting married."

Harry gave himself a moment. "I only found out today that John and Theresa Allgood were friends."

"They were more than friends. They were lovers. Does that trouble you?" Rebecca asked.

A test? Harry wondered. "I've learned recently that we're not supposed to refer to people like Theresa and John as mentally handicapped but as developmentally disabled. And I'm still trying to decide what, if anything, their marriage plans had to do with John's death."

Mark and Rebecca stared at him as if sitting for a portrait.

"What's your answer?" Rebecca asked, breaking a silence that had begun to echo.

"I haven't had time to form one. Martha says John didn't kill himself. Matthew says he did. So do the police, although less loudly. Harvey Bosco is certain he didn't. So is Theresa. I'm inclined to agree with the antis."

Mark nodded. "And the fact that John was planning to get married at the time he was killed makes it look as though Martha is right. But that doesn't mean he should have been marrying Theresa Allgood or anyone else."

"It's an old argument, Mr. Brock," Rebecca said sharply. "Like Matthew, Mark rejects interracial marriage and is disgusted by the thought of mentally—or developmentally handicapped—people having sex."

Harry had some trouble keeping his face straight. This woman had some edge.

"I think interracial marriages are difficult enough for those fully equipped to cope with the challenges," Mark countered. "Bunny was not so equipped. The idea of Bunny and Theresa bringing more mentally retarded individuals into the world did disgust me. Their having sex didn't."

"Retarded parents very frequently have normal children," Rebecca retorted, "but that argument's a red herring because Theresa said she did not want children. She was afraid she and Bunny might not be able to give them the kind of care and nurture they needed. Of course, she didn't use the word nurture, but it was what she meant."

"Then you don't think the conflict swirling around him and Theresa, added to his being implicated in that break-in at the Jiffy-Fix Automotive Supplies, might have proved too much for him?" Harry put in, fishing.

"Is that what you think?" Rebecca asked sharply.

"Your turn."

"I don't think two people could have been happier than Bunny and Reesie," she responded. "If John killed himself, I shouldn't be let back into a school room because it would prove

I didn't know the first thing about judging a person's state of mind."

"What do you teach?" Harry asked.

"History, one of the liberal arts, each of which conveys a distinct and essential perspective on the human experience. My conviction is that history is indispensable to knowing who we are. Do you have a problem with any of that?"

"Sorry," Mark said. "I should have warned you."

Rebecca didn't wait for Harry, who was enjoying himself, to answer. "Mark's the CFO for Bevel's Sand, Stone, and Gravel, which accounts for that unjustified air of superiority he wears like a stigmata."

"How do you see Martha fitting into all this?"

"Simple," Mark said. "She was the baby of the family and a spoiled brat. Growing up, she got her own way far too much. When John was found, and she didn't want to confront the fact he'd killed himself, she set out to change the world."

"By hiring me."

There was more of Matthew here than Harry wanted.

Mark opened his mouth but Rebecca responded first.

"It's not simple, Mark, and she's not spoiled. She's frightened. She's been frightened all her life."

"Of what?" Mark scoffed.

"Her father, Matthew, you, God, the sick world your parents put into her head. And she's frightened now. She thinks, and I believe with good reason, that Bunny was murdered. But she can't understand why. And when Rob MacDougal pulled him out of the Luther Faubus Canal, the world became a lot more frightening."

"Assume for a minute John didn't commit suicide. What then?" Harry demanded.

Rebecca gave a short, humorless laugh. "Then you're going

to earn your money. And I don't envy you your job."

Harry drove home wondering why Rebecca's closing comment had sounded so much like a warning. By the time he had showered and dressed, it was after six and he had worked through enough of the information his interviews had produced to come to some tentative conclusions. The one that troubled him most was that Martha Roberts had tried, by lying, to keep him ignorant of Theresa and John's wedding plans.

Next, it was clear the Roberts family was seriously fragmented. Except for Rebecca's probe about whether or not he was planning to go west to visit Luke and her defense of Martha and condemnation of Martha's parents, neither she nor Mark mentioned the rest of the family. The only time in his visit when Mark showed uneasiness was when Rebecca asked if Harry was going to see Luke. Finally, coming full circle, Harry still couldn't find any reason for thinking John Roberts had killed himself. Was it because he was missing something? And if not, why were Matthew and Mark so certain he had?

He was left in something of a muddle and did not like the feeling. There was nothing in John's life, aside from the robbery, that would provide anyone with a possible motive for murder. And, as far as he knew, John's role in the robbery had been so minor that it seemed unlikely anyone involved would have had a reason to kill him. As for his death being the result of a drunken or random attack, why would such an attacker have gone to all the risk and trouble of sinking him and his car in the Luther Faubus Canal?

The phone rang, and Harry answered it with relief.

"I'm hungry."

"All right, I'll pick you up in half an hour. How about Harborside?"

"Okay," Helen said in a flat voice.

"Or you could light the barbecue, and I'll pick up a road kill on the way in."

"Just get here," she said and hung up.

No snappy comeback?

Helen looked tired. He said so and got barked at, so he did not ask what was troubling her. But the white linen, the candlelight, the arrival of the wine, and his efforts at resuscitation gradually took the slump out of her shoulders.

"What's happening with the Roberts case?" she asked.

He was not fooled into thinking whatever was troubling her had gone away, but he knew it was too soon to ask about it. "I'm confused," he said. "I could use your advice."

"What's wrong?" she demanded, brightening slightly.

"Martha Roberts lied to me, and I don't know why," he said irritably.

She poured more wine. "Tell me."

He sketched his day for her and said in conclusion, "It's not possible she didn't know about Theresa and John's wedding plans, and lying to me about it makes no sense. She had to know I'd find out."

Helen looked out the window beside their table and seemed to lose herself in the flakes of orange and gold light flickering on the black water. But after a moment she caught herself and turned back to Harry.

"Rebecca's probably right. Martha's scared. We've done bird counts around Panther Trace. That's where she grew up. She lives in a trailer in Pecan Grove." She scowled at him. "So you should know you haven't been hired by Dianne Feinstein."

"She works for Arnell Property Management. She's been to college."

"Don't be misled by the diploma. In important ways she's probably still a little girl sitting beside her mother in a pew in that Bedrock Baptist Church. Say, wasn't it out by that church where we located those burrowing owls?"

"Yes. I did all the digging so we could count the chicks and you claimed them for your list."

She grinned.

"Well," he admitted, secretly admiring her reasoning, "you may be right. So far, they seem to be as different from one another as snowflakes."

"Maybe not. Maybe Martha isn't so much lying about Theresa and John's relationship as she is hiding from it. Both she and Matthew, and maybe Mark, seem to be fighting something where John's concerned."

"Possibly, but it's irrelevant. I'm not her shrink. She hired me to find out who killed John and why."

"I'm detecting some tunnel vision here, Brock. If you're trying to understand the dynamics of a family, even the cat box has significance."

The shrimp starter arrived, looking like a tiny green and orange island in a wide, white china sea.

"Nouvelle cuisine," Harry grumbled.

"The family has to be your starting point," Helen said, picking up her fork. "If you don't sort that out, I don't think you'll find out what happened to Martha's brother."

"Well, I'm reasonably sure Martha's right in saying John didn't commit suicide," Harry conceded. "But saying that only multiplies the difficulties. Aside from the robbery, there was nothing I know of in John's life that would provide anyone with a reason to kill him."

"What are the chances he just happened to be in the wrong place at the wrong time?"

"It's a possibility, but it's long odds. Mostly people are killed for a more specific reason."

Helen finished the shrimp and sat back. "That was better

than road kill," she said.

Sarcasm. Definite signs of life returning. Harry felt more cheerful.

The entrée was introduced with a modest fanfare of flashing covers, and conversation became desultory while they ate it.

"What's the 'Wall of Chocolate'?" she asked, when their plates had been cleared away and the dessert menus presented.

"More calories than Godzilla could cope with. And you know what it is."

She sighed. "I guess I'll have to settle for the *ile flottante* with the chocolate drizzle."

"We all have to make sacrifices." Harry passed the waiter his menu.

While they were driving home, Helen said, "Riga came to see me."

Harry took the hit fairly well, but there were more negatives in the news than he had anticipated. "How is she?" he asked, lashing himself to the mast.

"Beautiful as ever."

"Why is she here?"

"I'm not sure. She says she made a mistake moving to Tallahassee."

"Why?"

"She feels she abandoned me."

"Is that how you feel?"

The understanding friend role was not one he enjoyed.

She levered herself upright in the seat. "I don't know how I feel because I don't know what the situation is. Riga's not the world's best communicator about these things."

"What does she want?"

Helen bristled. "What could she want?"

"Of course, it couldn't be you."

It came out fast and nasty, and he despised himself for the

loss of control.

"Harry!"

"Okay. Has she come back for you, or is this a test drive?"

"Jesus, you never stop."

"That makes two of us."

10

On the way back from the restaurant, a chill settled over the Rover that was not due to the wind blowing through the rents in the canvas. Helen did not invite Harry to stay over, and Harry crossed the humpbacked bridge onto the Hammock without any improvement in his mood. In fact, he went to bed acutely aware of having let his jealousy of Riga Kraftmeier wreck the evening. When he finally forced himself into it, his bed seemed bigger and emptier than ever.

The next morning Harry made a peace of sorts with himself over Helen and decided to visit Tucker. But he had to wait to ask about Casanova because Bonnie and Clyde had raided the henhouse.

"It was a two-pronged attack," Tucker said, setting a plate of gingersnap cookies on the table. "Clyde began to tunnel under the fence, and Bonnie tackled the roof. Clyde did the digging because he's a little stronger than Bonnie, and she's a better climber."

"The roof has wire under the palm fronds, doesn't it?" Harry asked, postponing having to drink some of his tea.

Tucker nodded vigorously. He was obviously still worked up by the night raid. "That's right, and the bottom of the fence is buried a good two feet deep in the ground. But they'd been thinking about that roof because what Bonnie did was to drag off the palm fronds from the edge of the roof, get the edge of that chicken wire in her jaws, and start pulling it back so she

82

could burrow under it."

"I'm puzzled about how that fox could have clambered up onto the roof," Harry said, remembering she had done it once several years ago.

"Gray foxes can climb trees almost as well as a cat," Tucker said impatiently and then added, "That tea's going to go cold if you don't get started on it."

Harry held his breath and took a swallow.

"What happened up on the roof?" he asked, feeling the sweat break out along his sides.

"Well, she was pretty well into the coop when Oh, Brother! found them. He was making his rounds. Sanchez was on the back stoop asleep. He's not what he was, you know."

"What happened?" Despite himself Harry had gotten caught up in the story and did not want a sidebar on Sanchez's decline.

"Oh, Brother! routed Clyde," Tucker said with a laugh. "When he saw Bonnie up on the roof, he let out a bray that jumped me right out of bed and brought Sanchez roaring. I saw Bonnie go off the roof like a flying squirrel and land running. I never saw any living thing move faster."

"Bonnie and Clyde lost their suppers and the pullets get to grow up to lay eggs," Harry said with a laugh.

Tucker shook his head in a move toward seriousness. "We won a skirmish, nothing more."

"The war goes on?"

"That's it." Tucker brightened. "I've heard from Casanova. What we've got here is a consistent variant, maybe a subspecies, of the Florida Atala. How's that for a nice surprise?"

"Outstanding." Harry shook the old farmer's hand. "Is your name going to be on it?"

"I don't think that will happen for a while, if at all, and certainly not unless everyone agrees it really is a subspecies. The real question is how are we going to protect that colony of butterflies?"

"I guess you and I try to keep an eye on them until the state can take over."

"A lot will depend on whether or not the Covington estate sells off that land to Bevel's Sand, Stone, and Gravel. We'll wait and see. What's happening with your investigation?"

Harry recounted his most recent interviews and concluded by saying, "Despite Martha Roberts's comment that there wasn't much to know about her brother, I think he was more complicated than some of those around him were willing to admit."

"Are you saying he wasn't mentally defective?"

"Limited would be a better word, but his condition got him stereotyped. His mother said he was a sweet child who became difficult to manage. Martha thought of him as sweet and in need of care. Theresa, who loved him, thought of him as someone who had made a mistake. Althea Watson said he was a poor judge of people. Harvey Bosco, Theresa and John's minister, said he and Theresa were very brave. Rebecca Roberts told me she favored his marrying Theresa. Mark didn't. I know what Matthew thinks of him and that he doesn't want to talk about his brother, and he doesn't want the old story of John's involvement in the robbery brought up again."

Tucker reached for a gingersnap, pushed the plate toward Harry, and chuckled. "Sounds like that elephant the blind men went to see. Anybody you talked to a possible suspect in the boy's death?"

"Not that I can see, and I haven't heard anything that would make me think he was a suicide."

"Who are you going to talk to next?"

"Luke is the only one left."

"Oh, no," Tucker said. "You've forgotten Esther and Adam.

Of course, you can't talk to Adam because he's dead. Died in San Francisco in mysterious circumstances. I believe Luke and Esther are out west somewhere. One of them's in Arizona, I think."

"Martha didn't mention Esther or Adam," Harry complained, "and I forgot about them." The news made him careless, and he took a long pull at his tea and thought for a moment he was not going to breathe again.

"Doesn't surprise me. They both more or less disappeared after they left Avola."

"Do you know them at all?"

"Luke's married with a couple of kids. Esther kind of slid out of sight. There was some trouble there, but I don't know what it was."

Harry got to his feet. "I'm beginning to think I'm working from the wrong job description. Instead of, 'Find out why John Roberts died,' it should read, 'Write a book on the Roberts tribe.'"

Tucker walked Harry to the door. "They're a tribe all right. Just don't forget it."

It took Harry an hour or so of work online and the expenditure of a small amount of money to locate Esther and Luke. Esther was living in Phoenix at 3B, 13 Macey Street, in downtown Phoenix with someone named Angel Wing. Both women listed their occupations as artists. Luke was in Porterville, California, married, two children. His home address was 37 Sequoia Drive. For the past ten years he had been working for the Quality Real Estate Company, 76 East Olive Avenue.

Harry checked his watch and decided it was a little early to be calling that far west and decided it would be a good time to pay a visit to Bevel's Sand, Stone, and Gravel Company. John Roberts had worked for the company and somebody there might know something helpful.

"Keep turning over rocks," Harry told the gopher tortoise as he pulled it out from under the Rover where it was taking a shady break from its busy schedule.

The Bevel administrative offices were located in northeast Avola in the center of an enormous circle of devastation. Stripped to a huddle of squat, gray cement-block buildings, surrounded by mantis cranes, hills of gravel, rock, and sand, and crawled over by huge, lumbering, yellow earth movers rumbling on huge tires through clouds of dust of their own making, the place looked and sounded like the Tenth Circle of Hell.

The buildings moldered and the machines moved in a constant, bone-jarring roar emanating from the rock crushing towers. And from the towers poured a cloud of heavy, gray dust that fell back into the huge crater, slowly burying everything that could not move. Harry got out of the Rover in front of the personnel office and felt the earth shaking under his feet.

"Jesus," he said, partially in supplication, and walked quickly toward the door.

"You'll want to see Mr. Hawkins," the heavy woman behind her ancient desk said loudly and cheerfully, shoving a yellow #2 pencil into her piled-up black hair. "Grab a seat. I'll try to find him. You never know where anyone is around here."

The office waiting area was a space on the concrete floor to the left of the door with no files or pieces of twisted gray metal on it. There was a bare window in the concrete wall, looking out on a scene that would have made Dante tremble, and four wooden kitchen chairs so old their varnish had crazed and the bottoms of their legs were frayed like old toothbrushes from being dragged around over the cement. Harry sat down thinking hell's welcome wagon probably stood in a setting like this.

"I got him!" the woman shouted. She had to shout to make

herself heard over the incessant rumble that was shaking the floor. "He'll be right with you. There's coffee over there if you want it."

Harry waved and forced out a smile while shaking his head.

"Helps clear the dust out of your throat," she bellowed helpfully.

A big, rumpled man with no discernible neck and a bald head appeared beside Harry and said, "I'm Ralph Hawkins. Whatcha want?"

"To talk to you," Harry answered, levering himself erect.

"What about?"

"John Roberts."

"Come on."

Harry followed the broad back into a jungle of extra wheels, gears, packing cases, dust-covered five-drawer files and through a door into a room with a desk and two chairs, one behind the desk and one in front of it. Aside from the telephone on the desk, there was nothing in the room besides the four-foot shop light hanging from the ceiling.

"You sit. I'll make a call," Hawkins said.

Harry sat.

"It's Hawkins," he said. "Lemme speak to him." He put a beefy hand over the phone. "What's your name?"

Harry told him.

"Brock is here asking about John Roberts." He listened. "Okay."

The phone crashed into its cradle. "What do you need?" Hawkins demanded.

"Did you know John Roberts?"

Hawkins nodded. He had rested his forearms on the desk and laced his fingers in what Harry considered a very unaggressive gesture. Harry relaxed a little. "Did you hire him?" Another nod. "What kind of job did he have?"

"Tally keeper." Harry shook his head. "He kept a record of the loads of whatever the drivers delivered to the storage sites, the crusher, wherever we put him."

"And he worked for you right up to when he disappeared?"

Hawkins nodded.

"Was that Mark Roberts you called?"

"You got a problem with that?"

"No. Just curious." Hawkins sat like one of his rocks. "Was John a good worker?"

"He kept his tallies. He came to work every day."

"For how long?"

"About fifteen years."

"Did he have any serious problems with anybody?"

Hawkins shook his head.

"Do you think he killed himself?"

Hawkins shrugged.

"Care to elaborate?"

"He seemed happy enough. He was kind of a funny guy, considering."

"What?"

"His handicap."

"What kind of funny?"

"He liked to make jokes. Some of them were silly, but sometimes what he said let you know he saw more than you expected. Truth is, I kind of liked Bunny. I was sorry to lose him. It ain't everybody who can keep a tally book for fifteen years."

"Can you think of any reason anybody would have wanted to kill him?"

Hawkins shook his head. "Don't make sense to me. But, then, Bunny's killing himself don't make no sense neither."

"Did you know he was thinking of getting married?"

"Yeah."

"Did you know the girl?"

"I heard about her."

"And?"

"She was black. He was white. Both of 'em were dummies. What more do you need to know?"

11

With Jim Snyder's help Harry got the names of the three men who, along with John Roberts, had burglarized Jiffy-Fix Automotive Supplies. They were all guests of the state at the Everglades Correctional Institution in Miami. Harry got an early start and crossed Alligator Alley with the sun in his face, the Rover's driver's-side visor having been shredded the night Gideon Stone shot out Harry's windshield instead of blowing his head off, which had been the original plan.

Harry talked with Doby Schwartz first, a tall, gangling man with a turned eye and an ear that looked as if it had been bitten half off. With his neatly pressed uniform and cheerful smile, Schwartz looked, aside from his ear, more like a washing-machine repair man than a convict.

"I ain't thought of Bunny Roberts for a helluva long time," he said in a pleased voice. "I believe I heard something about his body being hauled out of the Luther Faubus Canal. That true?"

Harry told him it was. "You know any reason why anybody would have wanted to kill him?"

"Shit, no. Bunny never done nothing to make nobody mad at him, lessen you happened to be in a hurry while he was count-ing his change." Schwartz leaned back his head and laughed a wide, open-mouthed laugh and slapped his leg. When he had recovered his composure, Schwartz ran a big hand over his face and said, "When things got too slow, somebody would always reach into a pocket, haul out a handful of change and say, 'Hey, Bunny, count this for me.' It was always real funny."

Harry knew he shouldn't, but he asked why.

"Well, shit, he never could do it because, after he'd been at it for a while, one of us would ask him for a match, and by the time he'd found his matches and struck one, he'd have forgotten where he was and would have to start over." Schwartz leaned forward and looked at Harry with an expression of serious concern. " 'Course, you couldn't do that more'n once in an evening or Bunny would catch on and get mad. He was smarter'n most people figured. Sometimes, what he noticed would surprise you."

Hawkins, Harry recalled, had said the same thing about him.

"Do you think he might have shot himself?"

"Shit, no. He was too good-natured. 'Course, he would get mad over the change thing."

"Are you still here for the Jiffy-Fix business?" Harry asked, curious.

"There was another misunderstanding," Schwartz said without obvious rancor and scratched his head as if puzzled by life's complexities. "I h'aint quite got the knack of keeping out of jail. But, shit, there's worse places to be. You take what happened to Bunny. I hope you catch whoever done it to him. There ain't no way he deserved it."

Harry thanked Schwartz for his time and stayed on to talk separately with each of the other two men. They were not nearly as talkative or friendly as Schwartz, but they more or less repeated Schwartz's statement that they couldn't imagine anyone wanting to kill Bunny. Their similarity to the jocular Schwartz ended there, however, and Easy Blue's clenched fists and flat snake's eyes made Harry glad there was a solid barrier separating him from the convict. He wasn't sure Blue would need a reason to kill someone.

Driving back across the Alley, keeping himself awake by counting alligators in the canals and watching the black vulture cleanup crews disposing of road kills, Harry felt more strongly than ever that the sheriff's department was wildly off the mark in calling John Roberts's death a suicide. Aside from the possibility that the three jailbirds had been lying through their teeth, Harry was also at a loss to explain Roberts's death as murder. Where was the motive? Who could have wanted to kill him?

The next afternoon Harry parked the Rover under a Canary Island palm in the Fiddler's Pass parking lot and said, "We're here."

"Where is here?" Martha demanded with a scowl as she opened her door.

"Fiddler's Pass."

"Why did you bring me all the way out here?" she asked forcefully as they walked toward the beach.

Harry wasn't sure he wanted to tell her. He had set out to get her thinking a little outside of her box.

She was dressed in shorts, sandals, and an orange top that Harry thought made her look more like a kid than a salaried employee in a large and respected Avola property management firm. That thought was followed by another. Sarah was completing an MBA and working part-time for Rainy Lakes, a Milwaukee publishing firm. Paying for her education, he thought, was one thing he'd done right, but it had not, as he had hoped, brought them any closer together. As for Clive . . . He pushed that thought away. Boy and man, he had been as rigid as his mother.

"Do you like dolphins?" he asked, steering them toward a boardwalk on their left.

"I guess I'm supposed to, but I really haven't thought about it."

"If we're lucky, we'll see some out here."

She looked up at a glittering web that spread across the walk a couple of feet over their heads. "Are we going to get bitten by spiders?" she demanded uneasily.

"No. That's a golden orb spider's web. As big as she is, she can't eat you, so she's not interested in you."

"Oh, that's a big help, Harry. I feel a lot better now. Have you got any more good news?"

"Sure." As they walked, he plucked a thick shiny leaf from a branch of wax myrtle hanging over the boardwalk and passed it to her. "Smell it."

"So?"

"Is it familiar?"

"I guess, a little."

"Bayberry?" he suggested.

"Okay. Hey, you're right."

"The berries ripen later in the season. They're used to make bayberry candles."

"Do you charge extra for the nature notes?" she asked with a laugh.

He was glad to hear her laugh. He suspected there weren't many laughs in her days.

They stepped squinting out of the shadows of the shrubbery onto a foot bridge that spanned a fifty-foot-wide channel of churning green water, pushing inland from the Gulf. The late afternoon sun drenched the bridge and the white sand, darkening the green water with its buttery light.

"Is this thing safe?" Martha asked, coming to a full stop.

"Absolutely. Come on." He grasped her hand and led her out to the center of the bridge. Then he stopped and waved his arm at the surrounding scene. "How do you like it?"

"It's beautiful," she said a little hesitantly.

"It belongs to you," he said.

"Are you crazy, Harry?"

"No, Martha. It belongs to you. This is a state park."

She looked doubtfully at the line of roofs of palatial beach-front houses thrusting above the trees a quarter of mile to the north of the bridge. Then she looked down at the water just as a bottle-nosed dolphin exploded from the tidal race with a foot-long black mullet in its mouth and came entirely out of the water in a shimmering leap before crashing back with a resounding splash.

"Harry!" she yelled, "did you see . . ." But she didn't finish. A second and then a third dolphin, chasing the second, shot out of the water, each holding a fish. The second, a big male, threw his fish into the air and caught it again as he plunged back into the waves. The animal behind him turned a cartwheel and knifed effortlessly into the tumbling race.

"What are they eating?" Martha shouted.

"Black mullet. They come in on the tide to feed in the river. The dolphins chase them and have some fun while they're getting a meal."

A few minutes later the show ended and the pod fled away like shining gray arrows.

"Wow," Martha said when they were gone. She was beaming.

"They play a lot," Harry said, pleased with her reaction. It was the first time he had seen her express either enthusiasm or joy, and he felt like a conjurer.

"Hey, how come I've never been out here before?"

"Will you come back?" Harry asked.

She stopped smiling. "Probably not."

"Doing things like this takes a little effort," he said.

"I suppose it does."

"Why did you lie to me about your brother and Theresa Allgood?" he asked.

Martha was leaning on the top rail, staring down at the water. "Because . . ." she began strongly enough and then stopped.

"Keep going."

"You had no right," she said angrily, pushing herself erect and turning toward him, eyes snapping.

Harry ignored her challenge. "John's minister was in favor of their marrying. Rebecca supported the plan. Mark didn't. He doubts they could have coped with the strains of a mixed-race marriage, and he would still oppose the marriage because of the risk of their having mentally handicapped children. Rebecca disagrees on both counts and says Theresa had no intention of having children."

"Bunny . . ."

"I know. He was going to jail. But Reverend Bosco told me John and Theresa had factored that into their plans."

"Was bringing me out here to see the dolphins supposed to open my mind to new ideas?"

"I wish I'd thought of that. Actually, I wanted to get you far enough away from town to keep you from running away again."

"Is that what you think I was doing?"

"You tell me."

"Why are you poking around in my family, Harry?"

"You hired me to find out who killed your brother. Is that right?"

"Yes, and I don't—"

"—see how my digging into painful family secrets is going to help me find John's killer? Is that it?"

"Exactly."

"Wrong. But when I've answered that question, you may want to fire me. If you do, okay. But I hope you won't. Still, it's your nickel. Shall I go on?"

She struggled with something for a moment and then said, "I

guess you'd better."

Three people came onto the bridge at its north end and were walking toward them, talking and laughing as they came.

"Can we go back?" she asked.

By the time they stepped off the bridge, Harry had his thoughts arranged and he began talking but not without some trepidation. It was quite possible she would fire him, and he didn't want that to happen.

"The trinity of detection in most murders is means, motive, and opportunity," he said. "If your suspect has all three, there's a very good chance you've found the killer."

He paused to see if she was with him and was relieved to see that she was more interested than angry.

"Are you saying you haven't found anyone who qualifies in all three categories?"

"Not quite. In this case, means and opportunity hardly matter. So far, I haven't found anyone with a credible motive for killing John."

"If you're saying I should give up, I'm not going to."

Her voice was rising again.

"Fine, but if you don't, you may find what comes next very painful." He pulled open the door on the Rover, and she clambered onto the seat.

"I'm listening."

Harry left his door open to catch the breeze off the Gulf. "Up to now, I've been looking outside your family for a cause for John's death."

She had been sitting very quietly, listening intently, her face pale with a strain that told Harry how difficult this kind of conversation was for her.

"Where does my pain come in?"

"Given the way in which your brother was killed and the way in which the crime was hidden, I have to conclude it was carefully planned, almost a professional job. But so far, I haven't found a compelling reason for anyone to kill him."

"Someone did," she insisted.

"I agree. But right now I don't know enough about John. To find out more, I've got to ask a lot of questions of the only people who can answer them."

"Who?" she asked suspiciously.

"I'm going to shift the focus of the investigation to your family. Do you want to go through the discomfort it may cause?"

"Are you suggesting one of us killed Bunny?" she demanded, her pallor increasing.

To lessen the impact of what he was telling her, he lied a little. "Not necessarily."

"Then what . . ."

He moved away from the question of who might have killed John. "Who is Adam?"

Her eyes narrowed. "He's my brother." She hesitated. "Was my brother."

"Why didn't you tell me?"

"He doesn't have anything to do with Bunny's death."

"Who is Esther and who is Angel Wing?"

"Esther is my sister."

"And Angel Wing?"

"It's none of your business." She had turned away from Harry to stare out the side window. Her back was rigid.

"Maybe not, but a friend of mine said that in figuring out family dynamics, 'even the cat box has significance.' "

She swung around on the seat, her eyes wet with tears. "Only a damned Yankee would think of anything so foolish," she said, giving way to a brief laugh. Then her anguish returned. "You have no idea how hard it will be for me to do what you're asking, Harry," she said, bowing her head. Her voice was little more than a whisper.

He was shocked by the stress in her voice. "Maybe you shouldn't try."

She lifted her chin and fought back the tears. "I started this, and I'm going to finish it," she said with growing conviction. "What exactly do you want to know about the Robertses' cat box?"

12

The following morning, Helen called Harry. "Have I lost out to an indigo snake?" she demanded.

Harry had been writing up his notes on his prison visit and the long and sometimes painful conversation he had with Martha Roberts. For a moment Helen's question made no sense. Then the light came on. "Who are you?"

"Hillary Clinton. Who the hell did you think would be calling you at this time in the morning?"

"It could have been Hollywood."

"You're an idiot. Do you remember telling me that Tucker had located some rare butterflies or something like that on a piece of land belonging to the Lucy Mott Covington estate?"

"Yes."

"You did not hear this from me, but the Three Rivers mortgage department and reps from Bevel's Sand, Stone, and Gravel are down here, walking stiff legged around one another. I'm hearing that Bevel wants to buy that entire section along County Road 19 and is looking for backing."

Harry groaned. "That's why Bevel has opened what looks like the beginnings of a road just about across from the Hammock," he said. "Tucker's worried. The road's right on the edge of the butterflies' breeding area."

"My guess is that part of the Covington estate will never go on the block. If the bank comes in, and it looks as if it will, Bevel is going to buy it direct from the estate."

"Fred Casanova from the State Conservation Commission is saying that if the butterflies are a genuine subspecies, the state could step in to prevent any development of the land. That would be about thirty square acres, possibly more."

"Whoever's making the decision had better move fast. This thing is beginning to look like a bullet train." Helen went quiet for moment. Then she said in a much more subdued voice, "Want to risk my cooking tonight?"

"It works for me."

"Come over about six," she said and hung up.

Harry swore and asked the anole lizard climbing up the screen on the kitchen window, What would it have cost to say thank you for the invitation?

Neither of them smoked, so they pretty much had to talk.

"You look like that dead poet in the painting," Helen said, staring down at him as she pulled on her robe. "Or would, if you were twenty-five years younger."

The Death of Chatterton," he replied, "and not even then."

She fell back onto the bed and rolled against him, dropping an arm across his chest. "Are you okay about us?" she asked.

"I don't know what 'us' is. Do you?"

She pulled herself closer to him and pressed her face against his. "I was beginning to think I did."

"Until Riga showed up."

"Yes."

Harry kissed her, got his arms around her, and said, "Tell me what you're feeling and don't censor the report." He sounded a lot jollier than he was feeling.

"Kiss me again." He did. Riga's return had left him feeling like a squeezed lemon. "I'd like to stay right here with you and never get up," she said quietly.

Harry waited for the "but," and it came.

"But we can't do that. Tomorrow morning we'll get out of this bed. You'll still be in love with Katherine, and I . . ."

"Will still be in love with Riga," he said, struggling to keep the anger out of his voice. He had no right to be angry and he didn't want to be angry. He forced himself to go on. "Only I'm not in love with Katherine and haven't been for a long time. I still love her, but that's different."

"We both got left," Helen said.

"Katherine started leaving as soon as Thornton was conceived."

"Why?"

"She could never believe her father, Willard Trachey, and I were not the same person, an unreliable male."

"I'm sorry, Harry."

"So am I, but you and Riga currently have the spotlight. What are you going to do to entertain the crowd?"

"That's cruel."

"Yes. I'm sorry. Possibly it's none of my business, but what have you got in mind where Riga's concerned?"

A chill had entered the room. Helen grew very still in his arms. "I don't know, Harry."

"Are you still in love with her?"

She pushed herself out of his arms and onto her knees and leaned over him, one hand on each side of his shoulders. Her hair fell heavily around her face, and Harry could smell its warm fragrance.

"Why don't we forget everything else and just get married?" she asked him.

"Are you in love with Riga?"

It would have been easier and possibly more sensible to pull her against him and hang on until the sun rose. But some perversity or nascent masochism kept him marching.

"I don't know," she replied.

"Then how smart would it be for us to get married?"

She collapsed beside him and said, "Congratulations, Harry. You just won."

The bitterness that flooded him in the ensuing silence tasted more like defeat.

Driving home the next morning, Harry wondered what his answer would have been if Helen had said, "No, I'm not in love with Riga."

Instead of an answer, he got a question: Would you have said you love her?

He shrugged in the silence and drove faster.

There was more activity on the Covington property. Wetherell Clampett was putting out orange traffic cones along the road. A large, yellow dump truck was parked in the cleared area off the road. Harry slowed and stopped.

"What's going on, Wetherell?"

Clampett set down the stack of cones he was carrying and wiped his forehead with a hairy forearm. "Lord, I don't know. They sent me out here this morning with a load of gravel and a stack of these cones. You'd tell your dog more about your plans than what they tell me."

"Looks like they might be going to lay down a road in there with gravel for the wet spots."

"Well, if that's so, they're going to need a bulldozer, and they surely didn't say nothing to me about that."

"You heard any more about Bevel's Sand, Stone, and Gravel buying this place?"

Clampett's face lost its look of offended dignity, and Harry saw that he had said the magic word.

"Well, yes. It's a funny thing," Clampett replied, resting a thick arm on the window frame. "There's something about that in the wind. But the story that's growed the longest legs says that there's some butterflies or something in there the state might have an interest in. Sounds too foolish to mean anything."

"Could that be why you're here?"

"Somebody's getting awful anxious to do something, but I'm damned if I know what it is."

Harry let it go as if the subject had no particular interest for him, and the conversation wandered on for a while. Then he shook Clampett's hand and drove away.

"I think Bevel may be trying to preempt the state," Harry said.

They were in the Tucker's citrus orchard, and Tucker was trying to teach Harry how to use a scythe. Harry had insisted on helping Tucker mow the grass, and it was only after he'd stabbed one of the lemon trees that he agreed to be shown how to do it. It was hot work, and Harry's shirt was plastered to his back. It irritated him to no end that Tucker still looked as cool and dry as when they had started.

"You make it harder than it has to be," Tucker told him gently, taking the scythe into his own hands. "Just let the scythe's weight do the work. Draw back and let it swing through its arc." He swept the heft across the front of his body. The blade slipped through the hay with a soft singing sound as the grass fell smoothly behind the blade. "If the blade's sharp, and this one is, it will cut the grass without effort." He cut another swath. "Of course, I've had some practice."

Harry laughed. "When did you begin?"

"I think I was about eight. Here, try again."

Harry gripped the handles and started his swing, saw Oh, Brother! watching him from a safe distance, munching on the newly mown hay, and thought he saw the mule shake his head.

It's the flies, Harry thought and began again. Just then Sanchez, who had claimed a shady patch of cut hay to have a nap, sneezed loudly.

103

"Those two are laughing at me," Harry said.

"Ignore them," Tucker told him. "Now, you think they've got wind of the butterflies?"

"Yes," Harry said. "Wetherell doesn't know what's going on, but I'm guessing it has to do with the butterflies. Can you get in touch with Casanova?"

"I can call him."

Harry straightened up, breathing heavily. His face was glistening with sweat. "You'd better do it," he said.

The place where he had tried to cut the hay looked as if two tomcats had been fighting in it.

"Let me hang that scythe up here while we go in and have some cider. It's just the thing for haying. While we're in there, I'll call Casanova."

Harry sent up a silent prayer of thanks.

A breeze was blowing through the kitchen, billowing the gingham curtains, and to Harry, sitting slumped over his cider at the table, waiting for Tucker to finish his call, it felt like the balm of Gilead.

"Casanova was concerned, but he didn't think there was much he could do. He said he would try to persuade the supervisor to request a temporary restraining order to stop any further disturbance of the site, but without a final agreement that this is a subspecies, he doesn't think the department can act."

Harry struggled to his feet, feeling pain in every muscle. God, was he that badly out of shape? Tucker watched with a critical eye.

"I think it's a lot like snowshoeing," he said blandly.

"It's not anything like snowshoeing," Harry grated. "I can snowshoe all day. At least I could before the onset of premature old age."

"Let me get you some Tuttle's horse liniment. Oh, Brother!

and I swear by it." He started to get up but Harry stopped him.

"No thanks," he said, gripping the back of the chair to steady himself. "By the way, how hard is that cider? I'm seeing a couple of screen doors here."

"I put it down last October, so it's had time to find its feet."

"God help me," Harry said.

13

Harry went home, took a hot shower, then a cold one, and felt marginally better; at least he was no longer seeing double. He made himself some coffee and got out his file on John Roberts and reread the section on his most recent talk with Martha.

Reading it was almost as painful as taking part in it had been. At the age of thirty-four, Adam Roberts had died of AIDS in San Francisco, and Esther was the only family member who had gone to see him during his illness. She had been with him when he died. Martha had said she wanted to go, but her father and Matthew had forbidden it, telling her that if she went, no one in the family would ever speak to her again.

"And the rest of the family?" Harry had asked.

That had been seven years ago, she told him, before her father had begun his slow descent into Alzheimer's. Esther was already an outcast, for reasons Martha did not then understand, and she never knew why Luke had left Avola. No, she didn't know why Luke, who was also living in California, hadn't gone to see his dying brother.

"Sometimes, I'm sorry I didn't go," she had said and then added what sounded to Harry like an old excuse. "He was a lot older than me, and I don't remember much about him. By the time I was finished grade school he was gone." She checked herself. Her face hardened. "Leaving was Adam's choice," she said harshly. "He knew how Ma and Pa felt . . . how all of us felt. He knew what he was doing was wrong. He had to know.

That's why he went away."

"Was he taking drugs?" Harry asked, fighting off the temptation to blame her for the way the family had treated him.

"I don't know."

"Why did he leave home?"

"He . . . wasn't . . . normal."

"He was gay."

"Yes." She turned her head away and answered as if the word had been twisted out of her.

"You're an adult with a profession. You're educated." He stopped himself.

"Does that mean I should forget everything my family believes, what our people believe, what God wants us to do?"

"What does Esther think?" He knew he was being cruel.

"I don't talk to Esther. I asked you."

"It's not for me to answer."

That response, he knew, was as feeble as her reasoning. He had, in fact, already answered her question and not the way she would have liked.

"I just wish somebody would understand," she said.

"I understand more than I did," he said gently.

Harry leaned back in his chair and wondered now as he had then just how much he did understand the Roberts family. He dismissed, as oversimplifying, the old saw that in the face of ignorance even the gods fail. But he couldn't and didn't particularly want to free himself from the conviction that to some extent Martha was being deliberately obtuse. Saying that left unanswered how her belief system was coloring her judgment about John's death.

Dispirited by his thoughts, he watched Lady Godiva, the female red-shouldered hawk, pursue a black rat snake that had fled across the lawn into the coffee bushes like a length of black lightning. Repeatedly, she plunged without success into the tangle of leaves and branches, beat her way back into the air, and, screaming in frustration, dove again. At last, losing interest, she flew away. Harry wondered if, like her, he had embarked on a hopeless task.

He glanced at his watch, then went into the kitchen and made a call.

"This is Heather," a girl's voice said with a hint of the South in it.

"Do I have the right number for Esther Roberts?"

"She's one of my mothers," the girl replied.

"One?" Harry asked.

"Yes, I have two mothers," the girl answered patiently.

Harry heard an older voice. Heather said, "Some man wants to talk to Esther."

"This is Angel Wing. Who's calling?"

Harry wasn't sure, but her accent sounded like west Texas. It was a good voice, open and rich and full of music. He immediately liked Angel Wing.

Harry told her his name, that he was working for Martha Roberts, and that he was looking into John Roberts's death. Then he asked if he could speak to Esther Roberts.

"Why?" Wing asked, her voice no longer full of Texas sunshine.

"I'm not sure. I'm trying to talk with all the members of the family still living, looking for help. So far, nothing about John Roberts's death makes sense."

He apparently had said the right thing.

"Hang on. I'm not sure she'll talk to you, but I'll ask."

A different voice, flatter and harder, said, "So you're working for Martha."

"That's right." Harry took a chance. "Do you talk with her much?"

"No. I take it you don't think my brother killed himself."

Harry took the hint. "No. I can't find anyone other than Matthew, Mark, and the police who do. Of course, they could be right. I don't know if you know it, but your brother was being charged in a burglary and almost certainly would have gone to jail for a while."

"I hear from Rebecca—that's Mark's wife—often enough to stay in some sort of touch, although God knows why I bother."

Harry thought the qualifier lacked conviction. "Are you and Luke in touch with one another?"

"No. Have you figured out why?"

"There's no place for your sexual orientation in the Bedrock Baptist community?"

She laughed bitterly. "That's a bland way of saying it. Try this: Women shall defer to their husbands, and if they don't have a husband and stop obeying their fathers and their brothers, it would be best to kill them. But barred from doing that, put them where they can't be heard. Excommunicate them from the community of souls moving toward patriarchal heaven."

"That's a little more specific."

Esther laughed and Harry gave himself three points. "Will you talk with me about John?"

"I don't know much about Bunny, except that he was a sweet kid with a significant mental disability that my parents and siblings mostly refused to acknowledge or name. To Ma, he was a problem child. To Pa, a lazy good-for-nothing who needed a lot of knocking around."

"Did you know that at the time he died John was planning to get married?"

"Rebecca told me. I regret now I didn't call him to tell him how happy I was for him. But I didn't want to get him into any more trouble with Matthew than he was already in."

"Do you know who, if anyone, might have wanted him dead?"

She paused. When she spoke, she sounded weary. "Matthew for one. It's a terrible thing to say, and I never talked to him about Bunny. But after our father's mind began to go, Rebecca told me that Matthew refused to admit anything was wrong. When he couldn't deny it any longer, he began to act more and more as if he was James. He became obsessed about keeping everything just as it had been, tried to run everyone's life. Rebecca said his anger with Bunny became increasingly irrational, and then expanded to include Theresa and Rebecca and anyone else who supported their plans."

"You said, 'Matthew for one.' Who else do you think might have done it?"

"Just as terrible to say, my father. As I said, his mind was going, but nothing was being done about it. My mother was too afraid of him to say anything. Everybody else was waiting for Matthew, and Matthew was chin-deep in denial."

"Mark objected to the marriage, and so, I think, did Martha."

Esther made a dismissive sound. "Five years ago Martha was still under her parents' and Matthew's thumbs. Mark and probably Luke, although you'd have to ask him, objected on the grounds that Bunny was mentally handicapped. So is Theresa, as you must know. I suspect, also, that they objected because she's black. 'Sons of Ham' includes the daughters."

"Mark told me he thought interracial marriages had so many problems in this society that John and Theresa would not have had the skills to deal with the challenges."

"Maybe he's right, but the decision wasn't his to make. Bunny and Theresa were getting help and advice."

"Harvey Bosco."

"Yes."

"And you really think your brother and/or your father might have killed John?"

"Might have? Yes. Did they? God, Brock, I don't know. You'll have to figure that one out yourself."

Harry put down the phone and began processing what Esther had told him. Matthew and James murderers? Was it possible? Well, where people are concerned, most things are possible. But how likely was it? For that matter, was Esther Roberts an angry woman paying off an old score against the father and the brother who hurt her? Reluctantly, he admitted he didn't know enough even to guess, but he would certainly remember his talk with Esther and would look forward to talking with her again.

Restless and dissatisfied with himself and with the conversation he had just had, he walked out onto his lanai. Beyond the road, Puc Puggy Creek shimmered in the sun. Locusts were trilling in the oaks, and the breeze brought him the sweet, rich smell of hot earth and growing things. But the Hammock's midday peace did nothing to assuage his discontent.

Esther's suggestion that Matthew and James Roberts might have murdered Bunny may have been speculation. But to his disgust he couldn't dismiss it.

"Who owned the gun?" he asked the female cardinal, who was taking a rest from sitting on her eggs and looking for grubs in the wisteria vine on the south end of the lanai. He had almost forgotten about the gun.

Snapping up a caterpillar, she peered at him through the screen as if pondering the question and then flew off without answering.

"No time for anything but food and children."

He went back into the house and called Jim Snyder. "Anything yet from the lab on the gun that killed John Roberts?"

"The gun and slug match," Snyder said. "The case was still in the cylinder."

"Anybody get a serial number off the gun?"

"Sure, and that surprised me because the thing was a ball of rust when I saw it."

"Have you run the number?"

"Not my job. I don't know who did, if anybody."

"Can you find out?"

"Harry, do you know how swamped we are? And as a taxpaying citizen, why would you want us to waste our time?"

"Aren't you curious about where the weapon came from?"

"Why should we be? It's a four-year-old suicide, Harry. We have moved on."

"Who's got the gun?"

"My guess is it's gone to 10-30."

"The Evidence Section."

"Matthew's bailiwick."

"How do I get the serial number?"

"You could try Matthew."

Snyder was still chuckling when he hung up.

Harry thought he might call Helen, but checked his watch and decided she was still having lunch. He told himself he should write up his conversations with Esther and Jim, but his mind recoiled from the idea. Then he thought of the butterflies and, whistling with relief, grabbed his hat and went out to the Rover. He would find out what was going on with the Atalas.

The cleared area off the county road was deserted. Harry parked the Rover and walked into the woods. The sun beating almost straight down on the bulldozed ground was hot enough to make Harry blow out his breath with relief when he gained the shade of the pines.

He pulled off his hat and paused to look around and listen. Cicadas were trilling in the tops of the trees, their fiddling rising and falling with the rhythm of slow waves falling on a beach.

From deep in the trees a flicker gave a single, harsh cry and fell silent. He could see no movement in the grove. The silence was so complete the genius of the place might have been holding its breath in expectation of some immense event.

Harry stood motionless, caught in the spell. Then, with an effort, he broke free and began retracing the path he had walked with Tucker and Casanova. He walked quickly and quietly to the place where that had seen the butterflies. When he reached the first coontie plants, he paused and soon picked out the dark-winged butterflies flickering in and out of the shafts of sunlight pouring through the canopy. Dropping onto his heels beside a coontie plant, he watched a small colony of orange Atala grubs feeding on the succulent foliage.

He looked up and for a few moments watched the silent, dancing flight of the butterflies. Wakening again to his own affairs, he stood up and walked slowly back to the clearing.

He had seen nothing to suggest that Bevel's people had disturbed the area, but when he stepped into the clearing, Harry saw a silver Chevy Caprice parked across the entrance to the parking area. A man holding a cell phone to his ear was behind the wheel. Before Harry reached the Rover, the man pulled back into the road and drove away in the direction of the Hammock.

Harry, pleased he could take Tucker some good news, turned the Rover back toward the Hammock. He heard behind him the roar of an approaching truck but was not alarmed. Big trucks thundered along County Road 19 all day long. It was a shortcut to half a dozen construction sites between the county's two major highways.

Harry had just begun thinking again about ways he might get the serial number off that revolver without having to talk with Matthew Roberts when the racket of the rapidly gaining truck claimed his attention. Harry edged toward the shoulder, giving the driver plenty of room to pass.

The hurtling vehicle pulled a yard to the left, increased its speed, and smashed into the Rover just behind the left rear wheel. Harry's last impressions were of horrendous noise and being yanked violently skyward. The truck hurtled past, flinging the Rover end over end into the swamp.

14

Harry found he had no particular interest in the room into which he had wakened or the quietly spoken people who loomed over him from time to time. Feeling oddly detached from these meaningless objects thrown on the screen of his consciousness, he closed his eyes and slid away into darkness again.

"Mr. Brock. Mr. Brock. Wake up."

Harry swam slowly upward toward the light like an old bass rising to a fly. And when he broke the surface, he found he had more than a hook in his jaw. He had harpoons in every limb.

"I'm Dr. Thompson. You're a lucky man, Mr. Brock," the doctor said, beaming down on Harry. He was tall and bald with a short, grizzled beard.

Harry thought otherwise and tried to say so. All he managed was a rusty croak. A nurse lifted his head and gave him some water.

"The truck hit me," he said, remembering.

"Indeed it did. And you took a swim in Puc Puggy Creek. Not my idea of a good place to take a dip."

"We had to drive off a couple of alligators before we could pull you out of the water," a familiar voice said. Jim Snyder bent over him and grinned broadly. "We couldn't tell whether they were just keeping an eye on you or getting ready to eat you."

"Waiting for you to soften up is my thinking," Frank Hodges added, his moon face looming.

For the next few minutes the doctor, the red-haired nurse, and a pair of very strong candy stripers did things to Harry that hurt a lot without saying they were sorry. When they were finished, the doctor looped his stethoscope around his neck and said, "Some of those bruises are doozies. I'll see you later."

"If his eyes roll up while you're talking to him, you call me," the nurse told Snyder and Hodges and left.

Harry found the instructions disturbing, but he couldn't think why.

"How did I get here?" he asked, having already forgotten he was worried.

"You know somebody named Wetherell Clampett?" Snyder asked.

He and Hodges had found a couple of folding chairs and set them beside the bed. It took Harry longer than he liked to get to an answer.

"He drives a truck for Bevel's Sand, Stone, and Gravel." He reached up and felt his head. It was wrapped in a bandage.

"Something wrong?" Hodges demanded, already halfway out of his chair.

"Did Thompson say anything about my head?" Harry asked worriedly.

"Just that it was a good thing you landed on it," Snyder told him with a straight face. "It was Clampett who found you. You were jammed in the fork of a big willow branch that was dragging in the creek."

"You had to go through a lot of the tree to get there," Hodges said. "The passage didn't do you any good and you were stripped just about bare assed. I figure you traveled sort of like the fella that gets shot out of the cannon in the circus, only you got shot through the roof of your jeep."

"Sergeant! Watch your language!" Snyder said.

"They see a lot of bare asses in here," Hodges said, laughing happily at his joke.

Harry tried to laugh and groaned instead.

"I wouldn't try that for a while," Snyder said. "I saw what your rib cage looks like."

"Where's the Rover?"

"Rob MacDougal's got it," Hodges said with another laugh. "He was complaining that if he had to, he couldn't even sell it for junk."

Harry groaned again.

Snyder scowled at his sergeant and said to Harry, "Harry, was the man driving that truck trying to kill you?"

He wanted to deny it but lost track of his thought, closed his eyes, and went away for a while. When he came back, the room was empty. He had forgotten where he was and didn't care. It was very peaceful. For a while, he watched the light in the window. Then he slept.

Helen drove Harry home after she finished work on Friday afternoon. She had her suitcase with her.

"What about Riga?" Harry demanded.

"She's gone back to Tallahassee." And that was all she said.

Her insistence on staying with him over the weekend had him more worried about the sleeping arrangements than about Riga Kraftmeier or his admission that he'd been deliberately driven off the road.

In the hospital under Snyder and Hodges's grilling, Harry had, after exhausting all the alternatives, gradually come to the conclusion that someone really had tried to kill him. The clincher was remembering the man in the Caprice with the cell phone held to his ear. And while the possibility remained that he had no connection with the incident and that the truck driver had been simply drugged, drunk, or crazy, Harry had come with great reluctance to believe that somebody wanted him dead.

The police were making a serious effort to locate a dump truck that had damage to its right front end, but as of Friday afternoon they had found nothing. And, being driven by Helen over the hump bridge onto the Hammock much faster than he liked, Harry was not thinking about his assailant but how he was going to keep Helen out of Katherine's bed. Of course, it was his bed now, just as it had been his bed before Katherine slept in it, but clear thinking was not the horse pulling this wagon.

"Once we're in the house, I'm helping you upstairs and putting you right into your bed," Helen said, keeping her Camaro approximately on the narrow dirt road. "You're the color of old cheesecake and your chin's beginning to wobble."

Harry wanted to shut his eyes but refused to let himself. Neither did he grip the arm rest, although he wanted to. "My chin isn't wobbling," he protested. "It's your driving."

"You can't help yourself, can you? Every time you get into this car, I have to be criticized. Nobody else finds fault with my driving but you."

Harry shut his eyes and sought help in prayer. At the very, very last moment, she wheeled into his yard in a mushroom cloud of dust and planted the car in exactly the spot where he used to park the Rover.

For all of her threats, Helen got Harry bedded down with a minimum of fuss and discomfort and did not mention his chin again. He, on the other hand, continued to obsess about the bed, and even in the sleep that claimed him almost as soon as his head sank into the pillow, he dreamed of Helen in his bed. Actually, the dream wasn't all that bad. In fact, when Helen woke him for dinner, it was getting very interesting.

"Well, well," she said when he got up to go to the bathroom.

Red-faced, he tried to regain control by making for his destination in a spirited stride, but his stride turned out to be a crab crawl entirely lacking in either dignity or brio.

"Good try, Sport," Helen said encouragingly as she left. "Give a holler when you're ready to come downstairs."

The dinner was delicious. She had even brought a good bottle of wine.

"I'm impressed," Harry said when they were finished. "I owe you one. More than one."

She gave a cynical laugh. "Crawl over here and help me with the pans."

Later, surrendering to the inevitable, Harry said, "Let's go to bed."

"Okay," Helen replied. "Come on, put your arm over my shoulder. I'll help you up the stairs." But at the door to his room, she balked. "Are you crazy?" she demanded. "Do you think I'm going to sleep in Katherine's bed? Forget it."

He laughed.

"What's funny?"

"I am."

After Helen left on Monday morning, Harry called Luke Roberts at the Quality Real Estate Company in Porterville, California. The man who answered spoke in a gravelly voice washed clean of Panther Trace. Harry told Roberts who he was and why he was calling.

"I have clients," the man said following a long pause. "Call me at the following number after six this evening. Between now and then I'll decide whether or not to talk to you."

"A liar," Harry said to the hum on the phone that followed the click. He was reasonably sure that had he been looking across the desk at clients, he would never have said what he did.

By now Harry was accustomed to oddities in the Roberts

family and having noted the time difference, called at nine. Luke Roberts picked up on the second ring.

"What do you want to know, Brock?"

"I'm not sure. Let me tell you what I've been doing, who I've been talking to, and what I've found out. Maybe then you'll be able to tell me what it is I'm looking for."

Roberts laughed. Harry congratulated himself. He took Roberts through a quick review of the conversations he'd had with the other members of the family and told him what he'd learned from the police and the three men who had been involved with John in the robbery.

"You've been busy," Roberts said when Harry finished. "Despite the fact my parents and Matthew wouldn't see it, Bunny was a kid with real limitations. He had trouble making change. He could sign his name and read traffic signs. I don't want to go anywhere near his plans to marry the Allgood girl. Christ, Brock. Two retarded people having kids? Come on."

He paused and Harry waited.

"But I don't see him shooting himself. I doubt he had the coordination to drive his car into the Luther Faubus Canal and shoot himself at the same time. Hasn't anybody thought about that? No. I don't think he shot himself, if that's what you want me to tell you. And, yes, it means somebody killed the poor guy."

"For different reasons, your brother Matthew and the Tequesta County Sheriff's Department don't want the case reopened. What about you?"

"If you do force the police to take an interest in the case, my mother is going to suffer a lot more grief. My father is beyond all that. Do I think it's worth it?"

"That's the question."

"No."

"Okay. Do you think it's possible that either your father or your brother Matthew killed John?"

"Are you nuts?"

"Possibly. Your sister Esther thinks it's possible."

Luke gave a snort of derision. "Why would I care what she thinks?"

"I don't know."

"She's a fruitcake. She lives with someone called Angel Wing."

"Why didn't you go to see Adam when he was dying?"

"For the same reason I don't have anything to do with Esther. I'm done talking to you, asshole."

That was probably my fault, Harry told himself without remorse or regret. He also thought that Luke was probably angrier about being asked if his father or Matthew might have killed John than being exposed as a bigot. Harry picked up the phone again and called Rob MacDougal.

"Hey, Brock, you on your feet?"

"Yes. Is the Rover running?"

"I've got to say yes, but I hate to."

"When can I pick it up?"

"Tomorrow soon enough?"

"Great."

"You know, I've got half a dozen cars and trucks and SUVs on the lot that you could drive that would keep the dogs from chasing you."

"Nope."

"All right then. I got the snakes all out of it, but she still stinks of creek water."

"The sun will take care of that."

"While you're waiting, you'll want a posy under your nose."

15

Harry decided to test his luck by walking to Tucker's place. It was a lot farther than he remembered and the sun a lot hotter, but a quarter of a mile from the farm he met Oh, Brother! and Sanchez coming to meet him. He shortened the last part of his journey by resting his right hand on Oh, Brother!'s shoulder and telling him and Sanchez about the accident.

"I've been expecting you," Tucker said, tossing a basketful of garden weeds onto the compost pile beside the beehives and coming to shake Harry's hand. "The tea's ready."

"It's no more than I deserve," Harry said, making sure not to laugh. "I just spent five minutes telling a mule and a dog about my near-death experience."

"They said they were looking forward to hearing about it," Tucker said, heading for the house.

Harry gave up.

"And they haven't found the truck," Tucker said when Harry finished telling him about Snyder's decision to treat the accident as an intended homicide.

"No, but a warrant's been issued charging the driver with aggravated assault with a motor vehicle."

"And tomorrow you expect to be back on the road?"

"Those are my plans."

Tucker fiddled with the cookie plate and frowned. A quiet breeze was wandering through the kitchen, bringing with it the smell of hot pine needles. Beyond the back stoop, two pileated woodpeckers were pounding on a dead oak and screeching at one another. Tucker glanced out the door.

"Territorial dispute," he said, exchanging his scowl for a smile. "The inhabitants of the so-called animal kingdom are not as different from us as some people would like to think."

"Maybe that's why I got run off the road," Harry said with a laugh and wondered if the tea might have damaged his brain.

"Hold onto the thought," Tucker replied. "But I still want to know what steps you're going to take to protect yourself."

Harry pushed himself upright in his chair and winced. He was still sore just about everywhere. "Keep my eyes open. What else can I do?"

"Carry your gun. Stay off the road as much as you can."

Harry didn't want to talk about the possibility of being blown through the roof of the Rover again. It wasn't that he was frightened. His years had made him something of a stoic where personal risk was concerned. And if he did not think he was immune to dying, he was at least resigned to his mortality. He changed the subject.

"I've talked with everybody in the Roberts family except a couple of wives and some kids," he said. "I've got to say, they're a strange bunch."

He went on to tell Tucker about his conversations with Esther and Luke.

"Do you think there's anything more than unprocessed anger and resentment to Esther's saying her father or Matthew might have killed Bunny?"

"On whose side?" Harry asked, thinking of Matthew and Luke, both of whom seemed to have more anger and resentment in their makeups than Esther.

"I take it we can rule Luke out as a potential killer."

"Probably. He was in California when John died."

"But, like Matthew, he doesn't want the issue of Bunny's

death reopened."

"No. Neither did Mark, as I found out when I asked him who killed John. Rebecca, who seems more convinced than Mark that John didn't kill himself, very much wants a new investigation of the case. But Mark, like Luke and Matthew, claims to be concerned that it will cause their mother pain. As near as I can tell, Martha and Matthew are the only ones who ever see their mother. Esther and Luke haven't been in Avola in years."

"Have you told Martha that Esther said Matthew or their father might have killed Bunny?"

Harry made a sour face. "Not yet. She's not going to like it. She's almost as touchy about her family as Matthew."

"What is the likelihood that Matthew killed his brother?"

"Vanishingly small. And as for James having killed him . . ." Harry shook his head.

"Doesn't sound right, does it?" Tucker observed, then added with a sigh, "But you never know what's going on in a family."

"No," Harry agreed and thought, with a drop in his spirits, that he didn't even know what was going on with his own children because he had given up trying to find out.

As soon as Harry was able to drive, he called Martha.

"I thought you'd dropped me," she said.

"You're not that lucky. We need to talk."

"Let's meet at Fiddler's Pass," she said.

"Why?" Harry asked, caught off guard.

"Why not?" she demanded.

"No reason at all," Harry said with a grin.

He picked her up, and after they had been driving for a few minutes, she asked what smelled so bad.

"The Rover and I took a swim in Puc Puggy Creek," he said and told her what had happened to him.

124

"Should you be out like this?" she asked with a frown of concern.

"I'm okay."

When she clambered out of the Rover, she said, "I might just walk home."

She was dressed in green shorts and a white tank top. Harry had noticed with pleasure that she was wearing a new pair of narrow-framed sunglasses and what Harry thought were new leather sandals.

"I'm complimented," he said. "It's been a long time since a woman I was out with threatened to walk home."

Martha blushed a deep red and began walking very quickly toward the bridge. He guessed the blush was somehow connected to the upgraded outfit and asking to return to the Pass. He was very pleased.

"Hey," Harry called after her. "No fair running."

She stopped and waited for him to catch up. "What did Esther and Luke tell you?" she demanded.

He held his answer until they were on the bridge. The tide was just turning, and small waves and ripples were starting to run inland under the bridge. Martha leaned over the railing and began watching the water.

Harry stopped beside her. "What do you think of your sister?" he asked.

"I haven't seen her for a long time."

"That's not what I asked."

"I know, but you didn't answer my question either. Where are the dolphins?"

"They'll wait until the tide is running full. What you think of your sister will determine how I answer your question."

She turned to him in obvious surprise. There were moments, and this was one, when her resemblance to his daughter Sarah scared him. She was also very attractive, and entertaining those

125

two thoughts at the same time caused him some discomfort.

"I don't really know her. It's been a long time since I've seen her," she said sharply, frowning at him.

He shifted gears. "Luke doesn't like her. He won't have anything to do with her. Why doesn't he like her?"

"None of us do," she said, looking away from him.

"Rebecca does."

"She's not one of us."

It came back too quickly to have been censored. He wondered if she had noticed and made a quick decision. "Luke's a bigot."

"What do you mean?" she demanded angrily.

"He called Esther a fruitcake and made fun of Angel Wing's name. When I asked him why he didn't visit Adam when he was dying, he said, 'For the same reason I don't have anything to do with Esther.' Then he called me an asshole and hung up. He's got a name for everybody."

"Esther's a lesbian, and Adam was probably a homosexual," she said in a fierce whisper. "Adam was punished. He contracted AIDS and died. Esther and that Wing person have adopted a daughter. The child has two mothers! It's sick!"

I asked for it, Harry thought.

"I've talked with Heather. She's a bright, pleasant girl. You'd probably like her. She'd probably like you."

"I don't want to hear about her."

"Do you actually know any lesbians aside from Esther?"

"Of course not."

"How many women work in your firm?"

"Twenty-seven."

"Odds are that at least two point seven are lesbians and one or two more are bisexual."

"I don't want to talk about this." She turned her back to him.

It was going to hurt her, but he decided the shock might shake something more loose. "Do you think it's possible that

Matthew and your father had anything to do with John's death?" he asked.

She whirled to face him again. Tears were running down her face. Harry wasn't sure whether it was fury, fear, or anguish he was looking at.

"No!" she shouted. "Take me home."

That evening when she called him, Harry expected to be fired.

"Why were you so cruel to me, Harry?" she asked quietly. "I thought you liked me."

"You were right. I do like you, but I wanted you to hear the question when your defenses weren't all in place."

"Was it a serious question?"

"Yes."

"Do you think my brother and my father could have done such a terrible thing?"

"I don't know. What do you think?" He wasn't giving her any slack.

"But how could you have come up with such a terrible accusation?"

"I didn't."

"Then who?"

"Esther."

"Esther! Why would she . . . ?"

There was a long pause.

"You tell me," Harry said and hung up.

Martha called again the next morning before she went to work.

"This is a test, isn't it?" she demanded.

"Why would you think that?"

"You tell me."

Harry laughed. "Okay, I want you to take your blinders off."

"What does that mean?"

127

"Any good murder investigation begins with the victim. Who was he? What was going on in his life? Who might have wanted him dead?"

"No one could have wanted Bunny dead."

"Martha, your brother didn't die from sitting in a draft. Somebody killed him, and *somebody* includes John Roberts."

"Bunny didn't kill himself."

"Maybe not. But the only way we're going to find out is by getting to know everything we can about John Roberts. Step one is for you to stop insisting you already know it all. You don't. You're setting out on a journey. Begin thinking of John as the country through which we'll be traveling. And put on your body armor."

"What does that mean?"

"If you're right, and John's death wasn't suicide, whoever killed him is going to do everything possible to stop us from finding that out. It also means you're going to find out things you don't want me to know and don't want to face yourself. We're going to learn about the people with whom he was most closely connected. We're going to find things you will think are private. Some will be painful, embarrassing, and may shatter your view of John and your family."

"I wish you'd call him Bunny."

"The brother you loved and cared for all those years was Bunny. The man who died in the car Rob MacDougal hauled out of the Luther Faubus Canal was John Roberts. Learning that will be your first lesson."

"You're not very nice are you?"

"No. And I won't be able to find out who killed your brother unless I find a way into your family. Your mother and father are out. Matthew and Mark are doors that are shut and locked. Esther and Luke are too far away to be much help. As you said, Rebecca is not one of you. That leaves you."

Harry could hear Martha breathing, and for several moments that was all he heard from her. What he wanted to do was to say something that would ease her pain, but that was an indulgence neither of them could afford.

"I don't know how to begin," she said finally.

"Try answering the question I asked you last night. Why would Esther think Matthew and your father could have had something to do with John's death? And don't say what Luke did, that she's a fruitcake living with a woman named Angel Wing. Which translates into: Esther's a sexual pervert, and, therefore, nothing she says is of any consequence."

"I didn't . . ." she protested and stopped. "That's what I was doing."

"Yes."

"My father and Matthew were so harsh with her, and my mother did nothing to protect her, and the rest of us let it happen. I remember . . . Never mind. You want me to say that if they drove Esther and Adam away, they might have killed John because they couldn't send him away, and when he wanted to marry Theresa . . ."

She suddenly burst into tears. "No," she said, "I can't . . ." and hung up.

"You didn't call her back?" Helen asked, glowering at Harry.

"No. She needed time to think."

"Jesus, Brock, you treat women the way a butcher deals with meat."

"Hey, that's way over the top," Harry protested.

"Oh, good! There she is, seeing, probably for the first time in her life, that possibly her father and her oldest brother aren't the Old Testament prophets she's been brought up to believe. Also, it's dawned on her that Esther, who is her sister and deserves her love, had her butt kicked all over Panther Trace by those two crackers and might not have been the Whore of Babylon but just an abused girl."

She paused for breath. Harry shook his head in wonder. "You'd have made a fortune in a gospel tent or selling vegetable peelers at country fairs."

They were sitting side by side on Helen's couch with their feet up on her sky-blue coffee table, decorated with yellow, red, and orange butterflies.

"Don't try to distract me. You are a big time . . ."

"No, don't," he said putting his hand over her mouth. "I can't bear hearing you use dirty language. I become too excited."

She bit one of his fingers.

"I'm not as bad as I sound," he said, shaking his hand. "If I can't get her to cooperate with me instead of defending that family of hers, I may as well quit the case."

"You don't have to break her heart to do that."

"It's not her heart I'm trying to break. It's the hold that family has on her. She has a choice to make. If she can't create some psychological space between herself and her family, she won't be able to examine what went on and is still going on among them."

"What she said about the way her father and her brother treated Esther sounds like a good start."

"It's a beginning," Harry agreed.

Helen sat up and turned toward him. "I thought you had ruled out the possibility that someone in her family killed John Roberts?"

"I thought so too. It's what I told Tucker. But after talking with Martha, I'm thinking again that even if Matthew or Mark or James didn't actually kill John, there could still be some connection between all of them and his death. It occurred to me that they didn't kill Adam either, but they were involved in his death."

"I thought he died of AIDS."

"He did, but they drove him out of Avola."

"Oh, Harry, they didn't give him the disease. If they're going to be blamed for Adam's death, I don't see how any of us . . ."

"Exactly," Harry said.

"Well, I think you should be sure you really have exhausted all the other possibilities before you decide someone in the family killed him. Somebody tried to kill you. It's still possible you've missed something."

"True enough, but I just can't find anywhere else to look."

Helen regarded him with a guarded expression. "Harry, you said a while back that you weren't Martha's shrink."

"I'm not."

"Then just be careful you don't turn this investigation into an inquisition."

16

Harry decided Helen was being overly dramatic about his running a witch hunt, but he took seriously her urging him to think carefully about suspects outside the Roberts family. He came up with a single unexplored lead.

Jefferson Toomey lived on a dirt road in an unpainted shack nearly buried under an orange Florida flame vine and surrounded by a coyote fence made of ficus limbs, most of which had sent down roots into the damp, black earth and were sporting dark green leaves. The cabin was half a mile from the place where Rob MacDougal had hauled John Roberts's remains out of the Luther Faubus Canal.

Harry went through an iron gate in the fence and came back out just ahead of a large brown and white billy goat. The goat struck the gate with a crash and was backing up for another go when Toomey appeared in the door of his shack.

"Who's calling?" he shouted.

"Harry Brock. I'd like to talk with you about John Roberts."

"Charles! Stand away."

The billy goat lifted his head and backed away from the gate.

"Come along, come along," Toomey called cheerfully in the same booming voice.

"I don't fancy being spitted by your goat," Harry replied.

"Don't mind Charles," Toomey said, encouraging Harry by waving him toward the door. "He's just over-heavy on responsibility. Do you know what I'm saying? Just come right along.

You're gonna be fine."

Harry edged through the gate. Charles and three sleek, sloe-eyed nanny goats with swollen udders, who had come round the corner of the house, regarded him with interest. There was something louche about those female goats, Harry thought and found himself vaguely embarrassed by their attention. But he did not forget Charles while regarding his harem and walked briskly toward the door.

"I don't entertain a lot," Toomey said with a wide grin. He motioned Harry to one of the two chairs in the room. The house had only one room, and with a kitchen sink and a refrigerator and a small table at one end and a large brass bed at the other, the room was hard pressed to provide living room space in the middle. But given those restraints, Harry thought Toomey had made himself snug and comfortable. There was even an air conditioner rattling cheerfully in one of the windows.

"What do you want to know about Bunny Roberts?"

Harry waited to answer until Toomey had taken the other chair, his large, bony knees thrusting out in front of him and his gnarled hands folded peacefully across his chest.

"Almost anything you can tell me."

"You're working for Martha Roberts."

"That's right."

"Known the family a long time."

Harry gave Toomey time to think through whatever had furrowed his brow.

"I knew Bunny pretty well. He worked at Bevel's, but I expect you know that."

Harry nodded.

"Bunny had trouble making change and such like, but things he said sometimes surprised you. He knew more about what was happening than most people thought. Mr. Hawkins treated him like a dummy. So did most of the other brass. He seemed happy to let them." Toomey nodded. "He saw quick enough that it made things easier for him."

Harry had to reach to put a face to the Hawkins name and then remembered the personnel manager, but not with any pleasure.

"His brother Mark works there still," Toomey continued. "He got Bunny the job. It was either him or Matthew. Matthew was pretty tight with Mr. Bevel Senior. 'Course, he's passed over. Mr. Bevel Junior's in charge of things now. Much as anybody is. Last of my being with the company, there was days I thought Mr. Hawkins and Mr. Mark Roberts or nobody was running things."

"You're not working there now?"

"Nope. Two years ago I grabbed the gold parachute and jumped. Soon as I landed, I sat down and I've been sitting pretty steadily ever since."

His wrinkled face broke into a grin.

Harry grinned back, but he was wondering if Toomey was being ironic about the parachute, and if not, why would Bevel's have given Jefferson Toomey anything more than his last pay-check?

"So they made you an offer too good to turn down."

"You as surprised as I was?"

"I'm glad things worked out so well for you."

Toomey's grin grew a little sharper. "You work at a place a long time, you get to know things, things both good and bad. You know what I'm saying?"

"I'm not sure."

"Well, it don't matter. I heard Bunny took his life. You figure that's the way of it?"

"I don't know. What do you think?" Harry put aside the matter of the parachute.

"Why don't you just go ahead and tell me why you're here?

It might help me to find the answer tree."

Harry laughed. "I'm trying to discover whether or not someone killed John Roberts. His two oldest brothers think he committed suicide. So do the police. Martha, Rebecca Roberts, and Esther Roberts don't. I'm having trouble deciding what Luke Roberts thinks."

"You been busy." Toomey gripped his knees and looked out the screen door. Charles and two of the nannies were crowded together at the door, watching the two men. The third nanny was peering in a window. Toomey looked back at Harry and chuckled. "They's like me. Not used to company. Manners rusty. You know what I'm saying?"

"There's something about those nannies . . ."

"Fetchin', ain't they? Charles don't get much rest. I had one wife, like to run me to death. He's got three. There are whole days I feel sorry for him. Then he butts me, and I have to put the stick to him and lose all that fellow feeling. I think there's about as much chance that Bunny killed himself as that Charles is gonna give up butting or I'm going to get me another wife."

"He was getting married."

"A black girl from the Perkins House. I thought that might be a mistake. But he was happy about it as a bee in clover."

"Why would anyone have gone to all the trouble of killing him and putting him in the canal that way?"

"So they'd know where he was, and others wouldn't."

It was a while before Harry saw the full significance of Jefferson's Toomey's answer. It was the next day while he was driving to Tucker's that Jefferson Toomey's comment began to take on its full meaning.

"Toomey might have spoken more exactly than I thought," he told Tucker while he was turning over one of the old farmer's compost piles with a dung fork and repeated what Toomey had said.

"I'm thinking 'knowing where he was' meant knowing John was dead. 'And others wouldn't' could mean others would think John was still alive and wouldn't go around asking why he'd been killed."

Harry straightened up to rest. He was still not like the man who rejoiced to run a race. "If you're right, whoever killed John did it to put an end to something he was doing or might do and to stop anyone else from finding out what that something was."

"By way of Robin Hood's barn, I guess that sounds right. To shut his mouth is how I would have said it."

Harry felt the door he had been trying to open give a little.

"I'd better have another talk with Jefferson Toomey," he said.

He was finishing lunch when Jim Snyder and Frank Hodges drove into the yard.

"Have you been talking with Jefferson Toomey lately?" Jim asked as soon as he and Hodges were settled in the kitchen.

Jim looked to Harry as if he'd been a long while without sleep. Hodges, aside from the scowl of disappointment that clouded his face when he saw the table was cleared, seemed to be much as ever.

"Coffee?" Harry asked.

Snyder slumped into a chair and shook his head. Even Hodges declined.

"What's this about Toomey?" Harry asked, putting away the last dish he had been drying.

"The thing about old Jefferson," Hodges said, "is he's dead."

"And before he died," Snyder added, for once not criticizing Hodges for blurting out the news, "he scrawled your name in his own blood on the cabin floor. That's why we're here."

Harry pulled a chair out from the table and sat down. He felt a little sick. "I was out there yesterday, asking him about John Roberts."

"What did he tell you?"

"Nothing that should have gotten him shot."

"Whoever it was shot his billy goat," Hodges said in a disgusted voice. "The goat couldn't have known anything worth getting shot for either."

"Charles," Harry said.

"Who's that?" Snyder demanded.

"The billy goat's name was Charles. He butted people." Harry began to feel really bad. He thought about Toomey and his goats. "What about the nannies?"

"They're all right," Snyder said, his voice rising. "Can we stop talking about the goats? We've got a man down. He wrote your name in blood before dying. Let's try to focus."

"He didn't tell me anything new about John Roberts. I wish he had. I was planning to talk with him again."

"Did he know Roberts?" Hodges asked.

"He said he had known the whole family for years. He also said there was no way John Roberts would have killed himself."

Snyder leaned forward and planted his elbows on the table. "Did Toomey say anything to suggest he was worried or in any kind of trouble?"

"No. I'd say he was a man at peace with himself and the world."

"No enemies?"

"I wouldn't know. Aside from telling me he didn't plan to marry again, he didn't mention his private life."

"Why would he have left your name for us to find?"

Harry saw the CD officer come out, although he could also see Snyder trying not to be official. But, as Snyder had said, someone was dead.

"If old Jefferson wasn't naming his killer, he must have been leaving you a message," Hodges said.

Snyder was exasperated. "Sergeant, I believe I was talking to the . . . to Harry."

"Ha! Ha!" Hodges burst out, slapping his hand on the table. "You almost said 'suspect'! Harry, did you waste old Jefferson?"

"No, Frank. My 9mm is upstairs. You'd better have it checked out."

"I guess we'd better," Snyder said with a sigh and got up. "Harry, put your mind to work on this. Toomey must have been trying to tell you or somebody something."

17

Harry gave Snyder his gun to take away to be tested and saw him and Hodges into their cruiser. Then he began recovering as much of his conversation with Jefferson Toomey as he could remember. He had not misled Snyder, but he hadn't been completely forthcoming either. There were three things in particular he wanted to explore without the police trampling on his feet.

The first was what Toomey had called his golden parachute and the knowing grin that had accompanied his comment about having kept his eyes and ears open over the years about the workings of Bevel's Sand, Stone, and Gravel. The second was his suggesting that while he was working at Bevel's, John Roberts had been a lot more observant than people thought.

Finally, as a best guess, Toomey had probably not known the name of the person who had killed him, but he may have hinted that Bevel's was the place to look for his killer. Harry was less certain there was any connection between Toomey's murder and John Roberts's death.

The phone rang.

"Hi. This is Fred Casanova from the Conservation Commission. I can't get Tucker LaBeau to answer his phone. Is something wrong?"

"Probably not. Between his bees and the farm work, he's usually out in the weather as long as it's daylight. And if he's inside to eat or take a nap, he unplugs it. Call him after dark. If he hasn't gone to bed, he'll answer."

"I think I'd better tell you. The butterflies are certainly a variant. I've got to say, I'm pleased. This is a career first for me, and to have it happen this close to home is an added boost. Pass along my congratulations to Tucker and my thanks. He made the effort to follow up his hunch. Not many have the courage of their convictions."

"How do we get some protection for the Atalas's breeding ground?" Harry asked. "Bevel's getting ready to do something in there."

"That's bad news. It takes time to get the Commission to act. There a lot of bureaucracy to wade through, but I can make some calls. Who should I call at Bevel's?"

"Fontaine Bevel's the owner's name. Ralph Hawkins is the manager."

He gave Casanova the company's number and smiled while he was doing it. What would those three make of each other? As an afterthought, he also suggested talking to Mark Roberts and asked, "Can you actually get them to stop what they're doing by calling them?"

"I wish it were true," Casanova said ruefully.

"Where does that leave us?"

"About where you'd guess."

"Bevel's got equipment enough to clear-cut Southwest Florida and bulldoze the stumps. If they think an injunction of some kind is coming—"

Casanova cut in. "I'll file a report of my calls and tell them I'm doing it. If they go ahead and materially damage those Atalas or their habitat after the warning, they're opening themselves to a lawsuit."

"What will it cost them?"

"A couple of million, at least."

"Not enough. They'll swallow that without water."

"And there's the negative publicity."

"You mean their clients, the developers, won't call them afterward?"

"I'm trying to make us feel better here."

"It's not working."

Harry took himself to Tucker's with Casanova's news. Tucker was cutting back the clumps of fountain grass marking the north end of his vegetable garden.

"This ought properly to be done in the fall," he explained to Harry by way of a greeting. "But a strain of rust has afflicted them, and none of my remedies will touch it. There's nothing to do but cut them back to the roots and burn the stems before the plague spreads to something else. There's another machete in the shed in case you want to risk losing a finger."

Harry fetched the machete and, after watching Tucker chopping away with the wicked-looking tool for a moment or two, he set to work. In five minutes he was in pain from the back of his neck to his ankles, and his pile of shorn grass was pitifully small beside the stacks Tucker was building.

When they had worked their way to the end of the row, Tucker wiped the blade of his machete on the leg of his overalls. Harry tried to fluff his grass with the toe of his sneaker to make the pile look bigger, but nothing helped. He gave up.

"I'll let that dry for a day or two, then I'll burn it," Tucker said. "Thanks for your help."

"De nada. Literally. You got a call from Casanova. The good news is that the butterflies are a genuine variant. Whether or not that means they're a subspecies will have to wait a while."

Tucker's smile was as wide as his face. "That calls for a glass of plum brandy."

Sanchez and Oh, Brother! emerged from the woods behind the beehives and met the two men on their way to the house.

"What have you two been up to?" Harry asked, stroking the dog's head and then resting a hand on Oh, Brother!'s neck. The mule pushed his nose into Harry's chest by way of response.

"A female bobcat's got a den out there close to where the barred owls nested last year, and these two aren't going to rest until they find it," Tucker said, shaking his head disapprovingly. "I've told them they're courting trouble, but they won't listen. That lady's got kittens, and they're going to get their hides chewed if they keep poking around her."

Sanchez pretended not to hear, but Oh, Brother! snorted. Harry tried not to believe the mule had done it derisively and didn't succeed.

"He who laughs last," Tucker said.

Harry didn't know whether to feel vindicated or indicted.

When Tucker had put away the brandy jug, he came back onto the stoop and settled himself in the rocker beside Harry. "I can tell from your face you've been holding back some bad news. What is it?"

"It's going to take the State Conservation Commission a while to exempt from development that piece of the ground where the butterflies live. Casanova says he will make some phone calls to Bevel's, but my guess is that Bevel's will eat the cost of defying the warning and do whatever it's planning to do."

"Come dark, I may slip over there and pour a little sand into the fuel tanks of whatever they show up with," Tucker said grimly.

"Whoa," Harry said. "That's not like you. More to the point, you wouldn't like it at the Everglades Correctional Institution. For one thing, there's no plum brandy on offer."

"I might risk it. I've never discovered a subspecies of butterfly before, and I'm feeling about them a lot like that mother bobcat feels about her kittens. I'm ready to chew the ass off

142

anything that threatens them. As Sanchez and that smart-aleck mule are going find out."

Going home, Harry had to stop while a female raccoon and three young ones crossed the road. One of the cubs lingered to look at the Rover. Its mother trotted back and gave it a cuff to get it started. Spurred on by that moment of tough love, Harry decided he'd put it off long enough. He would beard Matthew Roberts in his den and try to get a trace started on the revolver that was used to kill John Roberts. But first he would give himself some cover by talking to Sheriff Robert Fisher.

The sheriff of Tequesta County was one of the top law enforcement people in the county. But more than that, having been elected to his post, he was a politician. Working to be reelected and being the community's leading representative of rectitude created strains. Like Caesar's wife, who, if she couldn't stay above suspicion, had to make damned sure not to get caught. So far, although there had been some close shaves, Fisher had made it out the window before the door opened.

The less reverent called him Hell-it's-a-vote Fisher. "Harry!" he said, striding around his desk to shake Harry's hand. "I hear you damned near drowned in Puc Puggy Creek. You trying for the weird way to die award?"

Harry returned Fisher's grin and shook his hand warmly. You couldn't help liking the man. He was big, open faced, direct, and while he was talking to you, it was impossible not to believe he really wanted to hear what you were saying.

"With some help from a very large truck," Harry said.

"I heard about that too," Fisher replied, losing his grin and dropping his voice half an octave. "We're looking, friend, and we're going to apprehend the son of a bitch who did that to you. I've got to do it," he added, his grin coming back, "or Captain Snyder will have my cojones."

143

He had a good laugh too.

"What can I do for you this fine morning?"

Putting a thick arm around Harry's shoulders, he walked him to a small conference area in a sunny corner of the office, set off with chairs, a Navaho rug, and a small stand of silk palms, to break up the light pouring in the window.

"I want to look at the gun John Roberts used to shoot himself," Harry said. "I think it's now in the Evidence Section. I'd like your permission to get the serial number on the gun and run a trace on it."

Fisher made a tent with his fingers and studied the results for a moment without answering. When he did respond, Harry knew he was talking to the sheriff's department head honcho.

"I'm not sure I should say yes to this. First off, you don't think John Roberts shot himself—or if you do, you're acting for a client who sure as hell doesn't think that's how he died. Next, one way or another, this investigation of yours is going to use up department time. That's money, brother, which you and other citizens of this fair county contribute in taxes. You following my drift?"

"I think I have a right to the information, Bob, and the only reason I'm in here spending the taxpayers' money by keeping you away from more important work—" Harry caught himself and didn't say, like raising money for your reelection campaign "—is that to get to that gun, I've got to go through Matthew Roberts, who thinks of me as something a lot lower than the angels. To get that serial number without a bloodbath, I'll need your help."

"I see your problem." Fisher slumped back in his chair and scowled at the rug. "Okay," he said brightening and pulling himself to his feet. "I'll say you can have access to the gun. After that you're on your own."

He chuckled all the time he was writing the note.

"Thanks. At least, I think so."

The Evidence Section's parking lot was deserted. The cicadas were shrilling in the oaks, dust devils were spinning over the gravel, and Harry stepped down from the Rover feeling that there ought to be a better way to make a living. The gatekeeper was still wearing her orange cardigan.

"He's where you left him," she said, when Harry stated his business.

"He still shouting?" Harry asked, trying to bridge the intimacy gap.

"Have you seen a new star in the east?"

"No."

"You've got your answer."

Harry sighed. "What are you working on?"

"You wouldn't understand if I told you."

"Okay. Then I'll go in," he said.

"Measure twice and saw once," she replied, attacking the keyboard with renewed violence.

Trying to figure out what that meant kept Harry from worrying about facing Matthew 10:30. "But the very hairs of your head are numbered," he said aloud to the empty corridors. No one answered, but he thought he could hear them listening. Matthew Roberts was seated behind his evidence table putting a ticket on a pitchfork.

"Murder!" he said loudly, printing a large black 3 on the tag.

Kicking his chair down the table, he slammed the pitchfork into a space already prepared for it and he pushed himself to his feet, glowering at Harry.

"What the fuck do you want?"

"I'm all right. How about you?"

Roberts doubled his hands into very large fists and planted them on the table and leaned toward Harry. "Are you hard of hearing or just plain stupid?"

Harry took Sheriff Fisher's note out of his pocket and passed it to him. For a moment, Harry thought Matthew was going to refuse to take it. Then the man pulled his weight off his knuckles and grabbed the note out of Harry's hand. When he had read it, he threw it onto the table.

"What do you want with that gun?"

Harry had just about run out of warmth and fellow feeling. "Just get me the revolver, Roberts, and cut the menacing bullshit."

Roberts's face cracked into what might possibly have been a grin. "Do you know how long it could take me to find it?"

"Do you think Robert Fisher would like it if Judge Jason Bryde had to come looking for it because you couldn't find it?"

Roberts studied Harry for a while, then turned and went out a door at the back of the room. When he came back, he was carrying the pistol by its barrel. He passed it across the table to Harry. Harry turned it over in his hands until he found what he was looking for. He wrote the number in his pocket notebook, then passed the gun back to Roberts.

"Serial number," Roberts said.

"That's right."

"You were warned, Brock."

18

Snyder groaned like a gored ox when Harry gave him the serial number of the gun that had killed John Roberts. "Now look what you've done," he said. "I suppose you want me to put a tracer on this."

"That's the idea," Harry answered.

"How did you ever get Matthew to give you the gun?" His curiosity defeated his disgust.

"I went to Fisher. He signed a release. Matthew wasn't too happy, but his choices were limited."

"You enjoy making life difficult." Snyder pulled a form out of one of his files and began filling it in as he talked. "Just how unhappy was he?"

"I could have come away thinking he was looking for a pound of flesh."

Snyder signed the form and leaned back in his chair. "I wouldn't worry. Matthew's too used to having his own way is all. And while we're talking about people who have you on their short lists, Fontaine Bevel is unhappy with you. He's had a phone call he doesn't like. He's equally pissed because some of his people got the same call. You know anything about it?"

"Yes. I meant to tell you. It's now official. Tucker's butterflies are true variants. And they're breeding on land that belongs, or did not long ago, to the Covington estate. Bevel wants to buy it or already has. I gave Fred Casanova Fontaine Bevel's number as well as Mark Roberts's and Ralph Hawkins's numbers. He told me he was going to warn Bevel's people that the Covington land holds endangered butterflies, and distressing or disturbing them is an actionable offense. Looks like he made the calls."

"Tucker's got to be happy," Snyder said, without looking pleased. "Why would Fontaine be so worked up over calls to his senior execs?"

"He can't deny he was called, which, I suspect, he was planning to do. If Casanova had called only him, it would have become a did/didn't standoff in a court case."

Snyder nodded, but it was clear to Harry that he was only half listening.

"You didn't hear this from me," Snyder said, running his hand over his face, "but there's some history with that company that suggests they can get rough with people who get in their way."

"You mean they might run me off the road with one of their trucks?" The possibility had not occurred to Harry before. It came to him as a joke but threatened to linger. He didn't like its company.

"I don't think they knew about the butterflies then," Snyder said.

"Before I was hit, Wetherell said he'd heard talk about the butterflies, but so far as I know, only Tucker and I and Casanova and his people at the Commission knew anything specific about them."

"We're still looking for that truck," Snyder said quietly, "but I'm sorry to say we've made no progress in finding it or its driver. It's beginning to look as if the thing may have been a drunken accident."

"I'd like to believe it."

"But you don't."

"It felt deliberate to me. I watched that truck coming straight as an arrow until it swerved just enough to catch the rear right end of the Rover. I didn't see any lack of control."

Snyder scowled. "But where's the motive, Harry? Without a motive, we're hopping on one leg."

"Maybe something will turn up."

"Very funny. It will take a week or so for a preliminary report on the serial number. That reminds me." He pulled open a desk draw and took out Harry's pistol. "Here. It's not the murder weapon. It hasn't been fired recently."

"Thanks. Anything on the Toomey shooting?"

"No. And don't say something may turn up."

Something usually does turn up, but it's not always welcome. This time Riga Kraftmeier turned up. Again.

"I'm thinking of going back to school," Helen said, pouring herself the last of the wine and shaking the bottle over her glass.

"To study what?"

"I'm thinking of becoming a veterinarian."

"What?" Harry had stopped thinking about the wine and was actually paying attention to what she was saying.

"You heard me. I want to become a large animal doctor."

"Why, for God's sake?"

She emptied her glass in one go. "When the time's right I want to have the knowledge and means to kill you and Riga without the racket and mess of shooting you."

"Oh, well, that makes sense."

"Very good sense," she said. She got up and walked almost in a straight line toward the kitchen.

"And now you're going to . . ."

"Get another bottle."

"Right, but before you do, let's talk about what's happened."

She steadied herself on the door frame and looked back at him. "What's happened?"

"You're supposed to tell me."

She came back to the couch and sat down like a beginner. "Riga's back," she said.

Harry waited for a while. "And?"

"What? Oh, she wants us to think about a trial reconciliation."

Harry reviewed his options without the endorphin rush he had hoped for. "What the hell is that?" he asked lamely.

Her focus when she got him in her sights was wobbly. "I think it means you fuck, eat out, and laugh more than you want to without mentioning whatever split you in the first place. At least, that's my take on it. How do you see it?"

"As my cue to leave," he said. And he did.

On his way home, Harry decided his relationship with Helen was once again in full klutz. Even allowing for the fact she had been, apparently, a lot drunker than he had realized, the reappearance of Riga was very bad news. As he bounced over the hump bridge onto the Hammock, he admitted that as much as he wanted to roll Riga up in a rug and ship her to Kurdistan, he couldn't do it. In fact, there was nothing he could do about the mess except avoid adding to Helen's problems. And he could do that best by staying away from her. Glumly, he admitted to feeling very badly done to.

As soon as he was home, he tried cheering himself up by making a fresh pot of coffee and a fried fish sandwich, trimmed with lettuce and horseradish. When he'd eaten that delicacy, he got out his tin of chocolate fudge brownies, which made it possible for him to drink the coffee. After the second brownie he felt strong enough to confront Snyder's warning about Bevel.

He had already dismissed the butterfly issue as a serious threat, but he was almost certain Jefferson Toomey had died for something connected to Bevel. And it wasn't much of a stretch to see a possible connection with John Roberts. As to what that connection might be, Harry had no idea. But if it had resulted in Toomey's death, it was worth investigating. He decided to talk to Wetherell Clampett.

The next morning, he found Clampett on the rock storage corner of the Bevel plant site, supervising the loading of huge yellow dump trucks by a giant machine that looked like a praying mantis. One scoop of its immense bucket filled each truck, making the dump body sag as the crushed rock plunged into it with a ferocious roar. Gray dust rose like a geyser over the area, and the sun shining through the haze looked withered and bleached to a deathly white.

"It's a work rule," the big man shouted at Harry. "You got to wear that hat they gave you at the gate. If a couple of tons of that rock was to fall on your head, some government fella would say you was killed because you wasn't wearing your hat."

Clampett laughed, but the racket around them was so loud, Harry couldn't hear him and only knew he was laughing because his florid face grew redder and his stomach shook.

"I'd like to have a talk with you," Harry shouted back.

Clampett looked at his watch. "I usually get to The Oaken Bucket by 11:30. I can talk and eat."

The Oaken Bucket was a no-frills diner a mile south of Bevel's plant. The chef and his two assistants wore T-shirts, dirty aprons, and greasy dungarees. The waitresses were in faded blue-denim dresses and blue aprons with pockets for their order pads. They were fast, efficient, and not to be messed with. Their smiles were wintry.

"Good food in here and plenty of it," Clampett said, slapping his plastic cowboy hat onto the bench beside him. His belly crowded the tabletop, but he was smiling broadly at Harry. "You're looking some better than when I found you hanging in that tree. What brings you in search of me?" he asked as he passed Harry a menu.

151

"I'm glad you came along when you did. How's your father?" Harry didn't know Hubbard Clampett, but he knew family came first in these lower latitudes. "I spoke to Tucker about him."

"He's a little better, and I'm obliged to you. Mr. LaBeau called in. My father had more to say to him in an hour than he's said to me in a month. Sprung him right out of his chair."

"I'm glad to hear it. Did you know Jefferson Toomey?"

"Hell, yes. Everybody knew Jefferson."

The waitress arrived. She did not give them her name, tell them she was going to be serving them today, or offer them a beverage.

"I'll have a Reuben and a half, a double side of sauerkraut, and a pitcher of coffee."

Harry ordered a cheeseburger on a dark bun and coffee.

"Cup or pot?"

"Cup."

She left as unceremoniously as she arrived.

"What do you know about him?" Harry asked.

"He's dead."

"Got any idea why?"

"Somebody shot him. At least, that's what the paper said."

"I was with him the day before he died. It kind of upset me when I learned he'd been killed."

"I can see where it might. He was an odd stick, you know. Kept to himself. Always brought his lunch in one of them old, round cookie tins. You know the ones I mean?" Harry nodded. "How did you happen to be talking to him?"

"I was thinking of buying some goats. I'd heard he bred them and thought I'd see if he had anything for sale."

Clampett laughed. "If you wanted to get rid of an hour, all you had to do was ask him about his goats."

"That's what I found out. He worked here a long time."

152

"Thirty years, I think it was." Clampett turned as best he could on his bench. "Where's that waitress? I'm hungry."

"How did Toomey get along at Bevel's?"

Clampett sighed and turned back to Harry. "Well, as I said, he'd been there thirty or thirty-five years. I've been there maybe ten. He was always pretty tight with the management. I figured he was a snitch, but then I asked myself, 'What was there to tell? I was spending too much time in the crapper? One of the drivers was napping in his cab?' " He gave a snort of disgust. "If anybody needs reporting on it's that crew of bandits in the front office."

"How's that?" Harry feigned surprise.

"Bevel's business is mostly with the big developers, putting in roads, pouring concrete, that kind of shit. Big jobs. Where the hell is our lunch?"

"Busy time," Harry said. He looked around the diner. The place was almost full. "What about the developers?"

Clampett settled down again. "This here's not on the record, is it? You're not trying to nail Fontaine Bevel or somebody up there?"

"Hell, no. I'm just interested in Jefferson Toomey." Harry decided it was time to reinforce his bona fides. "There were a couple of things he told me that puzzled me. He led me to believe he got a pretty big retirement package. He called it a golden parachute. I was surprised he even knew the phrase."

Clampett scowled and shifted uneasily on his bench. "There were rumors about that. I never believed it. Why should the company do for Jefferson Toomey what they sure as hell never done for anybody else outside of the top brass?" He paused and stared out the window a moment. "But Jefferson and old man Bevel were pretty tight. After Fontaine Senior, died, Jefferson began spending more time talking with Mark Roberts and Ralph Hawkins. That was when I began paying more attention to what

Jefferson was doing."

"Did you find out anything?"

"Yup. Old Jefferson was some kind of go-between. The old man had always used him as a fetch-it. I figured young Fontaine was putting some extra distance between himself and whatever it was Jefferson and his father had been up to."

"Any idea what that might have been?"

Clampett shook his head. "This here's one hell of a big operation. The developers have always got some kind of deal going to make a buck where the IRS won't shine a light. Each one of 'em's got six hands and not one of the six knows what the other five are doing. Hell, it's the same here. A while back one of those big dump trucks went missing. I reported it. Nothing happened. A few days ago it came back. I reported that. Nothing again."

Harry froze his face and very slowly let out his breath.

"So as far as you know," he said, "Toomey never quarreled with anyone here who might have waited for their chance and killed him? He wasn't pedaling dope or running a numbers racket?"

"Not to my knowledge," Clampett said. "Of course, I wouldn't necessarily know. Knowing things is dangerous, and I make damned certain not to know too much."

"Did Toomey and John Roberts ever work together?"

"Hell, yes. We used to call them the Bobbsey Twins. After Toomey retired, Bunny kind of took his place with Hawkins and Roberts."

Their food came, and Harry found that, despite his claim to the contrary, once Clampett began eating, conversation was finished.

As soon as he could, Harry called Snyder and got Hodges. "Frank, did your people run a check on Bevel's fleet of big dump trucks after I was hung on that willow?"

"Sure, what's up?"

"Do it again. One was missing when you made the check, and it's just reappeared."

"How do you know?"

"Can't tell you, but the information's rock solid."

"Thanks a lot. Jim's going to love to hear this."

Harry thought of telling Hodges more about his conversation with Wetherell Clampett, then changed his mind.

"Anything else?" Hodges asked.

"Yes, don't let them know you're coming."

19

"I'm not used to being taken out to lunch," Martha said a little glumly. She had stopped studying the menu to look out the window at the pelicans bobbing on the lagoon. She and Harry were at the Harborside in part because he had so little positive news to give her and also because he couldn't stop himself from trying to convince her that the world beyond Pecan Grove was worth exploring.

But now that she was seated across the table from him, he found he was far more worried by her pallor than the scope of her social life. There were dark smudges under her eyes, and although she had obviously dressed and made herself up with care, she looked exhausted and ill.

"Are you giving me the business?" he asked.

"No. I don't know what half of these things are." She dragged her eyes back to the menu.

"Choose whatever you want from the other half," Harry replied. "Or you can ask me about the rest. What I don't know I'll make up, and if you really don't know what something is, you won't know I'm lying."

Her answering smile came and went.

Harry put down his menu. He was going to have to work at this. The waiter hurried over. Martha had already brushed off the beverage query, but Harry said, "Bring us two glasses of the Newbury Chardonnay."

Martha started to protest, but Harry said, "Consider it as

medicine, which is how it will probably taste. Now then, what's the matter?"

"If anything was the matter, I don't think it would be any of your business."

Harry put his elbows on the table and regarded her sternly. "Do you have any idea how much you need a drink?"

She tried to say something but laughed instead. For a moment the lines in her forehead were smoothed away. "I wouldn't know where to begin," she said, her shoulders slumping.

"Tell me how you're feeling."

"Not great."

"I got that far on my own. Try again."

"The doctor says my father's dying." She paused. "But that's not really news. I feel really lonely and scared. I'm hardly sleeping at all, and I don't know why, Harry."

"I'm really sorry about your father. Has Matthew or Mark been talking to you or anybody else in your family?"

"I've been talking with Ma."

The wine arrived. Their waiter came back and they ordered. Then Harry pulled the napkin off the rolls and passed the basket to her. "Break up one of these and eat some of it while you're drinking your wine."

"I shouldn't be drinking this at all. I've got to go back to work."

"How many times have you gone back to work late?"

"Never."

Harry lifted his glass. "To Martha Roberts and the day she returned from her lunch break late with wine on her breath."

She blushed, but she picked up her glass and took a sip. "They've been giving me a really bad time, Harry," she said.

He didn't have to ask who "they" were. "Because of what I'm doing?"

"Yes. And the worst part is, I can see how much it's like what they did to Esther. Only now my father's not in on it."

It was not the time to mention the bullets through her window. "Have they threatened you?"

"No. Last night somebody let all the air out of my car tires. I'm not allowing myself to think one of them did it or put someone up to it. It cost me forty-five dollars to get my garage man to drive out to Pecan Grove and blow them up again. I was really pissed."

Harry worked on how he was going to handle that information while she drank some more of her wine. "I'm sorry about your tires, but given where you live, I'm surprised you even have a car in the morning."

"That's not funny."

"I didn't intend it to be. If Matthew and Mark aren't threatening you, what are they doing?"

"Telling me what a bad daughter I am and that my first responsibility is to protect the family. When I say I'm protecting Bunny by trying to prove he didn't kill himself, they tell me I'm being a selfish, disobedient child, and that I'm making Ma very unhappy at a time when she doesn't need any additional suffering."

While she spoke she demolished her roll without eating any of it.

"What does your mother say about all this?"

He put another roll on her plate and told her to eat some of it. She did, but Harry doubted that she tasted it.

"Ma won't say anything except that I should listen to Matthew. 'He's the oldest, and Pa can't tell you.' "

"But she doesn't say that she objects to what you're doing?"

"No, but she doesn't say she supports me either."

A seriously abused woman, Harry thought, feeling sorry for Ruth Roberts. She had probably learned to survive by keeping her head down.

Their food arrived and Harry said, "While we're eating, tell me about your job."

"You're not interested in my boring work."

"I am very interested in you and what you do."

She looked at him and for the first time since they had sat down, she smiled. Then she began talking.

When they finished eating, Harry asked her if she felt any better.

"I think so. Thanks for listening."

"I think they should make you a partner," he said. "It sounds as if you do most of the work."

She brightened. "Have you learned anything new?"

"Maybe. I've talked to some people at Bevel's about John. They agree with you that he didn't commit suicide. They also said he understood a lot more than some gave him credit for."

"I could have told you that."

"I know, but what I'm thinking is that he may have seen or heard something at Bevel's he shouldn't have. And it happened because people thought he didn't understand things."

"Like what?" she demanded.

"I don't know yet, but John may also have said something about what he'd learned and gotten himself in trouble."

"But you don't know what that something is."

"No. But even before Toomey retired, they used John as a messenger."

"Who used him?"

Harry hesitated and then told her. She flinched when he named Mark but did not protest.

"Is Toomey the man who was killed a while ago?" she asked.

"Yes. Jefferson Toomey. He was with Rob MacDougal when they pulled John's car out of the canal. His grandchildren had been swimming in the canal and found the car."

"And?"

159

"Toomey knew John. They had worked together at Bevel's."

"Did you talk with him?"

Harry said he had and gave Martha a quick summary of what he had learned from Toomey and what conclusions he had drawn.

"I should have a talk with Mark about this," she said quickly. "If it involved company money, he would have to know about it."

"No, Martha," Harry replied. "Don't say a word to Mark or Matthew or anyone else about this. Promise me."

"Okay. But why the cloak and dagger stuff?"

"Because if I'm right, two people connected with Bevel's have died, possibly for what they knew. I don't want you to be the third."

She looked at him with a shocked expression.

"My God, Harry," she asked in a choked voice, "What have I gotten us into?"

Harry sat on his lanai with his feet up, apparently enjoying the breeze and the light and shadows flickering in the oaks. A big, green spiny-tailed lizard, untroubled by the heat, darted back and forth across a sunny area of grass, catching crickets and grasshoppers. But Harry wasn't as relaxed as he appeared to be.

Since driving Martha back to her office, he had been trying to decide whether or not she was in any serious physical danger and whether or not he had any right to intervene in her quarrel with Matthew and Mark. By the time he was back on the Hammock, he had decided that as long as he knew nothing specific about how John came to die, she was probably safe. But what, if anything, he was supposed to do about the emotional abuse she was absorbing was proving to be a question not so easily answered.

When he pushed himself into a sitting position, his sudden

movement startled the lizard, and it sprang sideways just as one of the red-shouldered hawks plunged down from within the oaks, driving his talons into the earth instead of the lizard's back. Shrieking, the hawk flung himself back into the air in pursuit of the lizard, but the lizard, moving like green lightning, raced across the grass and vanished into the shrubbery.

"You owe me one," Harry shouted after the fleeing reptile.

Thwarted, the hawk swerved away over the lanai, cursing Harry as he went.

Harry laughed and as the bird flashed away went into the house and picked up the phone.

Heather answered the phone.

"Hi," Harry said. "How are you?"

"I'm all right. Do you want to speak to Esther?"

"Yes. Do you call anybody 'Mother'?"

"I call both Angel and Esther Mother. Do you always ask rude questions?"

"I'm afraid so."

"It must get you into a lot of trouble."

"It does."

"Hello," Esther said.

"Hi. Your daughter recognized my voice."

"So do I, Harry Brock. What can I do for you?"

"If you're willing to listen, I'll tell you a few things about where I am with John's death. Then I'm going to say something about Martha."

"And then you're going to ask me to forget we had the conversation."

"Yes."

"Well, there're no surprises so far. Go ahead."

"We'll talk," Helen said, "But it will cost you."

"Where do you want to eat?" Harry asked, resigning himself

to a cash hemorrhage.

"Forget restaurants. On Saturday you're taking me to the Swamp Buggy Races."

"You're smoking something really toxic," Harry said in alarm. "The people who go to swamp buggy races eat alligator meat and bark. You're not getting me—"

"And you're buying me chiliburgers and jambalaya with beer in a plastic cup. A lot of it because it's going to be really hot. Pick me up at ten, and don't forget the bug spray."

"Shit," Harry said when she hung up, but he laughed as he said it.

Whatever pleasure he got from the exchange with Helen, however, was balanced by the way he was feeling about her and Riga. After some waffling, he had decided that he was not interested in pulling on one of Helen's arms while Riga pulled on the other.

Helen had been right. It was hot. But nobody seemed to care. The place looked like a small fairground with tents crowded around the bleacher stands and raucous country music rattling the tent poles. Under a relentless sun, seven or eight hundred people were crowded into the stands overlooking the figure-eight track and shouting and laughing and stamping their feet and totally dedicating themselves to having a good time, cheered on by pails of beer dispensed in enormous plastic cups. Helen was holding hers in both hands.

"The water on the track is eighteen inches deep," she shouted, "but scattered around are sippi holes three-feet or more deep. And the bottom's all mud. So when the buggies get going, the mud and water are flying everywhere. Drink some of that beer before it boils."

Harry had to laugh when she grinned at him with a huge mustache of white foam stuck on her face. And for the next couple of hours he kept on laughing and shouting along with everyone around him. It was a cowboy-boots crowd, with the women dressed in chopped-off shorts and halter tops and the men in dungarees and white T-shirts. At regular and jarring intervals the music and the roaring of the crowd was drowned in the bellow of enormous buggy engines, bringing everyone to their feet as the monsters heaved and rocked up to the starting line.

The buggies raced in classes ranging from the relatively small, stripped-down jeeps to monsters with NASCAR racing motors and a roar like jet engines. But whatever their size, they all had tall wheels and thin tires to create as little resistance as possible to the mud and water through which they would soon be churning.

Helen and Harry had struggled to their seats between races and now more contestants lined up and plunged forward with a roar. Harry could tell Helen was shouting by her face, but in the enveloping thunder of the motors he heard nothing else. For a moment the drivers and their vehicles were in plain view, but an instant later they vanished in a sheet of mud and water ten feet high thrown up by their wild flight.

At the first turn, the leader suddenly vanished into one of the sippi holes and his buggy flipped like a water bug. The rest of the racers plunged past him, indifferent to his plight.

"He'll drown!" Harry shouted. "He's under that thing!"

"Just watch!" Helen shouted.

Harry was furious that no one was paying attention, but before he could even think what to do, two huge, yellow tractors with enormous wheels raced through the water to the spot. In an instant the drivers had pincered the buggy out of the hole and had the dripping driver on his feet, mudded but safe.

The crowd erupted in a rebel yell and went back to cheering their favorites. At some point that seemed to Harry outside of time, Helen said hoarsely, "I'm hungry." And Harry suddenly realized he could probably eat a whole pig.

Three quarters of an hour later they staggered out of one of the Cajun food tents. Harry had a fire in his stomach all the beer in Milwaukee couldn't quench.

"That jambalaya was to die for, and I may," Helen groaned, leaning against Harry as they made their slow way toward the viewing stands.

"You only ate three bowls of it and drank a quart of beer," Harry said.

"I never!" Helen protested, grabbing him around the waist. "It was two bowls and one cup of beer. You weren't exactly picking at your food."

"True," he admitted ruefully.

After the last race, a short, tanned man, dressed in a white suit and white, pleated-front shirt, stepped onto the judges' stand. His gold bracelets and a thick gold necklace flashed in the sun as he waved his white Panama hat at the crowd. The cheering grew louder as he turned to offer his free hand to a beautiful, tall, dark-haired woman in a lilac dress and spike heels who was making her way carefully up the plank steps to the stand.

"Fontaine Bevel the Second," Helen said when the shouting and whistling had died down a little.

"Who's the high-maintenance woman with him?" Harry asked.

"Belle Chance. Rumor has it he brought her back here from New Orleans. You just about never see him without her. And all that glitter on her is not glass."

Harry watched Bevel with interest. The man was a showman, apparently happy and at ease in front of the noisy crowd. He swung Belle past him. She twirled expertly under his hand, the lilac skirt swirling around her long, slim legs. The cheering increased. Someone passed Bevel a bullhorn. He released Belle's hand and shouted, "Y'all having a good time?"

He was answered with yells, whistles, and cheers.

"You ain't seen the best, but you're going to right now. This here's the prettiest little thing in this whole state of Florida. You know who it is?"

The crowd roared, "Cindy Lockerbie!"

"And who is she?"

"The Queen!"

At that moment a blonde girl in a scarlet thong bikini with a blue sash draped across her body with the words Swamp Buggy Queen blazoned on it in gold letters bounced up the steps and onto the stage. Bevel caught her hand as she bounded past him, stepped up beside her, and swung her hand up over their heads. Flushed and beaming, she planted a kiss on his cheek.

The next minute one of the yellow tractors wallowed through the water to the stand, and Cindy stepped aboard to renewed cheering.

"Now what?" Harry asked.

"Just watch," Helen said laughing and applauding.

"I sure hope she can swim," Bevel shouted into the uproar.

The tractor churned through the mud for twenty yards and stopped. Cindy hopped out onto the edge of the tractor's frame, and with a final wave dropped like a stone into the sippi hole and vanished in swirl of muddy water. Two muscular young men waded thigh deep from in front of the tractor to the spot where the Queen had plunged from sight. The crowd had gone suddenly quiet.

They reached down into the water, hesitated a moment, then straightened and propelled Cindy out of the muck onto their shoulders, bringing the crowd to its feet with a sudden roar. The next moment they handed her to two more men on the tractor who stood her on her feet. She looked as if she had been dipped in milk chocolate.

Shining with mud, she pranced about clasping her hands over her head. Belatedly, Harry noticed that she was bare to the waist. As the tractor reversed toward the stand, Cindy turned and waggled her bottom at the crowd. Then she twisted around and waved her breasts at everybody. Women and men cheered, whistled, shouted, stamped their feet, and applauded wildly.

Helen was shouting and applauding beside him, her face ruddy with sun, beer, and pleasure. It was, Harry thought, a genuine Southwest Florida moment, and Helen, good sport that she was, had thrown herself into it. But his own pleasure was dampened by the sudden thought of Martha Roberts and her lonely and increasingly painful struggle to find her brother's killer.

20

"When was the last time you saw people having that much fun?" Helen asked as they were driving away from the sports ground. "And wasn't Cindy great?"

"Yes, she was, and I don't remember," Harry replied. "But what I liked best about the whole thing was they didn't kill and eat her."

"Jesus, Brock," Helen said, falling back in the seat, "you're depraved."

"Possibly, but mostly I'm relieved."

She snorted in disgust.

"That was my first look at Fontaine Bevel and his playmate," Harry continued. "I had no idea."

"He's a winger all right, and he owes more money than the federal government," Helen said with a laugh. "He just about lives at the bank."

Harry filed that away and decided Fontaine was on his visiting list.

The sun was nearly down when they reached Helen's place. After that much fresh air, food, and jungle drums, Harry was ready to withdraw from the fray, but if he didn't settle some things with Helen, the peace and quiet when he found them weren't going to do him any good.

He followed Helen into the house feeling apprehensive. Mister Johnson, her green African parrot, greeted them with a blast of profanity for having been kept in his cage so long. Opening his door, Helen poured some beer into his green mug and gave him a quarter of a Snickers bar to quiet him down.

"You want any of this?" she asked Harry, holding up the can.

"No. I want to talk to you."

"I don't think I want to talk to you," she replied, taking a sip of the beer.

"Sorry about that," he said and sat down at the table. "What's going on with Riga?"

Helen slumped into a chair and ran her fingers through her hair as if she was looking for something.

"What do you want me to say?" She was not smiling and her voice was cold.

"What has to be said," he replied, trying to keep his own feelings out of his voice. For the first time in their relationship, he thought she was not being honest with him, and it hurt. It also made him angry.

"I don't like it that you're trying to corner me," she said.

"I don't like it that you're not telling me what's going on between you and Riga."

"It's none of your business."

"I almost said, I wish it wasn't, but that wouldn't be true."

She made a wry face. "I'm sorry, Harry. Of course it's your business. It's our business, isn't it?"

"It feels that way."

She reached across the table and put her hand over his, which were folded in front of him. "She's gone back to Tallahassee again."

"How about the trial reconciliation?"

"Harry, don't be sarcastic. It takes the hide off me."

"Sorry, but you haven't told me anything important. I don't care where she is. I do care about the rest of it."

Helen's face grew red enough to match the sunburn on her

nose. "I'm not going to say whether or not we're sleeping together."

"Fine." Harry stood up. "When you get this sorted out, let me know."

"Harry, don't be angry."

"I'm trying not to be, and I'm trying to give you whatever space you need."

"What do you want from me, Harry?" Her voice shook. "Do you know what you want? Have you asked yourself the question?"

Resentment, jealousy, and finally anger had shut him down.

At the door he turned and said, "I'll give it some thought."

"And you're not too pleased with yourself," Tucker said, pushing the plate of peanut butter and pecan cookies toward Harry.

"It's much worse, and on top of that I feel as if I've had a regression that's taken me all the way back to junior high."

Tucker laughed. "I can see why. But Helen's put you on the spot. Have you figured out what to do about it?"

"No. And I think I'm sorry I brought this up."

"All right, but if you can't tell her what you want from her, how is she going to tell you whether or not she's willing to give it to you?"

"Good question. I wasted a lot of last night trying without success to answer it."

"You sound like a couple of kids looking at a diving board, saying, 'You go first.' 'No, you go first.' "

Harry winced. "Let's move on. Tell me what you can about Fontaine Bevel the Second."

Tucker brought the tea. "I know considerably more about Bevel Senior than Bevel Junior," the old farmer said, "but I can tell you this for starters: if Junior follows his father, he'll be crooked enough to hide behind a corkscrew."

An outbreak of frantic squalling and screeching in the woods behind the house took Tucker and Harry to the door. Sanchez, who had been sleeping on the stoop, jumped up as Oh, Brother! appeared around the corner of the house, his head thrown up and his ears pricked. Despite the racket, Harry thought how regal the tall, black mule looked, standing as he was at attention.

"What is it?" Harry asked.

"It's probably that mother bobcat I was telling you about. It sounds as if another bobcat has wandered onto her hunting grounds. With cubs to feed, she won't tolerate the competition."

They all stared at the tangle of saw palmettos, oaks, and cabbage palms baking in the sun. There was another, louder outburst of screaming, followed by a brief crashing of brush, and then the woods sank back into silence.

"I hope you were listening to that," Tucker said to the mule and the dog.

Sanchez grinned at Oh, Brother! The mule waggled his ears but avoided looking at the door. Harry found himself thinking the mule was being polite to Tucker but wasn't taking the warning seriously. He quickly stopped himself and went back to the table where the dreaded tea still waited.

"Stubborn," Tucker grumbled, following Harry. "But if they keep on crowding her, they've got a painful lesson coming."

"What are they trying to do?" Harry asked, unable to quell his curiosity.

"They're looking for her den."

"How do you know this?"

"It was supposed to be a secret, but Sanchez can't keep his mouth shut."

"Okay, okay. Back to Bevel."

"His father spoiled him. And, at the same time, he treated him very badly."

170

"How's that?"

"Wouldn't let him near the business. Kept him hanging around like the Prince of Wales. The older the two of them got, the madder old Fontaine became about dying. He hung on as long as he could and made his son's life as miserable as he could. Then one day with no preparation, young Fontaine had that whole business on his hands."

"How long has he been running it?"

"Three or four years, I think."

"According to Helen, he's been borrowing money hand over fist."

Tucker nodded. "That's what I've heard too. Young Fontaine's no fool, but I think he's been listening too much to Ralph Hawkins and Mark Roberts, who pretty much ran the place the last couple of years old Fontaine was alive."

"I've met Hawkins. He strikes me as being tough as nails. I know Mark a little, but I don't have the feeling he's very aggressive."

"I don't know much about either of them, but Mark has sat on the top of Bevel's financial structure for a long time. My take is he enjoys the power the position gives him."

"Do you think Hawkins and Roberts have gotten greedy?"

"That's always a possibility. From what I hear the money's going somewhere."

Harry and Snyder were standing on the bridge between the county road and the Hammock. Harry had met Snyder turning onto the bridge just as he was leaving the Hammock. The bridge took one car at a time, so Snyder had backed up and parked. Now, to Harry's amusement, the gangling captain was picking up pebbles off the bridge and chunking them into Puc Puggy Creek.

"I've got some troublesome news," Snyder said between throws.

"You're making me dizzy with all this up and down," Harry said.

"Sorry. It's a bad habit. Done it all my life. It's sort of like starting in on popcorn. I can't seem to stop."

He leaned against the railing and scowled at the water. Morning flights of waders were drawing dark lines under the sun to the east of the bridge, and the colony frogs in the reeds below the bridge were getting in their last licks before calling it quits for the day.

"That truck of Bevel's is probably the one that hit you. Wetherell Clampett claims the truck was stolen. 'Borrowed' was his word. Do you know Wetherell?"

"Yes. But I'd say 'loaned' would be closer to the truth."

"By who to who?" Snyder asked. He was watching the water slip quietly under the bridge. "I'd sure like to throw a rock in there," he said.

"Have you taken up talking out loud to yourself?" Harry inquired.

"Sounds like it. Have you got an answer to the question? Wetherell says he doesn't know who took it. I don't think Wetherell's got it in him to lie to me and not give it away."

"I agree. I haven't got a name, but if the company management is involved, the list of people is short."

"That's a big if."

"Yes it is, but it would link the deaths of John Roberts and Jefferson Toomey and point toward why the company is floundering in debt."

"But is it?"

"I think Three Rivers Bank and Trust owns more of the operation than Fontaine Bevel does."

"You got any proof?"

"No."

Snyder pushed off the rail and shook his head. "We'll see what we can find out about this truck. I've already heard from your insurance company. It's only a matter of time before Bevel's backup will get involved. There's potentially some big numbers involved here. You may be on the verge of becoming a wealthy man, Harry." He sighed and started for his cruiser. "I don't think I could stand you rich. You're trial enough as it is."

Harry waved Snyder on his way and climbed back into the Rover. He was going to see Martha Roberts, and while driving to Pecan Grove, he allowed himself to wonder what he would do with the money if he were to get a major settlement. He thought he might buy a new Land Rover, and immediately he felt guilty.

"It's too nice to stay indoors," Martha called, coming out of her trailer as soon as he turned into the yard.

She was dressed in white sandals, white shorts, and a red top. Her dark hair was full of light as she ran toward the Rover. The sight of her drove all his worries about becoming rich out of his head.

"Are you always this good looking on Saturdays?" he asked, allowing himself to stray a little beyond the boundaries he had set between them.

"Only if I make the effort," she replied. "Stay in the Rover. We have to drive a little way."

The little way turned out to be two miles west on the main road and three miles down a rough, narrow track that dead-ended at a canal.

"Come on. We have to walk."

"Where are we?" he asked when she pointed out the way along a trail.

"Nowhere special. It's just a place I like to come to when I want to think."

Palms, willows, and lignum vitae, giant leather ferns, and the occasional mahogany tree lined the canal's bank. It was cool under the trees, and the water glinting beside them made a comfortable companion. Harry liked the place but wondered why she had brought him here.

"Are we going to do some thinking?" Harry asked as they started down the shaded path.

"No. I want to tell you what I've done. You're probably not going to like it, but I decided it was time I became a little more proactive."

"And?" He suspected she was right, and he wasn't going to like it.

She stopped and looked up at him, her fists on her hips. "I went to Mark and asked him straight out if there was some connection between Bunny's death and anything he'd been involved in at Bevel's."

Harry sucked in his breath and managed not to groan out loud. "What exactly did you say to him?" he asked, trying to keep his voice even.

She grinned. "Good control, Harry. I thought you'd already be swearing at me."

"I should be. What did you say?"

"Let's see. Something about your finding out that after Jefferson Toomey retired, somebody at Bevel's had been using Bunny to carry messages and maybe other things and probably paying him extra to keep quiet about what he was doing. Then I said, as if I'd thought of it and not you, 'I think he might have heard or seen things he shouldn't, and whoever had been using him had underestimated how much Bunny understood.'"

"That's it?"

"Well, no. Not quite." She paused and managed to look guilty and defiant all at once. "I said if I found out he had anything to do with Bunny's death, I would personally eat his liver. I got a little carried away."

Seeking guidance, Harry looked up at the sun scattering light through the trees and, finding no help there, forced himself to put his hands in his pockets because he wanted so badly to shake her. He cleared his throat. "Why did you do it?"

"I told you. I intend to become a lot more active in this investigation."

"No."

"No what?"

"No. You're not going to become more actively involved in this."

Her face darkened. "I am and you can't stop me."

That did it. She cracked his anger, and he couldn't help laughing. He scooped up her hands in his and said, "You must have been a terror on the school grounds."

Her face grew even redder. "I'm not going to let you go on treating me like a kid. Esther talked to me about growing up, and when we were done talking, I decided it was time I did."

Harry was pleased to hear she had talked with her sister and wanted to question her about the conversation, but he needed to settle this business of her taking a more active role in the investigation, if he could get to it. "I'm sorry you think I treat you like a kid. It's not my intention."

She looked at him, the anger dying in her eyes. "You don't treat me like a woman, do you?"

Before he could answer, she had freed her hands, stepped forward, and thrown her arms around his neck. Without thinking, Harry caught her in an embrace and found that she was indeed a woman.

"Well, don't just stand there, kiss me," she said.

"That might not be a good idea," he answered a little hoarsely, wanting very much to do as he was told.

"Harry. Kiss me."

He did and had no trouble making it a real kiss

"I liked that," she said, a bit out of breath.

She was still pressed against him with her head tilted back, regarding him judiciously.

"So did I. What are you looking at?" He was trying very hard to get his mind off how good it was to hold her and how quickly he had responded to her kiss.

"You. You're not bad looking, you know. And you kiss pretty good too."

"Are you an expert in these things?" he asked, releasing her.

"I don't have to be. I guess we're not just going to go on with this right now."

"That's right."

She let her arms slide away from him and glanced at the ground around them. "It's just as well. This place has more things that bite than a pail full of snakes."

Harry laughed. "Are you speaking from experience?"

"None of your business." She took one of his hands. "Come on, the walk isn't over yet."

When Harry felt he had recovered his composure, he said, "Getting back to treating you like a kid."

"You're showing improvement," she said.

"Never mind. My first responsibility is to see that no harm comes to you. And you've just made that part of my job a lot more difficult. Next, you've told everybody at Bevel's we're coming after them. I wish you hadn't done that. And one last thing. To investigate a murder properly, you do need some experience."

"Okay," she replied, giving him a knowing smile, "let's make a trade. You tell me how to investigate a murder, and I'll teach you some more about kissing."

21

When Harry got home he sat down on his lanai with the intention of thinking about his walk with Martha, and found he was worried, amused, and frustrated in more or less equal proportions. He admired her dash, and he was flattered by her physical advances, even if he did suspect it was mostly a case of having decided to be more aggressive and trying it on with Uncle Harry.

But she had said plenty to worry him. He began by reviewing what she had told Mark. From what he knew of the man, he doubted he would put his sister in any real danger. But he couldn't be sure. That meant he was going to have to treat the threat to Martha as real. Reaching that conclusion justified his frustration because Harry knew that it was almost impossible to protect anyone from a determined attacker.

Troubled, but unable to find the answers he wanted, he checked his watch and went to the phone.

"Hold on. She's around here somewhere," Angel Wing said.

Esther Roberts came on the line.

"Hi. I called Martha, but I don't think I made a lot of headway. Getting her to talk with me was like pulling teeth. I feel bad about it, although I know I shouldn't."

"You helped, believe me, but I doubt she knew how to say so. Now I want you to do something else. I want you to ask her to visit you."

Esther was quick. "Is she in danger?"

"I don't know. She may be."

"Why?"

Harry gave her a sanitized version of John's job at Bevel's, about his own run-in with the truck, and about Jefferson Toomey's murder, and concluded by telling her what Martha had said to her brother Mark.

Esther sighed like a mother and said, "Sure, I'll try, but don't count on my getting her out here. And it sounds as if you had better start being extra careful yourself."

"I'm taking steps," Harry said, finding talking with Esther had made him feel better. Something, he thought wryly, about a cleaner, greener land and then laughed. Where Esther lived wasn't greener unless Christo had painted the desert.

Fontaine Bevel's office was in the same concrete building Harry had visited when he talked to Ralph Hawkins. It was on the second floor with double-glazed glass in the windows, a Turkish carpet on the floor, and desks and chairs made of some almost black South American wood that shone like polished marble and looked a lot more expensive. Once the door closed behind Harry, the noise of the mills and the heavy equipment was reduced to a low background rumble.

"Come in here and have a seat," Bevel said, shaking Harry's hand and steering him toward one of the black wood chairs fitted with maroon leather. "What are you drinking?"

He was already on his way to the liquor cabinet, glittering with crystal decanters and glasses, backed up by rows of bottles.

"I've got some single malt here that would make a Scotsman drop his kilt. But if you're a bourbon fancier like me, I can do that too."

"I'm going to pass," Harry said. "I appreciate your taking the time to talk with me."

"Hell, think nothing of it." Bevel came back with a serious drink uncontaminated by ice. He dropped into a chair and grinned at Harry, displaying a full set of very white teeth. "I've been told one of my trucks ran you off the road. That's a damned shame. I'm sorry for it. Of course, my lawyers would howl like tomcats being cut if they knew I was talking to you. Screw them, however. I wasn't driving the goddamned thing. I'm just glad you're still around to talk to."

Bevel was dressed in stone chinos, Italian sandals, and a black silk shirt open at the neck. He was trimmed like a Christmas tree, with a thick gold chain around his neck, a gold watch, a heavy gold bracelet on his right wrist, and a solid onyx and gold ring on his right hand. He wore his thinning blond hair down to his collar and sported a pair of rose-tinted designer glasses. Despite the youthful turnout, Harry thought, judging from Bevel's weathered face, the man was about his own age. Harry remembered Belle Chance and tried hard to dislike his host.

Bevel took a long drink, said, "Aha," grinned at Harry again, and asked what he could do for him. To his disgust, Harry found he was actually getting to like the raffish idiot, if he was an idiot. Well, anyone who began drinking at eleven in the morning must be something of an idiot—unless that was what he wanted Harry to think. Now he was making up stories. Harry moved on.

"What can you tell me about John Roberts? He worked for Bevel's for about fifteen years, right up to the time he was murdered."

Bevel set his glass on the stand beside his chair. "You know, I don't believe I ever met the man. He went missing didn't he?"

"I'm surprised you remember," Harry said, thinking that if this man's a liar, he's a good one.

He had hoped he might stir up something with the comment, but Bevel only nodded.

"I'm surprised too, when I think how much booze I've drunk. Say, didn't I read somewhere that he or what was left him was pulled out of the Luther Faubus Canal? How long had he been in there?"

"Four years. How long has your father been dead?"

Bevel paused and looked past Harry, a shadow of something crossing his face. "A little over four years."

"What did John Roberts do here?"

"You'd have to ask Ralph Hawkins about that. He's the head honcho in personnel." He paused to chuckle. "We've got a name for everything."

"I've talked with Hawkins. Perhaps I'd better talk with him again."

Harry was getting more and more puzzled by Bevel. Had Hawkins really not told him about their talk? If not, what did that signify?

"Then you never used Roberts as a personal messenger or anything like that?"

He shook his head. "Do you think something this guy did while he was working here had something to do with his death?"

"Probably not," Harry said and got to his feet.

"How did he get in that canal?" Bevel asked.

"I don't know. That's what I'm trying find out."

"Maybe I could ask around, see if I can turn up anything, but it's been a long time. I'm sorry not to have been more help."

They shook hands.

"Thanks for your time, Mr. Bevel."

"You're welcome. And call me Fontaine. That way I know I'm not my daddy. He was Mr. Bevel and with any luck, I won't ever be."

Snyder's call caught Harry just as he was leaving the house.

"I'm not too happy telling you this, Harry," the policeman said. "And I don't want you doing anything about it until we've

180

talked, you hear?"

"How can I answer that, Jim, when I don't even know yet what you're talking about?" He could never resist needling Snyder.

"Well, just hold your horses and I'll tell you," the captain said, bridling. "I never get to have just a plain conversation with you. Talking to you is like driving on a road full of sharp corners and chickens trying to cross it." Then he saw what had happened and stopped himself. "Very funny, Harry. I've got a good mind not to tell you."

"You're going to tell me."

"Yes, I am. Now listen. The gun that killed John Roberts was used in a homicide seven years ago." He stopped.

"I'm waiting," Harry said.

Snyder sighed heavily. "Here's the bad part. After the trial, the assistant district attorney turned it back to Evidence."

"Matthew Roberts."

"That's right."

"I'll be there in twenty minutes."

"Where is the gun now?" Harry asked.

He and Jim Snyder and Frank Hodges were in Snyder's office, which was one step up in décor from the interview room in the county jail. Hodges insisted that the flimsy chairs and skinny brown rug had been made in Louisiana by prison labor. Snyder denied it.

"We hope Old 10-30 still has it," Hodges answered with a broad grin.

"Sergeant, this is no time for jokes. And now that Brock's here, let's just let him fill the joker role."

That was pretty good for Snyder, Harry thought. He must be taking this gun business seriously. Hodges put both hands up, palms facing the captain, but his broad face expressed no contrition.

"What we've got here," Snyder went on, "is a very sensitive situation—"

"Maybe," Harry interrupted. "But more to the point, we've got our first real window into John Roberts's death. What do you think the chances are that he stole that gun from his brother's Evidence Section and shot himself with it?"

"None," Hodges said flatly.

"Hold on," Snyder said, rapping on the desk with a pair of handcuffs lying on its battered metal surface. "Let's not get carried away. It's way too early to be drawing conclusions."

"Are you sure Matthew's got the gun?" Harry asked, thinking about Hodges's comment.

"He must have," Snyder said, in a slightly calmer voice. "Didn't you give it back to him after you wrote down the serial number?"

"Yes," Harry said, "but I need to know that it's still there and that it won't suddenly disappear."

Snyder ran his hand over his cropped, pale hair. "That's the sensitive part."

Hodges made a snorting sound and started to say something, but Snyder told him to save his remarks for later. Hodges subsided with a rumble of disgust.

"I either get what I want here, Jim, or it goes to the judge."

"Harry, there's no need to bring Judge Bryde in on this. We're going to make sure the gun's where it's supposed to be. Then . . ." His voice trailed off.

"You just realized there's no other place but the Evidence Section to keep it. I think it's time you had a talk with Sheriff Fisher."

Snyder pushed his chair back as if Harry had dropped a timber rattler on his desk. "Are you out of your mind? Do you know how hooked up Matthew Roberts is in this county?"

"Martha's lawyer isn't going to argue with you about this, Jim. Somebody with access to the Evidence Section either shot John with that revolver or gave it to somebody else to use. And what jury is going to believe that last option?"

Snyder groaned, and Hodges pushed onto his feet and said, "I think we ought to go over there right now and tell the son of a bitch to hand it over."

"We're not going to do any such thing!" Snyder shouted. "We're not going anywhere near the Evidence Section, not without a release order from either Fisher or the ADA."

"That tears it," Harry said and stalked out.

Harry went from Snyder's office to Arnell Property Management. Martha was talking with her boss. Bob Arnell saw him through the glass wall and waved. Harry waved back and forced himself to smile at Mr. Wonderful.

On their way back to her work area, Martha said, "When you waved to Bob, you looked as if you were trying to swallow a peach seed. What's was that all about?"

"My ex-wife," Harry said before he thought, then added quickly, "but it's not what that sounds like."

She started to ask another question, but he interrupted her. "Forget Bob Arnell. The gun that killed your brother came from the Evidence Section of the county sheriff's department. More than that, I don't know, but you need a lawyer, a good one. I suggest Jeff Smolkin. He's smart, energetic, and best of all, he's got plenty of trial experience."

Martha went milk white. He pulled a chair around and, taking her by the arms, eased her into it. "I'm sorry," he said. "I sprang that on you too fast. I wasn't thinking. Are you going to faint?"

"Maybe. Your wife worked here, didn't she?"

"Yes. Do you want some water?"

"No. Just talk to me."

"And she wanted me to give up my work and learn property management," he said a little desperately. He was feeling very guilty. "I heard about how safe I'd be working here and what a great husband and father Bob Arnell is until it was running out my ears."

"He really is a great guy," Martha said in a shaky voice.

"Sounds familiar," Harry said. "Are you feeling better?"

"This is good news, isn't it?"

"Yes."

"Why do I need a lawyer?"

"Because finding out where that gun came from means it's almost certain your brother didn't shoot himself."

"Tell me more about the gun." She had regained some color in her cheeks.

Harry relaxed a little. "The gun had been used in a crime. There was a trial, and after the trial the gun was returned to the Evidence Section. Somehow, someone must have taken the gun out of the Evidence Section, and then it was used to kill your brother."

She stood staring at Harry, her dark eyes full of pain. "Bunny couldn't have taken that gun. Matthew would never have let him. Bunny wouldn't even have known it existed."

"No, probably not," Harry said quietly. "That's one reason you need a lawyer. That gun has to be located and made secure. I probably can't do that, and the sheriff's department is going to tiptoe around the problem as long as they can."

"Why?"

"Demanding custody of the gun is tantamount to accusing Matthew of some kind of wrongdoing." He hesitated. "Possibly murder."

"Where is the gun now?"

"It was in the Evidence Section. Then it went to the state labs. After they determined it was the gun that killed John and that it was also the same gun that had been used in the crime I mentioned earlier, it should have been sent back to the Evidence Section in the sheriff's department."

"To Matthew?"

"Yes. He should have checked it back in and refiled it."

"Then it must be there. Matthew is the most careful person I know. He doesn't make mistakes."

"We all make mistakes."

"Not Matthew."

Harry backtracked. "Matthew and the other people working in Evidence are responsible for it now and were responsible for it when it was taken. Do you understand what that means?"

She narrowed her eyes at him. "I can't do this," she said and dropped back onto her chair.

"Let me call Smolkin."

She shook her head slowly as if her mind was having trouble processing what she had heard. Harry waited.

"There has to be another answer," she protested.

"Hire Jeff," Harry said, "and then try to find it."

22

Martha looked as if she had walked into a wall. Harry wanted to put his arms around her and tell her everything was all right. But it wasn't, and until she decided whether or not she was willing to accept the consequences of pursuing her brother's killer, there was nothing more he could do for her. He sat with her until she said she was ready to go back to work. Then he left.

Half a dozen years ago, Jeff Smolkin had represented Luis Mendoza, a client of Harry's, wrongly charged with murder. Thanks to Harry, Smolkin cleared Mendoza of the charges. In those days, Smolkin was a struggling lawyer working out of a third-floor walkup office in a rundown section of Avola where you could walk for a long time without seeing a gold chain. It was still rundown, but Smolkin no longer worked there. His office was now on the top floor of a new complex with a view of the Seminole River and an elevator that wafted its occupants up and down in silent comfort.

"Harry! Get in here! Man, it's good to see you. Betty, hold my calls." Smolkin was shaking Harry's hand and herding him through his inner office door, talking and laughing as they went.

"How have you been, Jeff?" Harry said, grinning in spite of himself. Although the lawyer was older, balder, and thicker through the middle, his energy was as high and infectious as ever.

"Sit down. Can I get you anything to drink?" Harry shook

his head. "What brings you out of the woods? You and Old La-
Beau still on Bartram's Hammock, making the place safe for
the wild things?"

"We're hanging on. I heard you're married. Congratulations."

"Thank you. Nice of you to mention it. Anything new with
you and Katherine?" He slowed down to ask the question, and
his round face grew serious.

"No. That's pretty well behind me." Harry thought that
answer had probably lengthened his nose.

"I'm still sorry."

"Thanks."

"What brings you up here?" He had settled into a green
leather chair beside Harry.

"We're off the record for a few minutes. Okay?"

"Sure thing." Smolkin locked his fingers in front of his
stomach and leaned forward to listen.

"If you have to charge me for this talk, fine, but what I'm going to say to you is confidential. It involves what I think is a
murder masquerading as a suicide. It happened four years ago."

Harry told Smolkin he was working for Martha Roberts and
laid out what he had learned and what his speculations were
about the death of John Roberts, concluding with the events
surrounding the gun that had been found in the car with the
man's remains. When he was finished, Smolkin ran a hand over
his vanished hairline and gave a low whistle.

"You don't know where that gun is now?"

"Not for sure."

Smolkin nodded. "If Roberts will call me, I'll take the case. If
she won't, I'll give you what help I can. We can sign a contract
if that will make you feel better about protecting our conversations, but I won't take a cent from you. I owe you, Harry. The
Luis Mendoza case made my name in this town, and without

you, it wouldn't have happened. As it was, it damned near got you killed."

"I'm still here."

"Yes you are and stubborn as ever. Which is good." He got up. "Give me a couple of days. I'll see what the law is on this and get back to you. And don't be such a stranger. You do eat lunch, don't you?"

Harry admitted he did, shook hands again, and left feeling that he had some reliable backup. He remembered that Smolkin had always had that effect on him. If they were going to clone people, they should begin with the Smolkins of the world.

When Harry got home, Tucker was just turning out of his driveway. Oh, Brother! was pulling the green buckboard Tucker favored now when he wanted to get around the Hammock. He still walked the woods, but if he could ride he did. It gave Harry a twist in his stomach to see his old friend perched on the buckboard's padded seat. Tucker was not, as Harry wanted to believe, immune to time's passing.

Sanchez met Harry with a grin as he stepped down from the Rover and led him toward the buckboard. Oh, Brother! waggled his ears at Harry and then went back to munching from his nosebag.

"Hubbard Clampett rang me this morning," Tucker called to Harry. "Next week Bevel's going to start bulldozing a road right through that Atala breeding area. I've been trying to call Casanova, but all I get is his voice mail. I can't think what else to do."

"I'll try talking to Fontaine," Harry said. "It can't hurt and might do some good. Don't get too worked up over this. We've got four days to resolve this in our favor."

"I'll wait while you call," Tucker answered, "and I'm not 'worked up.' I'm damned mad. I'll tell you one more thing.

Those people are not going to bulldoze a single shovel full of dirt in there. I've got enough dynamite to blow the treads off a dozen of their damned bulldozers. And if we can't stop them any other way, I'll do it with dynamite."

"Just go on being calm while I make the call," Harry said. "If you want to come onto the lanai, I could find a glass of lemonade for you to drink. It's hot enough out here to fry eggs on a rock."

"Just make the call," was Tucker's answer.

"Hello, Harry Brock," Fontaine said. "I haven't had time to find out much about your John Roberts."

"This is about something else," Harry said. "It has to do with that piece of land you bought from the Lucy Mott Covington estate."

"Hell, yes. Three Rivers damned near busted my balls over that deal. What about it?"

"There's a section of it close to the county road and just about west of Bartram's Hammock that's got a colony of Atala butterflies living and breeding in there. Those butterflies are a subspecies with some markings that make them unique. The state is going to protect them. That means protecting their habitat. What I hear is that you plan to go in there next week and bulldoze a road right through their breeding site."

"Whooee," Fontaine said. "You know more about what this outfit is doing than I do. Some biologist or bug man did talk to me a while back saying something about some butterflies on my land. But, you know, Brock, I don't remember much about it. Can I get back to you on this?"

"Fontaine, this is serious. If your company does anything to harm those butterflies, you're going to court."

"You're not threatening me are you, Brock?"

"Of course not. I'm trying to warn you, but I can't tell how much of what you say to me is you and how much is bullshit."

189

"I know just what you mean. Half the time, I can't tell either. Give me half an hour."

"Tucker, you'd better come in," Harry called from the lanai. "Bevel's got to talk with somebody."

"Just like his father," Tucker grumbled, collapsing into one of Harry's white lounges.

Sanchez was stretched out like a dead dog on the cool tiles, and Oh, Brother! with a pail of water for comfort was dozing in the shade of one of the oaks with his nosebag slung from a hame.

"How's that?" Harry asked, passing Tucker a sweating glass of lemonade.

"Whenever you asked him anything, especially if it might cost him a nickel, he always had to talk with somebody."

"I got the idea Fontaine didn't know anything about a plan to bulldoze a road through that piece of ground."

"Don't trust him any farther than you can carry Oh, Brother!," Tucker said after taking a long drink. "The genes in that family all come in a triple twist."

A moment later the phone rang.

"I don't like telling you this, Brock," Fontaine said cheerfully. "It sounds downright unfriendly, but my financial people tell me it would cost us less to pay the fine for messing up the Atala's breeding ground than it would to develop an alternative route into the new land we've just bought. Brock, you wouldn't believe what I had to pay for that chunk of dirt and rock, and unless I develop a return on it PDQ, my ass is going to be on fire."

"Why not talk to Fred Casanova at the State Conservation Commission?" Harry countered. "There might be a way to work out a plan that would give Bevel's access and protect the Atala's habitat."

"I hear you, Brock. It's a good idea, except for one thing. If I start talking to Brother Casanova, and the first thing you know, six months will have turned to dust and ashes, and I'll still be standing out on the county road looking for a way into my property. Mr. Casanova's just found out we've got maybe another eight weeks before the Commission can review our proposal. The bank has hired the sheriff, and he's formed a posse. My checks are bouncing all over Southwest Florida. And, as I said before, Brock, my ass is on fire."

Harry hung up.

"The worst thing about it," Harry said as Tucker was climbing into the buckboard, "is that what he said makes a certain amount of sense."

"As the fox said to the chickens," Tucker replied, picking up the reins.

"Don't even think of opening that box of dynamite," Harry shouted after the old farmer as the buckboard jingled out of the yard.

"I'm not," Tucker called back.

Later that afternoon, Harry called Martha Roberts before driving to Pecan Grove. The sun was going down between two towering thunderheads like a red giant, streaking the clouds and the sky vermilion. More heat coming, Harry thought. A very safe forecast.

"How are you feeling?" he asked her as he got out of the Rover.

She managed a smile. "I'm not sure," she told him, leading him into her trailer.

In her green shorts and white jersey, she looked to Harry way too vulnerable to deal with what had been piled on her plate. It also occurred to him that after being brought up in the protected center of the Roberts family, she was probably about to be ejected from it. He hoped Esther called soon.

"Have you thought any more about hiring a lawyer?"

"Maybe. I don't know."

"Smolkin will take you on if you want him. He's good, Martha. They don't come any better. And you'd like him."

They were sitting together on the couch, and she was leaned forward, her chin in her hands and her elbows on her knees. She straightened up and turned to face him, her dark eyes wide with some private pain. "But somebody's made a mistake," she said. "The gun can't be the one Matthew had charge of. He'd never let an unauthorized person take anything out of the Evidence Section. Everybody says how careful he is."

"Martha, listen to me. A year or two before your brother died, the gun that killed him was used in another crime committed here in Tequesta County. The person who committed the crime was arrested, tried by the district attorney, convicted, and sent to prison. The gun was returned to the Evidence Section. Someone took it out of there and used it to kill John. There's been no mistake. I'm sorry this is so painful for you, but what happened, happened."

"But what if Matthew is somehow blamed for what happened. I can't . . ." Her voice failed. Tears spilled down her cheeks.

There was a box of Kleenex on the stand beside him. He pulled several from the box and passed them to her. Then he put his arm around her and pulled her against him.

"You don't have to do anything more than you've already done. But you now have information that probably establishes that John didn't kill himself. And if he didn't, someone else did. What you do with that information is entirely up to you."

She had mopped herself dry and blown her nose while he talked. Now she rested her head on his shoulder and appeared to him to be struggling with what he'd told her. He kept his arm around her shoulders and waited. A moment or two later, she sighed and raised her head.

"I'm going to have to do this, aren't I?" she said as though it was making a statement rather than asking a question.

"It's whatever you say. Unfortunately, there are costs for you both ways."

"You'd go ahead, wouldn't you?" Another statement.

"Probably. But that doesn't mean you have to."

"No, but how would I live with myself if I didn't?"

"Any answer I make, Martha, will put pressure on you. But whatever you do, go where your heart takes you. This is about Martha Roberts and who she is."

He took his arm away, giving her space. He didn't want her to begin thinking she needed holding up.

She gave a brief, harsh laugh. "I'm not sure I know who I am, Harry." She looked at him with a rueful smile. "But I know who I want to be."

"That's a start."

"Are you with me?"

"Yes."

The smile had died but Harry saw a new determination in her dark eyes.

"I'll call Smolkin," she said and added, "I may not want to but I will."

23

Two days later Jeff Smolkin called Harry. "I talked to Martha Roberts. From what I know so far, it's none too soon. You did some good work, Harry. There's at least a wrongful death suit here, but right now I'm focusing on Harley Dillard."

"The new district attorney?"

"Right. Since Eric Smith left for Tallahassee."

"We lost a good law man to politics when he was elected to the state senate."

Smolkin laughed. "They're all honorable men."

"What about the gun?"

"Here's how it works. If Dillard decides there's grounds for reopening the Roberts case, he or one of his people or any officer assigned to the case can go to the Evidence Section and sign it out. That would remove it from Matthew Roberts's custody. The gun can then be held by whoever signs it out for as long as necessary to do whatever he needs to do with it."

"I'd sleep better with that revolver in Dillard's office."

"I hear you. Stay close to me on this. Getting Dillard to reopen quietly might not startle Roberts or whoever in his section spirited that gun out of there in the first place."

"Are you going to speak with Sheriff Fisher?"

"Not yet. Bob's a good man, but he is not going to want this case reopened. Admitting your department called a murder a suicide and having it get out that the gun used in the shooting was taken out of your Evidence Section is not the stuff great reelection campaigns are built on.'"

"He wouldn't mess with evidence."

"No, but he's got Matthew to deal with. Let's not put temptation in his path."

"Okay, I'll keep digging, but I'm not sure there's much more I can do."

"What about Martha Roberts? She at any risk?"

"She may be. In fact, I'm trying to get her sister Esther to lure her to Arizona for a while. Until then, don't tell her things that could get her into trouble if she repeats them. She's a leaky boat where her family's concerned."

"Okay, but I've already told her how I'm going to go about recovering that gun. Talk to you later."

Harry thought that over and decided the sooner Martha went to Esther the better. He checked his watch. Tucker had caught up with Fred Casanova, and the Conservation Commission's entomologist was coming for another look at the Atalas. Harry agreed to accompany him and Tucker on the survey.

Casanova, looking more and more like a heron to Harry, listened carefully while Harry recounted his conversation with Fontaine Bevel.

"It doesn't sound good," he said. "Let's have a look."

When they reached the butterfly site, he leaped out of the Rover, strode into the woods, and set up a howl of protest. When Harry and Tucker caught up with him, Harry saw the yellow grade stakes poking out of the ground cover and his heart sank. "This hundred-foot-wide swath we're looking at here," Casanova shouted, waving his arms to indicate where the proposed road would drill west through the woods, "is going to take out almost the entire stand of coonties in the area."

"And that means," Tucker put in grimly, "an entire generation of these butterflies now in the larval stage is going to be exterminated."

"That's right," Casanova continued in a loud voice, his hawk bill nose sweeping back and forth like a scythe as he swung his head around surveying the ground. "And that means, good-bye Atalas."

"Can you do anything?" Harry asked, his mind filling with the picture of Tucker and his box of dynamite.

"I'm doing it right now," the tall man said.

He was wearing a sleeveless canvas vest covered with pockets. Fishing deeply in one of them, he pulled out a purple cell phone with silver stars on it. Tucker and Harry stared at him.

"It's my daughter's," he said uneasily. "And I'm in big trouble. This morning mine had a dead battery. I took hers while she was still asleep."

Harry returned the mandatory smile, but with a twist of pain he thought of what he was missing with his own daughters, Sarah already an adult and Minna almost ten.

"It's worse than I thought," Casanova said to the person who answered. He listened briefly, then said, "Call Figuel. Tell him the grade stakes are in and the colony is in Bevel's crosshairs. Don't take any shit from him, Patricia. Tell him to do it."

He followed up the comment with several instructions and the names of people to be called and put the phone away. "I've done what I can," he said glumly.

"Who's Figuel?" Tucker demanded when Casanova snapped the phone shut.

"Figuel Miranda," Casanova replied. He was frowning and obviously thinking of something else.

"He's the Fish and Wildlife Conservation Commissioner," Harry said.

"What's he going to do?" Tucker asked.

Casanova fidgeted with his vest, walked three paces away, turned, and strode back like a stork on a leash. "The system isn't perfect," he muttered, scowling as he spoke.

"Meaning what?" Tucker asked, his voice tight.

Casanova stopped and stared at the old farmer. "We can order Bevel's to halt operations here, but we can't actually stop the company from doing anything it wants to do."

"The Commission only has any real teeth after something is done," Harry said.

Casanova made a sour face. "Bevel is going to get a warning notifying him that to take or harass a protected species is a criminal offense. If Fontaine Bevel thinks driving a road through these Atalas will result in nothing more than a civil action, he's been living in dreamland."

"Who's issuing the warning?"

"I am, just as soon as the commissioner gives me the authorization."

"Has he given it?"

Casanova shifted his feet a little. "No, but he will just as soon as Patricia tells him what's going on here."

"Is he the one Patricia's not to take any shit from?"

"You never heard me say that."

Tucker still wasn't smiling. "When will Bevel get the notification?"

"Tomorrow or the next day. It will be sent express mail."

"If Patricia gets hold of the commissioner."

"That's right."

"Is he hard to find when a notice of this sort has to be sent?" Harry asked.

"Never has been," Casanova said and looked at his watch. "Got to go," he said, setting off with long strides for the Rover. "I've got another stop in Everglades City. Somebody's been robbing eggs from alligator nests. It's a first. I figure they've adapted a chicken incubator. Shouldn't be all that hard to do."

"I'm not feeling all that much better after hearing that,"

Tucker grumbled as they trailed after Casanova. "How about you?"

"The threat of criminal prosecution might be enough to stop Fontaine, even if a civil suit isn't," Harry said without much conviction.

"I don't like the odds," Tucker said in a level voice.

"Neither do I," Harry agreed, "but I like the idea of your vigilante alternative even less."

Tucker snorted and picked up his pace.

Harry went home and called Martha at her office. The receptionist picked up for her and said she had just left on her lunch break. He asked where she usually ate lunch.

"At Murphy's over on Third and Central."

Harry thought he might catch her, and if he didn't, he could at least get something to eat. But before he left, he made another call.

"You wreck it, we fix it," a loud voice answered.

"Hello, Rob. It's Harry Brock."

"You haven't put the Rover into a creek again, have you?" MacDougal replied with a roar of laughter.

"No. I've got a question for you."

"Let's have it."

"Where would you take a truck if you wanted to have scratches patched and some paint put on it, and you didn't want it talked about?"

"I'd do it myself, and that's what I think they did," MacDougal answered several decibels more quietly. "They've got their own shop."

It took Harry a moment to make the connection. "We're talking about the same thing here?"

"Sure."

"How did you know?"

"Avola's a small town in lots of ways. I know pretty well everybody here in my line of business. People talk to one another."

"And you're sure that's what happened?"

"No, but I put two and two together. Remember, I saw the color of the paint that had scraped off on the back of the Rover."

"Is there somebody I should talk to?"

"You know anybody at all over there except the brass?"

"Yes." Harry had thought of Wetherell Clampett.

"Here's another name, but you didn't get it here."

"Understood."

"Freeman Todd."

Harry thanked MacDougal and hung up.

Martha was sitting alone in a booth toward the back of the diner, reading a book with a cup of coffee looking neglected in front of her.

"Mind if I sit down?" Harry asked.

She waved him into the booth and greeted him with a welcoming smile. "You bringing me more bad news?" she asked, putting down the paperback.

Harry noticed she didn't look very worried and wondered if it was just more of her flight into health she had begun that day they walked beside the canal. She was wearing a blue, long-sleeved silk blouse with a square onyx locket on a gold chain. Fleeing from reality or not, she was looking very good. He said so.

"Thank you, Harry. You're showing all kinds of improvement."

That was a change from when she blushed and became angry whenever he paid her a compliment.

"Have you heard anything from Esther lately?" he asked.

A thin-lipped waitress, looking fed up with God's arrangements, appeared at the table and asked Harry if he wanted to order.

"How about a grilled grouper sandwich, hold the tomatoes?"

"You want it on a kaiser roll?"

"No, dark bread."

"Drink?"

"Water with lemon."

"It's getting so you can't give the beer away," she said wearily and left.

"To go back to Esther, yes, she called the other day and invited me to go out there for a visit."

"And?"

Her cheerfulness had left with the waitress. "And nothing. I'm not going."

"Why not?"

"Why should I? There's some movement in the investigation . . ." Her voice trailed off and she stared at the coffee.

"Jeff Smolkin and I can handle what needs to be done."

She raised her head to scowl at him. "Why the sudden interest in having me leave?"

"Because I think your asking Mark about whether or not John had learned things at Bevel's he shouldn't have known could have put you in some danger."

"Mark wouldn't harm me."

"Mark doesn't worry me. Whoever killed John does. And somebody killed Jefferson Toomey. I suspect the same somebody tried to kill me. I'd be a lot happier if you were in Arizona for a while."

Martha shook her head. "I can't go out there, Harry."

"Can't or won't?"

"Both."

Okay, he thought, I'll give her a few days to change her mind. He wasn't really happy with this plan, but he knew Martha well enough by now to know that trying to push her would be point-less, and he thought the odds were that she would be safe for now.

24

Harry spent the afternoon catching up on work that had collected like dust under the bed. At four-thirty he pushed back from his desk, stretched, and found his mind suddenly full of Helen Bradley. Putting Martha temporarily on hold had apparently provided space for Helen to reassert herself.

His first impulse was to push her away as quickly as she had arrived, but he resisted the impulse. He knew he had behaved badly in their last meeting, and he knew it was time he answered the question she had thrown at him. What did he want from her?

He wandered from his office onto the lanai and stood with his hands in his pockets watching a pair of mottled ducks make a noisy landing on Puc Puggy Creek and gradually settle down to feeding. He pushed open the screen door and crossed the lawn to the sandy road, absorbed in his thoughts. Around him the Hammock hummed and buzzed in the heat.

It was not a problem he wanted. It was tempting to rid himself of it by saying it was her problem to solve by choosing between him and Riga Kraftmeier. But it left her question unanswered. Tucker was right. She had a right to know what he wanted from her. All right, he'd tell her. The answer couldn't be all that hard to articulate.

After a few minutes of staring blankly at the water meadow beyond Puc Puggy Creek, he pulled his hands out of his pockets and strode purposefully toward the house, confident that he was not running away. If thinking wasn't going to solve the problem, he would talk to Helen and thrash it out with her.

"This doesn't have anything to do with lack of commitment," he said, carefully monitoring his voice level. "I just don't understand the question, Helen. My first response would be to say I don't want anything from you. But if I said that, you'd deliberately misunderstand me."

After dinner they had driven to the Peninsular and were walking through Admiral Park to watch the sunset over the Seminole River Pass. The sun was throwing long shadows across their path, and the royal palms lining the walk were glowing softly in the saffron light.

"Can I get in on this conversation?" she inquired. "Or do you want to go on having it with yourself?"

It was not an auspicious beginning. He threw up his hands. "Why do you think I'm here?"

"God may know. I certainly don't."

Harry laughed. What else could he do? Arguing with Helen was like stepping on a fire-ant nest and then trying to deal with the onslaught by swatting one ant at a time. "Go ahead," he said. "I'd bare my throat, but I know you'd cut it."

"And drink the blood," she answered. "If you don't want anything from me, why are we here?"

"Why are you here?" he countered.

They stopped to face one another.

"Because I love you, Harry," she said in a steady voice. "Because I'd do almost anything for a free meal. Because my calendar was empty. How are those for answers? Now, what brought you out of the woods?"

Harry looked at her and reminded himself that he had spent the past hour and a half with someone who never bored him, whose honesty and courage gave her clear-eyed beauty depth and a kind of gravitas. He knew where he was with her. Except when Riga Kraftmeier walked on stage. His heart lurched at the reminder.

"I lied. I do want something from you. I want your company."

He was stuck for a moment, but she saved him by kissing him and whispering in his ear, "What about my body?"

"That too," he said.

It was no use. He laughed and thought, She treats intimacy like castor oil. But what about his own laughter? What was that about? He winced and left the question unanswered.

By the time they reached the point of land bordering the pass, the sun had changed from saffron to vermilion and was melting into the Gulf in a blazing finale of purple and scarlet light. They picked their way among the rocks that formed the point until they found a place to sit down together and watch the day's fiery ending.

"There's still Riga," Harry said when the ceremony was over.

"Should I take notes? Will there be more new and startling information?"

Harry did not respond.

"Okay. I'm sorry. I don't think I can do anything about it."

"Meaning?"

"She's in my life, Harry, and she doesn't wash out."

Her answer startled him. It was not what he was expecting. And, to his irritation, the more he thought about what she'd said, the more opaque it became.

"I don't know what you mean by that," he said in disgust, as if his cognitive failure was her responsibility.

She shrugged. "I'm not surprised. I don't understand it myself. Maybe this is something that just has to work itself out."

"While whatever neither of us understands works itself out, what do we do?"

She leaned her head against his shoulder. "Take the milk in, and spend as much time as we can in bed."

Driving home the next morning, feeling better than he had for a while, Harry recalled Helen's comment about taking in the milk. He tried to dismiss it as another of her eccentric remarks, but it kept tugging at his mind the way a broken tooth attracts the tongue. He gave up and thought about it.

"Eliot," he said triumphantly as he bumped over the bridge onto the Hammock. "Something about the dark night of the soul." A shadow, black as a crow's wing, passed over him, leaving him chilled, and he told himself he could look up the reference, but the uneasiness lingered.

You never knew what she was going to come up with.

The first message on his answering machine came from Snyder.

"Harry, call me."

He did not like the sound of Snyder's voice. Instead of calling, he drove to the Headquarters Building.

"Martha Roberts is missing," Snyder said when Harry entered his office. "The duty officer took a call late last night from someone in Pecan Grove. The caller was probably a woman. She said Martha's car was standing beside the mailboxes at the entrance to Pecan Grove and that she wasn't in her trailer."

Harry experienced a rush of anger mixed with fear, but fought them down. If he was going to be of any help to her, he needed to think clearly.

"Of course we don't know anything is wrong," Snyder added quickly. "Mostly, in these kinds of situations it's nothing life threatening. She could have just gone somewhere with a friend."

"Jim, we're talking about Martha Roberts."

Hodges, red faced and sputtering angrily, got up from his chair, his hand outstretched. "I'm sorry, Brock," he said. "This is bad news. I'm not contradicting the captain, but when they go like this, they're usually gone. But we'll do all we can to find her. And if get my hands on the—"

"Frank," Snyder said, "don't go on. Harry knows we'll do everything we can . . ."

"That's right, Brock, even if she is probably already . . ."

"Frank!" Snyder shouted, coming out of his chair.

"Thanks, Frank," Harry said, shaking the sergeant's hand. "Who else knows about this?"

"Matthew Roberts. I called him just before I called you. He's calling Mark and his mother. He particularly didn't want me calling her. The officer on duty last night didn't know the family. He sent a deputy out to check out the situation. There was no evidence of a struggle. The keys were gone and the car was locked. No one answered calls to her home. No one he talked to out there knew anything."

"I don't think she just walked off," Harry said.

Snyder made a face. "I'm sorry to have to agree. But she's a strong, healthy woman. If somebody had dragged her out of the car or grabbed her while she was out of it, you'd think there'd be some scuff marks on the ground."

"Might have tapped her on the head and then just picked her up and carried her where they wanted to put her," Hodges said. "Lock up the car so as not to arouse suspicion. Keys are probably lying out there in that swale grass. Either that or she knew whoever went off with her."

"Who does she know who'd do anything like that?" Snyder asked in a dismissive voice.

Harry just shook his head. He did not want to waste time making the case to Jim that Matthew or Mark or both of them might have done what Hodges suggested.

"I've got one place I want to look," Harry said, "and it's easier for me to do it than to try to tell you how to get there. I'll keep in touch."

"No Lone Ranger stuff, Harry," Snyder protested. "I don't want to haul you out of Puc Puggy Creek a second time."

"That's right," Hodges put in. "This time they'll probably put a bullet in your head."

"Thanks, Frank," Harry replied, going out the door. "That makes me feel a lot better."

The odd thing was it did.

Harry parked the car where he had the day Martha had brought him here. He stood in the path and looked and listened. The morning was bright with snowy white thunderheads pushing up from the east into a cerulean sky. A breeze rattled the cabbage palms and hissed softly in the Fakahatchee grass bordering the canal. Two scrub jays were squabbling in a stand of pin oaks. Aside from those sounds, the woods and the water hung quietly, waiting to see what the day would bring.

Reasonably sure he was alone, he set off along the path, searching for trampled weeds and ferns or any other signs of a struggle. It had seemed just possible that she had brought someone else out here, and it had turned nasty. The path ended at the edge of a water meadow of head-high grass. Harry straightened up with a sigh, took a final look around, and went back to the Rover, relieved the search had left him empty-handed.

Driving home, he tried to develop a sequence of events that would account for her disappearance, but he came up with nothing compelling. And although one part of his mind told him she was dead, another and more stubborn part said, No, she's not. Accepting that idea was, disturbingly, more difficult to deal with because there was no logical reason for believing it was true.

Harry did not have a lot of faith in his intuition, but it refused to be silenced, and its persistence finally drove him to try to justify its persistence. Five miles from the Hammock, he suddenly slapped both hands on the steering wheel, made a U-turn, and drove back to Pecan Grove. Driving past the trailer park, he went on to Panther Trace.

The closer he got to James and Ruth Roberts's house, the more he doubted himself, but he knew he'd have no peace until he did what he'd come to do. There was an old, white Lincoln Town Car parked in the driveway. He wondered if it could be a doctor's car, but there was nothing on the plate to suggest that. Harry crunched up the path to the front door, and had one foot on the steps when the door swung open. A tall, square woman in her early forties with cropped black hair shoved back the screen with her left hand and said, "Stop right there."

She was wearing dungarees and a man's white shirt, knotted at the waist. In her right hand she held a Colt Frontier model revolver pointed at the floor. Harry saw by the way she held it and the way it fit her grip that she was not holding it for the first time.

"I'm Harry Brock," he said.

"I know who you are," she replied in a harsh voice, the scowl on her dark face growing more threatening. "It's your fault all this has happened."

He started to say that he hadn't kidnapped Martha, if that was what she meant, and checked himself. The look of hatred on the woman's face was as clear as a painted poster, and he decided he had better step carefully.

"I agree I'm partly to blame. Right now I'm trying to find Martha. Who are you?"

"Matthew Roberts's wife." She hesitated, and then said, "Felicity Roberts."

"Pleased to meet you," he responded. "I'm sorry about all this. Is your mother-in-law here?"

"Why?"

"I'd like to speak to her."

"That's not going to happen. What is going to happen is that this family will deal with Martha's situation. If we have to, we'll deal with you. This is going to be straightened out by us, and from now on, if you know what's good for you, you'll leave us alone. Now get out of here."

Harry took a chance. "Are you threatening me with that gun?"

She raised it high enough for him to look down the barrel and asked, "Why would you think that?"

That was when Harry turned on his heel and left.

25

Harry left Panther Trace and drove to the Bevel's plant. He half expected to be stopped at the gate and told to leave. But the bored man at the gate with a clipboard and an earphone radio wrote down his name and the time and waved him through. Harry didn't know whether to be pleased or insulted.

Gradually adjusting to the racket of the place, Harry drove around the yard until he found Wetherell Clampett.

"Christ, Brock," Clampett said, his head swiveling, "are you nuts? Bevel's put a goddamned bounty on your head."

"I hope he took a number and found the line," Harry said. "Can I talk to you?"

"Make it quick, and give me some kind of excuse that won't put my ass in a sling."

"Tell them I had a message for your father from Tucker La-Beau."

"Say, you know, I owe you one there. Mr. LaBeau's calling my father has made a big difference. They jaw away one or twice a week. I'm obliged to you. My father's a lot more lively these days."

"I'm glad to hear it. What can you tell me about Freeman Todd?"

"You know what he does for a living?"

"I've got an idea. I think he touched up that Bevel dump truck that damned near punched my clock."

"That's right, but don't you go over there and say so. We're

210

talking real mean people here."

"Where's 'over there'?"

Clampett blew out his cheeks, obviously stressed by the question. "They's a green half barn on Dooley Road. You cain't miss it. But if you're going over there, you go carrying, and don't let nobody get 'tween you and the door."

"Will I find Todd there?"

"Not if you're lucky, but, if not, yes. You go careful. Yuh hear?"

Harry found the place, and, sure enough, it looked as if the barn had been cut in half lengthwise and the front half hauled away. But to say it was painted was an exaggeration. Streaks and tatters of what had arguably once been green paint still clung to the building. But mostly it was bare wood, bleached and stained in grim streaks of rusty brown and mottled, yellowed gray.

Two wide overhead doors in the front of the barn were separated by a narrow door with a dirty window protected by heavy gauge screening. Remembering Clampett's warning, Harry stepped inside, being careful to leave the door slightly ajar. The huge floor space under the blackened roof was littered with pieces of machinery in various stages of disassembly. The air reeked of paint remover and a dozen other noxious chemicals. Harry tried not to breathe and failed. The blue flare and crackle of welding and cutting torches bloomed in half a dozen places in the dark interior.

"If you're selling anything, I ain't buying. If you're not, you've got the wrong place. Leave."

A grease-stained man with a shaved head disentangled himself from a road grader and came toward Harry holding a wrench at least two-feet long. He was tall, broad-shouldered and heavily muscled. His swift approach suggested to Harry that he intended to put the wrench to a new use.

211

"I'm looking for Freeman Todd. I'm not selling anything. I could be buying."

The man stopped and regarded Harry with a flat stare. "I'm Todd. What do you want?"

"My name's Harry Brock. I'm a private investigator in search of some information. If I get it, no one will ever know it came from you. A little while ago you did some work on one of Bevel's dump trucks. I'll pay to find out who brought the truck in and who picked it up."

Harry had not quite stopped speaking when the wrench left Todd's hand and flew straight at his head. Harry spun away on his left heel and saw the steel shaft flash past his face. By then Todd was reaching for him, but Harry decided he would have a better day if those hands didn't grab him. He bolted out the door, slammed it shut, and sprinted for the Rover. He blasted out of the parking area, leaving Todd in a swirl of dust.

"Jesus," Harry said in thanksgiving when he was safely off Dooley Road with no one behind him.

Being thrown out of two places before lunch seemed excessive to Harry, but the experiences had pretty well settled two questions: where Martha was and who had repaired Bevel's truck. A third as yet unanswered question was what he was going to do with the information.

Harry had intended to talk over his options with Tucker, always a good way of finding the holes in his reasoning, but when he reached the place where Bevel had put a road into the woods, he found a trailer truck unloading a very large, noisy bulldozer into the scraped-out parking area. Harry pulled off the road and went to find out what was happening. Wetherell Clampett was driving the trailer truck.

"Well, I'm glad to see you're still upright," the big man shouted over the roar of the tractor.

"It was a close thing," Harry replied. "Todd's not too sociable. What's going on?"

He was reasonably sure he knew, but he wanted Clampett's version.

"Tomorrow the road's going in."

"But not today."

"Nope. Don't forget to tell Mr. LaBeau how much I'm obliged to him."

"It's already done."

"Where's Oh, Brother! and Sanchez?" Harry asked, as Tucker walked him toward the house. Around them Tucker's gardens bloomed and bore with a profligacy that sometimes scared Harry.

"In the barn," Tucker said, giving way to a wicked chuckle.

"What are they doing?" The last time he arrived at the farm without being met by them, someone had just tried to burn Tucker's house down.

"Recuperating."

"The mother bobcat?"

"That's right. You want to see them?"

"Yes."

They were in bad shape. Sanchez was stretched out on a bed of straw in a corner of the mule's box stall. One of his ears was wrapped in white cotton and his snout was lacerated with nasty scratches. Patches of hair revealing bloody skin were torn from his back. He managed a feeble thump of his tail but would not look at Harry.

"Ashamed of himself. As he ought to be," Tucker said in a censorious voice. "And look at the other one."

Oh, Brother! had several deep scratches on his left shoulder. One of his ears looked as if it had been chewed, and his hat, sitting on the shelf beside his manger, was in tatters. Harry walked

213

over to the big mule and carefully put his hand on the animal's neck. Oh, Brother! waggled his good ear but kept looking into the corner. The wounds had all been treated, but they still made Harry shake his head. They looked painful.

"Pride goeth before a fall," Tucker said.

Harry seldom had cause to be critical of his friend, but he thought Tucker was being much too hard on his . . . Harry stuck. What were they? Not his pets, not his animals.

"You're being awfully hard on your friends," Harry said as they left the barn.

"Probably," Tucker replied, "but I'm taking good care of them, and I'm just getting a little of my own back. They were pretty rough on me when I was warning them about her. Making sarcastic remarks and snickering behind my back."

Harry had gotten in too far. "Did they find the den?"

"Yes, and they were playing with two of the kittens when Mrs. B. came home. By God, I wish I'd seen it. First she laid out Sanchez, and then before Oh, Brother! could get out of the way—he said he was afraid of stepping on one of the kittens—she climbed him like a tree and ripped into his hat and then his ear before sliding back down his shoulder with all her claws out for another go at Sanchez."

Tucker stopped to laugh. "His being a dog was against him. By now, they were running full out, but she rode first one then the other, putting in the rowels before finally dropping off and going back to her kittens. These two got back here bleeding like a couple of stuck pigs."

"They told you all that," Harry said, struggling to climb out of the rabbit hole.

"Oh, yes. They said they never heard such blood-curdling sounds as came out of her. Scared them worse than the licking she gave them. I heard her squalling and guessed what had happened."

By now he and Tucker had reached the back stoop.

"Wetherell Clampett says they're going to start that road through the Atala patch tomorrow," Harry said, having decided there was no gentle way to pass on the information.

"Hubbard's already told me. He feels bad about it. If this is Fontaine's doing, he's a skunk. If it's those other two gully shooters Ralph Hawkins and Mark Roberts, he's a coward for letting them run him that way. And I'm telling you this. They're not going to do it."

Tucker got Harry into a chair and for once, to Harry's relief, didn't offer him tea.

"Have you called Casanova?"

"I have, and he says he'll do what he can. That will probably be damned little."

Harry was startled. Tucker spoke with a bitterness that was new and worrying. "What about calling Figuel Miranda, the commissioner?"

"I tried. He's off in Washington, trying to influence some Everglades legislation. I'm thinking these butterflies are pretty far down on his Important Things list."

"Then I guess we'll have to leave it to Casanova. He's been pretty active so far." Harry was really hoping to get Tucker's mind off the dynamite. "I've got a couple more things to run past you."

Tucker eased himself into his rocker. "Let's hear them." He seemed to have recovered some of his good spirits.

Harry told him about Martha's disappearance and his visit to her mother's place. They talked about that for a while and then went on to Harry's Dooley Street visit.

"You've been busy," Tucker said with a chuckle. "But going to see this Freeman Todd seems right up there with Sanchez and Oh, Brother! deciding to play with Mother Bobcat's children. You didn't have that cannon of yours with you."

215

"No. That was probably a mistake."

"Now you've got somebody else with a reason to shoot you in the head, as Hodges would say. You know, his whole family's like that. Blunt as a stump."

"I'm thinking everything that's happened from John Roberts's death on is all tied together," Harry put in quickly, not wanting a tour through the Hodges's generations.

"Unified theories are seductive."

"What do you mean?"

"You're trying to pick the corn before you've planted the seed."

"I don't like the analogy." He was a little stung by Tucker's demolition of his shining edifice. "But there's probably some truth in it."

"Find Martha. We'll argue the analogy later."

Harry went home and called Esther Roberts.

"My God, I hope you're right and nothing bad's happened to her," Esther said. "But from here, your thinking seems pretty heavily laced with wishful thinking."

"Possibly. I see the problem. What I don't see is how to solve it without doing a lot of damage."

"A lot's already been done."

"That's true, but I've got an idea."

"I'm not going to like it, am I?"

"No," he said.

26

Harry had expected that. He called Jeff Smolkin. "Do you know Martha's missing?"

"Goddamn!" Jeff exploded. "Who's got her?"

"Somebody who wants this investigation into her brother's death to go away."

"You don't sound too upset. What's going on?"

"I may know where she is, but right now I can't do anything about it."

"Call Jim Snyder. Jesus, Harry, what's holding you back?"

"Jim can't help, at least not yet. I'm working on it, Jeff. As soon as I get this figured out, I'll let you know."

"That's not good enough, Harry!"

Harry broke the connection.

Forty-five minutes later he had Snyder and Hodges at his door.

"We got a call from Jeff Smolkin," Snyder said through the screen door.

"Something about withholding information on the whereabouts of Martha Roberts," Hodges added, sounding offended.

"Come on in," Harry said and pushed open the lanai door. "I knew I should have kept my mouth shut."

Once in the shade, Hodges pulled off his hat and mopped his face with his blue bandanna. "Hot," he said, "but when ain't it?"

"One or two mornings in January," Snyder answered, folding

217

himself onto a lounge chair. "What's going on here, Harry?"

"I may know where Martha is, but there's no way you can get to her."

"Brother, have you been smoking some bad shit," Hodges said and laughed loudly.

"Hold on, Frank," Snyder said, raising his hand. "Is this some kind of joke, Harry?"

"No."

"Then tell us where she is."

"I don't know. I'm only guessing, but right or wrong, if it's not handled very carefully, a lot of people could be hurt unnecessarily."

"So what are you saying?" Snyder did not sound pleased with what he'd heard.

"Your department goes on looking for her, and I try to find out if she's where I think she is."

"And if she is there, you'll tell me. No playing games."

Harry nodded. "No playing games."

Snyder blew out his breath and stood up. "Okay. You don't know where Martha Roberts is. If you find out where she is, you'll tell us."

"Right."

Harry didn't say when.

Harry was wakened by a very loud CRUMP which rattled his windows and sounded as if a heavy roof had fallen in.

"Oh, shit!" he groaned. "He's done it."

Flinging himself out of bed and into his clothes, he was reaching for the lanai screen door when he saw Sanchez in the road, coming at a run from the direction of the bridge. A huge moon was hanging in the oaks, flooding the yard with light. An instant later Oh, Brother! appeared in a full gallop, hooves pounding, pulling the buckboard with Tucker crouched forward over the dashboard, gripping the mule's reins and urging him on.

Harry ran toward the road, but before he got there the ghostly racers had vanished, and he was alone with only the flecks of mica in the swirling dust falling through the moonlight and flickering like tiny glow worms. He started for the Rover, then stopped.

Much as he wanted to see what had happened, the last place he ought to be, he realized, was anywhere near that bulldozer. Or near Tucker, he told himself, checking another strong impulse to drive after Tucker to ask him what the hell he had done. As if he didn't already know. Reluctantly, he went back into the house.

The problem was he couldn't fall asleep. As soon as he managed to stop thinking about what Tucker had probably done, his head filled up with Martha Roberts. Then, when he had gone over everything he had done and planned to do about her disappearance and persuaded himself he was doing the right things, Helen's unsmiling face filled his screen. For some reason he felt worse than he had when he was thinking about Martha. He was reasonably sure he knew what needed doing in her case. And there was no guilt involved.

"Why am I feeling guilty?" he demanded of the moon in his window as he clambered out of bed.

He had remembered that he had not looked up her Eliot quotation. Going downstairs was an evasion, and he knew it. But he definitely did not want to lie in bed thinking about Helen. At the same time he was busily assuring himself that this was all nonsense. There was no reason why he should feel guilty about Helen, and it was only to satisfy his curiosity that he was taking Eliot's *The Complete Poems and Plays* down from the shelf over his desk.

He found the line in "Fragment of an Agon." Sweeney is telling Snow, Swarts, Dusty, and Doris about the man who murdered a woman and kept her in his bathtub in a gallon of Lysol.

"This one didn't get pinched in the end / But that's another story too. / This went on for a couple of months / Nobody came / And nobody went / But he took in the milk and he paid the rent."

Then Swarts asks Sweeney, "What did he do?"

Another line of Sweeney's caught his eye. "Talk to live men about what they do."

Harry snapped the book shut and shoved it back onto the shelf as if it was suddenly too hot to hold. He almost ran back up the stairs, wishing very sincerely he had stayed in bed, and got back into it as quickly as he could. Then he managed to laugh at himself. Leave it to Helen to say something no one else would think of. "Talk to live men . . ." indeed.

Sure enough, at seven a.m. two uniformed deputies knocked on Harry's lanai door.

"Deputies Dan Springer and Berker Szalay," the blond one said.

"That's S-Z-A-L-A-Y," the taller one added, spelling slowly, as if Harry was deaf or borderline senile.

"Harry Brock," Harry said and pulled open the door.

"Is that with a C or a K?" Szalay asked, when the two men had sat down and Harry could see what they looked like.

"Both. What's up?"

They were painfully young and very serious, with cropped hair and their hats tucked under their arms. Szalay made a note of the spelling.

"We're investigating an incident involving a bulldozer belonging to Bevel's Sand, Stone, and Gravel Company. It's parked in a clearing on the west side of CR 19," Springer said.

"That's County Road 19, intersecting with the unsurfaced

road out here," Szalay interrupted, pointing with his pen at the road.

Springer nodded and continued. "The clearing is only about a half mile south of where this road—" Szalay pointed again at the road "—intersects with CR 19."

"I know where the clearing is," Harry said. He wished one of them would say something deliberately funny so he could laugh.

"Sometime between approximately four p.m. yesterday . . ."

Szalay checked his watch and said, "That would be the eighteenth."

". . . and seven a.m. this morning . . ."

"That would be the nineteenth," Harry said.

Szalay nodded.

". . . the bulldozer sustained damage that appears to have been deliberately inflicted."

Harry feigned surprise. "What happened to it?"

"Looks like the perp put some dynamite under the tracks and blew the suckers right off the wheels," Szalay said with obvious satisfaction.

"Inflicting serious collateral damage on the bulldozer in the process," Springer added.

"That's too bad," Harry said.

"Probably covered by insurance though," Szalay said quickly.

"Except for the deductible," Springer said.

"I wonder how much . . ." Szalay began, but Springer stopped him.

"We should probably . . ." He pointed his pen at Harry.

"Oh, sure."

"Did you hear anything last night, Mr. Brock?" Springer asked.

"No. I sleep pretty soundly."

"So do I," Szalay said. "But my wife, she's up and down half the night. So she tells me. I'm asleep so I don't . . ." He stopped himself.

Springer had been writing in his notebook. Szalay had his notebook open on his knee, but he was ignoring it.

"There's one thing Deputy Szalay and I are puzzled about," Springer said and scratched his head. "Does somebody around here drive a horse and buggy?"

"And have a big dog?" Szalay put in. "There's tracks all over the road."

Springer started to point, but Szalay beat him to it.

"It's a mule," Harry said.

"What is?" Szalay asked.

"It's a mule pulling the buckboard. The dog is a big bluetick hound. The man driving is Tucker LaBeau. He lives farther down the road."

Szalay and Harry both pointed. It was a dead heat.

"That's right," Harry said.

"We'd better talk to him," Springer said, looking at his partner.

The two men got up.

"We might be back," Springer said. "Thanks for your time."

"You're welcome." Harry wondered what they would make of Sanchez and Oh, Brother! and what Tucker would say to them. He dreaded to think. Probably make them drink some tea.

"I'm sorry you saw me," Tucker said, shaking his head. "It was my plan not to get you involved in any way."

"One of us in the state prison at a time would probably be enough," Harry replied.

"Nobody's going to jail, Harry," Tucker said, looking very relaxed. He pushed back to get his rocker moving. "That dynamite is stashed in an empty super in one of my beehives. And there's nothing else to tie me to the bombing."

"Do you think what you've done is going to solve the

problem?" Harry was so concerned about Tucker's breach of
the peace his voice had grown sharp.

"No, but it's given the Commission time to get itself
organized. And the police are looking at Bevel's. The two tall
trees who visited us aren't as dumb as they appear. The dark-
haired one, when he stopped pointing at things, asked some
good questions."

"Did he want to know how Oh, Brother! spelled his name?"

Tucker laughed. "He did. Then he asked how upset I was
over the threat to the butterflies."

"You told them about the butterflies?" Harry's voice rose.

"Don't get aerated. Of course I did. If they pursue this, and I
think they will, they'll find out all about the Atalas and my
involvement. There's no way they won't. Now let's change the
subject. What about Martha Roberts?"

The next morning at eleven-thirty, Harry was waiting for Esther
Roberts at the Southwest Florida International Airport. From
Avola the airport was a half-hour drive north on Interstate 75,
originally built through a wilderness of swamp and slash pine
but now steadily being converted into malls, golf courses, and
housing estates, separated by sprawl. He had no trouble
recognizing her. In her white, beaded doeskin vest and
dungarees, western boots, and braided hair, she stood out like a
Fiji Islander among the shorts and chinos and pastel jerseys
crowd hurrying through the security check points.

Harry liked her the moment he saw her. She made him think
of Martha. Her handshake was firm, and her clear gray eyes
took him in with an expression of tolerant appraisal. If it was
true, he thought, greeting her, that by forty we have the face we
deserve, this tall, solid woman with the Robertses' high cheek
bones and dark hair, in her case streaked with gray, was worth
knowing.

"You look about the way I expected," she said.

"So do you," Harry replied. "I'm sorry you couldn't bring Heather."

" 'He travels the fastest who travels alone,' " she said with a grin.

" 'And races are won by one and one . . .' " he added, returning the grin.

"If we live, we might become friends," she responded, hitching her backpack into a more comfortable position as they started for the escalators.

"How do you want to do this?" Harry asked as they turned onto the Interstate.

"You set me down while we're still out of sight of the house, and I'll just walk in," she said.

Harry suddenly wondered if he had made a mistake. "If you want some time to think about it, there's plenty of room at the house. And I'm far enough back in the woods that no one's going to know you're there."

"How much good am I going to do hanging out with you and this Tucker LaBeau?" She paused and laughed. "Although I would like to meet Sanchez and Oh, Brother!"

"Neither of us knows what you'll be walking into," he said, his concern growing.

"You're forgetting something. I was born there. It's my mother's house."

"It's not your mother I'm worried about."

"I know. Would it make you feel better to buy me lunch?"

"It might."

Over their pear and roasted walnut salads she told him something more about what led up to her leaving Avola. She had, Harry thought, been putting on a brave front that actually driving back into Avola had been shaken by what he guessed were unpleasant memories.

"Nothing much has changed in that quarter," Harry said quietly.

She smiled ruefully. "Not with them, maybe. But I'm not the person I was."

"I think I see pretty clearly who you are."

"And?"

"They've lost more from your absence than you have. Your coming back here at all, Esther, is a major act of charity."

She finished her coffee. "Let's go find out."

She climbed down from the Rover and shrugged into her backpack. "Panther Trace hasn't changed by so much as a wild-pig track," she said with a bitter laugh and scuffed the heel of her boot through the sandy dirt under her feet.

Harry came around the Rover to stand beside her. "If you want out of here, call me," he said. "If anything even begins to look dangerous, call me."

She thrust out her hand. "Thanks, Harry. The worst part of this is going to be seeing Pa. I'll handle the rest with no sweat."

Harry didn't believe the "no sweat" part, but she strode away like a woman on a mission. He hoped it wasn't something worse.

27

"I'm not apologizing for blowing the whistle on you, Harry," Smolkin said defensively, leaning across his desk and trying to scowl at Harry.

"Not required," Harry responded. He dropped into a chair. "Esther arrived this morning, and she went home. I set her down on Panther Trace where nobody could see us from the house, and she walked in." He said it as if he had just sent Daniel down to the lions.

"So you think Martha's with James and Ruth Roberts?" Smolkin asked, coming around the desk wide-eyed.

"And with Matthew's wife, Felicity, who was carrying a Colt .45 the last time I saw her."

"Where was that?"

"At Ruth's house. She was glaring at me and telling me to get out of there."

"Ouch."

"That's what I thought."

"Did you ask if Martha was there?"

Harry nodded. "She said 'this family' would deal with Martha's situation. Then she told me, 'if we have to, we'll deal with you too.' I also asked to speak with Ruth. She said that wasn't going to happen and told me to leave."

"Do you think she was threatening to kill both you and Martha?" Smolkin asked in obvious alarm.

"I don't think Martha's in much danger, but I'd bet heavily

she was threatening me."

"And you think Martha's there?"

"That's my guess."

"And she's being kept there against her will?"

"Possibly not in the way you mean."

Smolkin let that pass. "What's going to happen now Esther's with her?"

"The cat's amongst the pigeons."

"Meaning?"

"I don't know. I just hope . . ." He did not want to finish the sentence.

"They don't finish what they started a long time ago?"

"Yes."

On the way back to the Hammock, Harry spent most of his time trying to settle on what he should do next. He considered having another go at Freeman Todd, then discarded the idea almost as soon as it formed. The man was too dangerous to confront without heavy backup, and even then . . . He moved on, trying one approach after another without success until he reached the disabled bulldozer.

When he had left the house that morning, he had been in too much of a hurry to do more than glance at the tractor as he drove past the parking area. Now he pulled into the parking area and got out of the Rover, glad to be distracted from his frustrated efforts to find a way to crack the puzzle of Matthew and Mark Roberts's involvement in John's death. He did not doubt they were involved, but how and with whom and why, he had not a clue.

He walked around the bulldozer. Berker Szalay was right. The tracks had been blown completely off the wheels, leaving the wheels oddly bare and useless. Harry grinned in spite of himself and chuckled. Tucker had done a very good job. But what would happen next?

A big, yellow dump truck rumbled into the parking area and stopped with a hiss of brakes. Wetherell Clampett swung down onto the ground and gave a rebel yell. "This some of your doing?" he shouted and gave a loud laugh.

"I wouldn't know how to begin," Harry replied and shook the fat man's hand. "Have you been sent out to do something about this?"

"Make a report," he said. "It appears the state and the sheriff's department arrived all at once and cooled somebody's interest in cutting this road. You know anything about it?"

"A little. Somebody bought the butterflies some time."

"Looks that way." Wetherell grinned happily.

"Remember my saying I dropped in on Freeman Todd?" Harry asked, wiping the happy look off Clampett's face.

"Sort of."

"Then you'll probably recall that he tried to take my head off with a two-foot wrench. Before this thing goes any further, Wetherell and somebody else gets killed, don't you think you'd better stop pretending you don't know what's going on here?"

There was a moment when Harry thought Clampett might be going to jump his bones, but it passed and Clampett pushed his hat back on his head and blew out his breath as if he'd just surfaced from a deep dive.

"My father's been after me about it," the big man said with a sigh. "But it's not as though I know a hell of a lot."

"Who was driving the truck that hit me?"

"I don't know."

"Who took the truck and who brought it back?"

"How much cover can you give me?"

Harry looked at Clampett's broad, open face and saw an essentially honest man in a bad place. "I won't lie to you, Wetherell. I can protect my sources up to a point. But if you give me information that shines a light on the people you're protecting and I act on it, they may know it had to have come from you."

"That's about what I thought. Ralph Hawkins took the truck, and he brought it back."

"Do you figure he was the driver?"

"Who went after you? I doubt it."

"Todd?"

"That would be my guess, but it's only a guess. What are you going to do?"

"First, I'm not going to mention your name. After that, I think it's better if you don't know."

Clampett nodded. "I think I'm going to start traveling with my shotgun."

Harry drove to Tucker's and told him what Wetherell Clampett had said about Bevel's putting a hold on the road.

"If you stay out of jail, you may be up for a good citizen's award." Harry was feeling very proud of his friend and more than a little protective. "But I'm counting on you to put away your vigilante costume."

Tucker laughed. "Don't count on the good citizen's award. You know what comes of good deeds."

"They never go unpunished?"

"There you go. What made you tackle Wetherell?"

"I'd been wrestling with the problem just before he arrived. I don't know why I didn't think of it sooner."

"What are you going to do with the information?"

"I'm going to start by talking to Mark Roberts and kind of lay it out for him."

"To see which way he jumps."

"Yes."

"What about Martha and Esther?"

"I've thought about that. I'm hoping Esther's being home

and my confronting Mark will shake something loose."

"The question is what."

Tucker's comment troubled Harry. He didn't think Martha was in danger, but he was less sure about Esther, and until he heard from her, everything was still in play. Wetherell's information had temporarily boosted his spirits, but Tucker's wintry face had killed Harry's optimism. Worse still, thinking about Martha and Esther brought to mind Esther with her backpack, hiking off alone toward the home which had, apparently quite early, stopped being a home.

He thought of Warren's comment in Frost's "The Death of The Hired Man": "Home is the place where, when you have to go there, / They have to take you in." And his wife's replying, "I should have called it / Something you somehow haven't to deserve."

He shook his head, in part because the picture of Esther walking so purposefully along Panther Trace reinforced his concern for her safety. How could any outsider know what she was walking into? Did she know? He thought of his own conflicted relationships and escaped from that painful subject by turning his mind again to Esther.

It was certain that she had walked into a hostile environment, possibly a dangerous one. He recalled Felicity Roberts, her eyes black with hate, and swore silently at the recollection. But her hostility toward him didn't necessarily extend to Esther. Nevertheless . . . God, he hoped he had not made a mistake he couldn't correct.

Harry pushed back from his desk and put away the file he had been working on. Esther had been home a day and a half, and there was still no word from her. He had her number and the number of her parents' house, but if she was in any trouble, calling her would only make her situation worse.

The phone jumped him out of his thoughts.

"Progress," Jeff Smolkin said loudly. "I'll tell you about it at lunch."

Smolkin favored the Thai restaurant across the street from his office. "It's quick and cheap," he told Harry as they slid into a booth.

"I could use some good news," Harry said after they had ordered.

"Here it is. Harley Dillard, good new broom that he is, has taken custody of the gun."

"Matthew just handed it over?" Harry thought he must be hearing wrong.

"Yup."

"I don't understand. Why didn't he drop it in the Seminole River and say it must have been stolen? What the hell is he doing?"

The news, which should have been good, alarmed Harry. It didn't make sense that Matthew would put his head in a noose that way, especially if he had been the one who shot his brother. "He didn't do it," Harry said.

"Yes he did. Dillard, our intrepid district attorney, has the gun. I've seen it."

"It must be another gun."

"Harry, the serial numbers check. It's the gun."

Their food came, and as they ate Harry told Smolkin about Felicity Roberts and Esther. Smolkin made Harry repeat what he had said.

"What if she gets popped?"

"Don't say that," Harry replied.

"Okay, I won't, but all the same . . ."

They finished eating in silence. Smolkin stopped in the middle of putting his credit card on the bill and said, as if a light had just come on, "I must be losing it. Why did Matthew give Dillard the gun?"

"I asked first."

Esther called Harry at four that afternoon.

"She's here. She's all right," Esther said in a guarded voice. "So is Felicity."

"Can you get Martha out of there?"

"She won't leave. Pa's very ill. She's bought into the guilt trip Felicity's been laying on her. I think she's regressed to about twelve."

"How are you?"

"I'm okay, but things are a mess here. Ma is running on some kind of autopilot. Nothing goes in and nothing comes out but, 'Ask Matthew.' It's seriously bad. I can't talk anymore."

Harry tried and failed to feel encouraged by what he had just heard.

28

Snyder was not pleased with Harry.

"So, you went to see this Freeman Todd and almost had your head pulled off. You did all this without telling me what you had learned from Wetherell Clampett, and on top of that you sent Esther Roberts into a house where a woman had recently chased you away with a gun."

Harry had lied and said he didn't know who the armed woman was. "That's about it."

"I've got to say this, Brock, you've got balls." Hodges was grinning merrily.

"Balls, maybe. Brains, no," Snyder barked. "What else haven't you told me?"

"I forgot to tell you about the gun."

Snyder's ears turned red. "What gun are we talking about here?"

"The one that killed John Roberts. Jeff Smolkin persuaded Harley Dillard to take it out of Matthew's keeping. And the thing I can't figure is why Matthew gave it to him."

"As a senior officer in the justice system, the district attorney can't be stopped from requesting and getting access to a piece of evidence. You know that."

"Not my point. If you were Matthew and had been involved in your brother's murder, what would you have done with that gun after you got it back into your hands?"

"I'd've dropped it in the Seminole River where God Himself

couldn't have found it," Hodges said in his best bullfrog voice.

"What makes you think Matthew Roberts had anything to do with John Roberts's death?" Snyder demanded.

"Easy," Hodges blundered on. "That gun was in Matthew Roberts's custody."

"I don't know how I got from one day to the next before I got to know you, Sergeant," Snyder said, pushing himself out of his chair and looking as if he might bite an arm off Hodges.

"Jim, what makes you think he wasn't involved in John's death?" Harry put in.

Snyder took a deep breath and appeared to be counting fly specks on the ceiling. When he was finished, he said, "Matthew Roberts is a lot of things, a nutcase about his family being one of them, the Evidence Section for another, but there's no way he could have killed his brother."

"Somebody killed John Roberts," Harry insisted. "And it was done with that gun. Without wanting to start World War III, I think Frank just about made the case."

Snyder shook his head. "Not a chance."

Hodges was keeping his mouth shut.

"I'm pretty sure Dillard's going to reopen the case," Harry said, trying another approach.

"I hope you're satisfied," Snyder retorted.

"I'm not following you." Harry's patience was fraying. It wasn't like Snyder to behave as if he'd lost the ability to draw a line between two dots an inch apart.

"If Dillard does reopen the case, this department is going to shred itself." Snyder was leaning across his desk on clenched fists. Harry had never seen him so upset. "What's this going to do to Bob Fisher's hopes for reelection? He's the best lawman we've had in the job in my time on the force. What's it going to do to the department's reputation? Also, Matthew is probably going to be charged with negligence, and God knows what else will shake loose. The Roberts family could be torn apart."

Harry and Hodges exchanged a quick look.

"Jim," Harry said quietly, "we're talking about a murder here. Matthew isn't going to be charged with negligence. Unless he can explain how that gun got out of his possession without his knowing it, he's going to be charged with murder."

Harry got himself out of Snyder's office before his friend exploded all over it. Hodges caught up with him as he was getting into the Rover.

"Martha Roberts is out there on Panther Trace, isn't she?" he asked, mopping his face with his bandana.

"Yes," Harry told him.

"I thought so. Who put her there?"

"I don't know that yet, but she hasn't been harmed."

"Esther tell you?"

"That's right."

Hodges hitched up his belt. "Esther and I were in school together. It's been a while. Tell her I was asking after her."

"I'll do that. Frank, you and Jim and your SWAT team can't go out there. Not yet anyway."

"I expect that's why the captain didn't ask about her," Hodges replied. "I also expect it's one of the reasons he's so cranked up. You've got to see he's in a bad place, what with the DA on the prowl and all."

Actually, Harry wasn't sure he did, but he was sure Hodges couldn't reduce his confusion. "Sure," he said and left.

Mark Roberts kept Harry cooling his heels for twenty minutes before he let him into his office. And when he did see him, he was no longer the smiling, easygoing guy who had welcomed him into his house to talk about John Roberts's relationship with Theresa Allgood. Harry thought again how much the rawboned man in front of him looked like his older brother, especially now with his face screwed up as if he was sucking a lemon. He did not ask Harry to sit down and stood himself behind his desk as if he was glad of the distance.

"What do you want, Brock?" Roberts asked in a harsh voice.

"I'm pretty sure I know who ran me off the road," Harry began, ignoring the question.

"So?"

"I also know who took the truck off your lot to get the job done and who brought it back."

Harry caught Roberts's involuntary flinch that told him the shot had gone home.

"Then you know a lot more than I do. What's all this in benefit of?" Mark asked in an effort to cover himself.

"The district attorney's office has the gun that killed John safely stored," he continued. "Harley Dillard's probably going to reopen your brother's death as a capital murder case."

"What's this got to do with me?" Roberts said loudly.

Harry walked to the door and paused. "You were too late with Jefferson Toomey. He and I had a long talk before he died."

When Harry was out of Roberts's office, he looked at his watch. He had an appointment with Fontaine Bevel.

"Are you serious?" Fontaine demanded when Harry stopped talking.

Harry took a deep breath. "For Christ's sake, Fontaine, wake up. You are in serious trouble. And unless you want to find yourself in front of a grand jury being questioned about the murder of John Roberts, you will call the biggest and best accounting firm on the East Coast and hire them to audit your books. Hawkins and Roberts have been stealing you blind, and with the help of Freeman Todd they probably killed John Roberts and Jefferson Toomey and tried to kill me."

"Why kill Roberts and poor old Jefferson Toomey? That's crazy. I can understand their wanting to kill you and that wild man neighbor of yours."

"Very funny, Fontaine. Toomey and John found out somehow about how they were skinning you. So Mark and Ralph killed them. But they were slow, and I talked to Toomey before they got him."

Harry sat back and thought with a quaking in his stomach that if he had made a mistake, not even the dogs would eat him.

"Sweet Mother of Jesus," Fontaine said and gave a long sigh as he stared into his whiskey glass from which he had drunk nothing.

Harry waited.

"You can prove all this?"

"No, but by the time I can, it will be too late for you."

Harry quickly laid out his theory of what had led to John Roberts's murder in a little more detail. He then tied in what Jefferson Toomey had told him, Toomey's killing, the temporary theft of the Bevel's truck, Freeman Todd's attempt to kill him, and the kidnapping of Martha Roberts.

"That last move was so feeble I don't really know what to do with it," Harry concluded.

"How do you know she's not dead?" Bevel sounded genuinely concerned.

"Because she's in a house with her mother and father, her older sister Esther, and a sister-in-law." He left out the bit about Felicity and the gun that won the West.

Bevel scratched his chin and frowned. "Why are you telling me all this? I'm the guy who tried to bulldoze those fucking butterflies," Bevel grated, scowling at Harry. He banged his glass down on his desk as if he was disgusted with the desk, the whiskey, and himself.

Harry relaxed enough to grin. "Have you given up on that effort?"

"Oh, hell, yes. The Commission's all over me. I'm glad, sort of. I didn't really want to do it, but the goddamned company's in such shit I thought I had to make a try. Now tell me why you're giving me this heads-up?"

"Because a lot of your people are going down, and I wanted you left standing. That's one reason. The other is, I'm staking everything I have on the auditors finding what I've said they'll find."

"And I can't tell anybody what I'm doing."

"No one. Not even your secretary. You make that call to the East Coast yourself."

"I'm at some risk here?"

"Not unless Hawkins or Roberts think you suspect them."

"They'll know you came to see me."

"If it comes up, tell them I was trying to get you not to bulldoze that road. Make a joke of it. Say you pretended you were still going to do it just to hear me holler. Laugh about it."

"Behave like an idiot, as usual." There was a world of bitterness in the remark.

"If this all goes right, you'll come away from it your own man."

Bevel absorbed that in silence and walked Harry to the door. He put out his hand. "I'll do it," he said.

Harry thought he had about forty-eight hours before someone came after him. There was no point in sitting around waiting for it to happen. He decided it was time to get Esther and Martha out of Panther Trace. But when he got home, he had a call waiting for him from the district attorney's office. He returned it and was asked to come down as soon as he could. He called Jeff Smolkin.

Smolkin met him at Dillard's office. The district attorney was a short, fat man with a grip like a vice. He was bald, wore rimless glasses, and did not smile a lot.

"Good of you to come, Brock," he said, waving him and Smolkin toward chairs arranged around a wooden coffee table with a stained top.

A tall, slender, and dark-haired young woman in a black suit was standing behind one of the chairs, holding a briefcase.

"Jennifer Fortunato, my assistant," Dillard said.

She nodded at Harry. Harry looked at her and felt a chill run across his shoulders. She looked so much like his first wife in the early years of their marriage that he stared at her, unable to speak. Smolkin saved him.

"Hello, Counselor," the lawyer said.

"Hello, Jeff," she responded with a smile that lit up the room.

Her smile broke the spell. Harry pulled his eyes away from her and sat down.

Fortunato opened her briefcase and produced a tape recorder and passed it to Dillard, who set it on the coffee table and kept his hand on the machine as he looked at Smolkin.

"We're going to record this conversation. Any objections?"

"No. I may need to confer with my client off the record from time to time."

"Fine. Okay, Brock?"

Harry nodded.

"No more nods," Dillard said. "This thing can't see."

"Okay." Despite a major effort not to, Harry kept glancing at Fortunato and at the same time telling himself to quit it.

Dillard recited names, a time, and a date and sat back on his chair. "Ms. Fortunato will begin the questioning."

"Mr. Brock, please give us your full name and address."

He did, and when they were finished, Dillard gave the time and said they were finished.

"I think between them they got everything but my liver," Harry said as he and Smolkin got off the elevator.

"If Dillard's not a judge in ten years, I'll eat a deposition."

"How much of what I said do you think they believed?" Harry asked.

By now they were putting on their sunglasses and still squinting in the blaze of midday light.

"Let me answer you this way. If Bevel doesn't have that audit underway within a week, he's going to be one sad puppy."

"What's Dillard's next step?"

"I think he and Jennifer will start with a review of the investigation following John Roberts's disappearance and come up from there. After that, I think Matthew will be in for a grilling. The connection to Bevel's people will depend on the outcome of the audit."

"Which he will subpoena."

"Sure."

Harry experienced an adrenaline rush that felt as if a cat and a dog had tangled in his stomach, but he also felt vindicated . . . at least he would if the audit struck oil.

29

Harry drove home and put on his shoulder holster. Then he headed out to Panther Trace with no clear idea of how he was going to get Esther and Martha out of their parents' house or even if he was going to get them out. With James Roberts seriously ill and Felicity playing Calamity Jane, both of them might choose to stay.

Esther met him at the door. There were dark circles under her eyes, and Harry guessed from the way she held herself that she was exhausted.

"Where's Felicity?" he asked.

"Matthew took her home this morning." She motioned him into the house. "No explanation. He told her to get her things, and she did."

"What did he say to you?"

"Nothing."

"You okay?"

"Yes."

"You don't look it."

"Thanks."

"What's going on, Esther?"

"Pa's really low. The doctor was here yesterday and said there was nothing to do except try to keep him comfortable. He wanted Ma to call hospice, but she refused."

"I'm sorry. How long?"

"Ten minutes or a week. He doesn't know."

"Has Matthew been told?"

Esther nodded.

"Mark?"

Another nod. Harry did not like it. Why had Matthew taken Felicity away? What was he planning? He pulled his mind back to Esther and her situation. The house, along with a pervasive smell of Lysol and stuffiness, was uncomfortably silent.

"Where's Martha and your mother?" he asked.

"Probably with Pa. Harry, the news with Martha isn't good. She's not going to want to see you. Felicity hammered her into blaming herself for everything here."

"Your mother?"

Esther's eyes filled with tears which she made no effort to hide, and when they ran down her face, she ignored them and went on talking. "She's shut herself off from everything. She's doing the things she has to do, but it's as if she's not here. God, it's awful."

He put a hand on her arm. Outside, a red-bellied woodpecker began its raucous call. "I came here to take you and Martha away. I don't like your being out here."

"I can't go. Not the way things are."

"Before you decide, there are some things you have to know. The district attorney is reopening John's case as a murder investigation. You've got to be prepared. Matthew and Mark are going to be involved. I won't go into it all now, but there's a possibility that your brothers were implicated in John's death. What, if anything, your father knew about it, I can't say."

"I think I'd like to sit down," Esther said in a weak voice.

She did not make it to the chair, and Harry caught her as she was going down. As he was easing her onto the floor, Martha charged into the room. Her hair was uncombed. Her clothes looked as if she had worn them for a week, and her eyes didn't seem to belong to the Martha Roberts he knew.

"I heard voices," she began before she saw Harry. When she did, she looked as if she'd seen a ghost. "What are you doing here?" she shouted. "What have you done to Esther?"

Harry thought she looked half out of her head. "She fainted. Get some water," he said as he pulled a pillow off the sofa and put it under Esther's head.

Martha turned and ran out of the room. But it was Ruth who came back with the water and a wet face cloth.

"What happened?" she asked.

"She fainted."

"Were you troubling her?"

"No, Mrs. Roberts, I would have no reason to do that. We were talking, and she said she thought she ought to sit down and fainted before she could. I caught her."

"You ought not to be here," the woman said in an all but expressionless voice as she knelt beside Esther and began to wipe her forehead with the face cloth. "Matthew wouldn't want you to be here."

"I am sorry about Mr. Roberts," he said.

Esther stirred and groaned softly. Mrs. Roberts sat back on her heels and looked at him. The vacancy in her gaze was replaced by an acute and unsettling presence.

"You don't need to be," she said in a wholly different voice. "I'm not. Two of my sons are dead because of him."

"So they're both still there?" Helen asked.

Harry had picked her up after work and driven to the Stickpen Nature Preserve, where the National Audubon Society maintained a mile and a quarter of raised boardwalk, winding through a black-water swamp with enormous old-growth cypress trees towering over the trail.

"That's right. I think Martha has had something close to a nervous breakdown and thinks it's her fault her father's dying.

243

Esther is just about worn out by the work that's fallen on her, but she can't bring herself to leave her mother and her sister to look after themselves."

He and Helen had just stopped to watch a flight of white wood storks with black-edged wings pass over the water meadows. Now they walked out of the still fierce sun into the cool shade of the cypress forest itself.

"Why did she come back?" Helen asked. She leaned on the plank railing. Below them a black and white speckled limpet waded delicately through the water and ferns in search of frogs.

"In part because I asked her to," Harry replied, leaning beside Helen. "I thought her sister was in danger. It turns out she was, but possibly not for the reasons I thought."

"She was free," Helen said, "and she put herself back in a nightmare."

The anger in her voice startled Harry. "Esther knew what she was getting into," he said a little defensively. "I didn't deceive her about anything."

Helen pulled away from the railing and pushed past him. "I'm not talking about you. God, sometimes you're like a child. Me. Me. Me. I'm talking about Esther."

"So am I," Harry protested, catching up with her. "What are you angry about?"

Helen shrugged. "Nothing. Nothing at all."

"It doesn't sound that way. Don't you think she should have come home?"

It had been Helen's idea to come to the Stickpen, and Harry had jumped at her request. Since their day at the Swamp Buggy Races, he had found it increasingly difficult to arouse her interest in anything.

"No, I guess I don't." She spoke as if she found the subject distasteful.

"Why not?"

"What's the point of putting your hand back in a fire once you know it burns?"

"I think she came back for Martha and her mother. That much of her family still drags on her mind."

"Does she live alone?"

"No." Harry thought about whether or not he wanted to go on and decided he had to. "She lives with a woman by the name of Angel Wing. They have a ten-year-old adopted daughter named Heather. The second time I talked with her, I asked her if she called either of the women she lived with Mother. She said both of them as if I wasn't playing with a full deck."

"Maybe I should go live with Riga," Helen said harshly. "I could be Cheryl's Aunt Helen. Or, even better, I could visit a sperm bank and become a mother on my own, even steven."

Harry cursed himself for having taken the lid off that jar.

They walked out on an arm of the boardwalk to a small viewing platform with wooden seats. Surrounding the platform were water plants and scattered stands of slender swamp maples trailing their branches in the narrow rivers of light pouring through the towering cypress. In one of the stands of maple twenty or thirty yards to their right, four big, nearly fledged yellow-crowned night herons were squabbling loudly and crashing around in the tree where their nest was located.

Helen dropped onto one of the benches to watch. "Maybe I'll skip the kid," she said after watching the fight for a while.

"I didn't know you wanted children," Harry said.

"No? Why am I not surprised?" She jumped to her feet. "Let's get out of here. I'm not fit company even for those wretched herons."

Harry knew it was coming, but not when or where he would be when it came. A little thought, however, about how *he* would do it, led him to conclude that it would probably happen at night while he was at home, preferably asleep. So he decided to pretend he had the answer and acted accordingly.

Before going to pick up Helen he had collected some pieces of clothing and equipment and laid them out beside his bed. Later, he asked himself why he had assumed he would not be staying the night with Helen and spent some unpleasant moments in the company of that question. In any case, he didn't sleep with her. She drank too much at dinner and drank more when she got home. Then she threw up. After that part was dealt with, he helped her into bed, and when she stopped groaning and fell asleep, he left, wondering if two swallows made a summer and decided to believe they didn't.

Harry was back on the Hammock by ten. He let himself into the house, and being careful not to stand in front of windows, he worked at his desk and did the things he usually did. But after getting into bed and shutting off his light, he snaked back out again. Lying on the floor, he pulled on the dark coveralls and watch cap he had laid out earlier. Next he pulled on a pair of black sneakers and strapped on his Luger. Last, he checked the side pockets of the coveralls for his pen light and extra cartridge clips.

The waning moon was up when he crawled to the window overlooking the back lawn and scanned the edge of the woods for any movement. After two or three minutes, one of the gray foxes appeared from the shadow of the oaks and began hunting for mice in the grass. Harry couldn't tell whether it was Bonnie or Clyde. He stood up slowly and leaned against the wall watching the fox. The animal crisscrossed the lawn, frequently pausing to listen. Suddenly it spun around to face the house. It held itself still for a moment and then trotted toward the woods, looking back over its shoulder.

"Company coming," Harry whispered and raised the sash, tossed a rope ladder over the sill, and eased himself out the window into the night. Once on the ground he ran quickly and silently over the grass and into the shadows of the oaks. Keeping out of the moonlight as much as he could, he slipped into the woods and began to move toward the front of the house. Whoever had spooked the fox was there somewhere.

Harry had two sheds to go around to put himself where he had a clear view of the front of the house and the moon at his back. Even before he reached the place he was aiming at, he could hear something moving in the shadows on the other side of the Rover. Harry was puzzled but went forward as quietly as he could.

From what he was hearing he thought the person was doing something with the door on the rider's side of the Rover. Suddenly there was a loud ripping sound. Shit! Harry thought and stepped clear of the trees. The dim figure had his head poked through the Rover's torn door.

"Back out," Harry said. "Very slowly."

The bear pulled its head free, gave a snort of alarm, waddled backward two steps, dropped onto all fours, and exploded away from Harry as if it had been fired out of a cannon.

"Jesus!" Harry gasped, his heart in his throat. Then, as the surprise subsided and relief washed over him, he broke out laughing. In the oak over his head a barred owl hooted in disgust and ghosted away through the trees.

"What was it looking for?" Tucker asked.

"I'd left half a sub sandwich on the rider's seat. I'd forgotten all about it."

Tucker was planting some plumbago bushes at the sunny corner of the hen run, and Harry was digging the holes and shoveling in rotted horse manure and black humus as footing for the root balls. Tucker was holding the garden hose, waiting for Harry to finish.

"Well, you probably scared him out of the county," Tucker said with a chuckle. "I expect if he had a taste for eggs, he would have been over here next. Are you going to go on staying up nights?"

"No. If they were coming, they would have come last night. I think I've misjudged their intentions."

Tucker, turning on the water, asked, "What's your plan?"

"Not to have one. I'm going to wait them out."

"Be careful," Tucker cautioned.

As they were putting away the tools, they talked about the butterflies and Bevel's decision not to go on with the road. "It looks as if they're safe," Harry said.

Tucker made a sour face. "We've won a battle, not the war. How's Helen?"

Harry told him what had happened.

"She doing that often?"

"No, not when I've been with her. It's happened twice in the last month or so."

Tucker hung the hose on its peg on the barn wall. "If it's happened twice with you, it's probably happening without you. It's a radical change in her behavior."

Harry agreed it was. He really did not want to think about it, much less talk about it.

"Then she needs some help."

"It's not easy," Harry said.

"What does that have to do with it?"

"It's not my business," Harry protested, not liking the way Tucker was pushing him.

"Listen here," Tucker said sharply. "You know better than that."

Harry felt his face burn and started to argue, then stopped himself. "You're right, but . . ." He stuck.

"You might as well say it as choke on it."

"She got herself into this mess."

"Maybe she did. How does that change anything?"

"Then let Riga . . ." he began and stopped. He was very angry, but not so angry he couldn't hear himself, and he did not like what he was hearing.

"Another issue heard from." Tucker spoke gently but firmly.

Harry studied his shovel. "It looks that way," he said.

30

Harry now thought he knew the answer to Tucker's question, but he was still struggling with its implications. He knew that his anger was clouding his thinking where Helen was concerned, but he couldn't see how to help her unless she decided what she was going to do about Riga Kraftmeier. That made two questions he had no answer for. The second was what he was going to do about Esther and Martha stuck out there in Panther Trace.

For the next few days, Harry did not have much time to think about either situation. Dillard had moved quickly. He impounded the sheriff's department's Evidence Section's records and dispatched Snyder and his CID people with a warrant for Freeman Todd's arrest. But, of course, the chop shop was stripped and Todd gone.

Bevel had put Digby & Walters, his East Coast accounting firm, in place just hours before the police arrived. The district attorney's office had issued a restraining order, denying Mark Roberts and Ralph Hawkins further access to Bevel's books. Dillard put a couple of his own people into Digby & Walters's team as monitors and told the firm to get on with its work.

Within four days Dillard issued subpoenas ordering Fontaine Bevel, Matthew Roberts, Mark Roberts, and Ralph Hawkins to appear before a grand jury convened to look into the murders of John Roberts and Jefferson Toomey and the attempted murder of Harry Brock. In a separate filing Todd was charged in absentia with two counts of murder, one count of attempted murder, and one count of operating a chop shop. The sheriff's department issued an APB on Todd.

Then Harry got a call from Mark Roberts's wife, Rebecca.

"I need to talk to you," she said.

"Where do you want to meet?" Harry asked, instantly thinking that he was being set up.

"You say. I really need to feel safe," she said in an unsteady voice.

"How about Blackfin Park? It's public, but there are some quiet corners where we can talk. If that's what you want to do."

"Can you do it now? I can get away for a couple of hours."

"Yes. Give me half an hour. I'll meet you in the pro shop next to the tennis court. If either of us sees anything wrong, we don't have to speak."

"All right."

It was hot, and the courts were beginning to empty. Business was picking up at the drinks counter, and a fairly steady coming and going of laughing or complaining players made the place lively. Harry was buying a root beer when Rebecca appeared beside him. She tried to smile and didn't make it, but stressed or not, she had taken pains to brush her hair, and her red blouse and tan slacks were pressed and immaculate.

"Can I get you something to drink?"

"Diet Coke."

"Here we go," he said passing her the can. "We've just met by accident and are looking for a place to sit down and talk."

"Okay."

He led the way out of the shop and along a path lined with ficus trees and stopped at a bench. "This all right for you?" he asked.

She looked around nervously. "I guess." She dropped onto the edge of the bench and clenched her hands around her Coke and stared at it as if she was waiting to be executed.

He no longer thought she was baiting a trap. "Whenever you're ready," he said.

"He's done something awful," she said in a cracked voice. "Something really awful."

"Mark?" Harry asked as gently as he could.

She nodded. "I'm afraid."

"What of?"

"What's going to happen!" she said in sudden anger. "For Christ's sake, Harry, he's going to jail, and he's so deeply into denial, he can't see it."

"What's he done, Rebecca?"

"I thought you knew." She shot him a glance stiff with suspicion.

For a moment he wondered if Rebecca was on a fishing expedition, then dismissed the thought. "Are you looking for help?" he asked.

"Yes, I guess I am. And I don't know why I turned to you. It's because of you he's in all this trouble."

"Speaking of denial," Harry replied.

"I know." Her shoulders slumped. "He and that waster Hawkins, who was supposed to have been Mark's friend, have been stealing money from Bevel. Of all the stupid . . ." She checked herself. "Harry, I swear to God, until last week I didn't have a clue. All the trips, the boat . . . I don't know how I could have been so blind."

"Blaming yourself is a waste of time and won't do Mark any good at all."

"Will anything?" The desperation had crept back into her voice.

"Yes. But he has to go to Harley Dillard, the district attorney, and tell him everything he knows. And he has to do it before he appears before the grand jury."

"And that's it?"

"No. Two people have died because of what's been going on at Bevel's, and I was almost killed." He did not want to be more brutal than he had to be, so he left it to her to make the connections.

She stared at him white faced. "Are you saying . . . ?"

"Yes. Hire the best attorney you can find and if he's any good, he will run with Mark to Harley Dillard."

"I don't know if . . ."

"Rebecca, it's his only hope."

Without answering, she sprang up and hurried away.

Harry watched her until she was out of sight. Then he got up from the bench, tossed his root beer into a trash barrel, and left the park. He drove to Harley Dillard's office. Dillard was out, but Jennifer Fortunato took him into her office.

"What can I do for you?" she asked.

Harry hated being asked that question, and, coming from someone who looked like Jennifer One, some of his negative feelings found their way into his answer. "Nothing. But I've just done something for you."

She looked so startled that Harry immediately felt guilty. This young lawyer was only trying to be professional. He softened his voice. "Rebecca Roberts called me. We met and talked. When I'd heard what she had to say, I told her that her husband should hire an attorney and talk to Harley Dillard as soon as he could. She may call Dillard herself, but that's only a guess."

"Did she tell you anything we need to know?"

"Nothing I want to repeat. It was all hearsay. But make sure everyone who answers the phones around here knows who she is and doesn't brush her off or scare her away if she does call."

Fortunato frowned. "You came in here to give us a heads-up

on office procedure. Is that it?"

Harry took the hit. The city streets had made a spirited entrance. "Let me try again. You've looked at the case. How strong is it?" He did not wait for an answer. "Rebecca Roberts might be able to force her husband to cooperate with your office. She came to me asking for help and expecting confidentiality. I told her to talk to Dillard. I hope she will."

"Okay," Fortunato responded a little hesitantly. "I'll pass the word around. But be careful, Mr. Brock. I think you're walking very close to the edge of a cliff. You know what I mean?"

"Withholding evidence, Counselor?"

"It's a long fall."

Harry stood up. She was right, but he had said all he intended to say for the moment.

She stood up with him. She was almost exactly Jennifer's height. "Can I ask you an unprofessional question, Mr. Brock?"

"It's Harry, but sure."

"Why do you dislike me?"

"Does it matter?"

She stepped around the question. "As a rule, men don't, unless I put them in jail."

"You could be the twin of someone I once knew."

"There's not much I can do about that."

"Neither can I."

On the way home, Harry reviewed his conversation with Fortunato and decided he had not covered himself with glory. He did not exactly let himself off the hook, but he did acknowledge that Jennifer One had been enough Jennifers to last him a lifetime. To his surprise he found Wetherell Clampett and two other men in the butterfly parking lot putting the treads back on the tractor. He turned in behind them. They were nearly finished with the job, and Wetherell walked over to greet him, wiping his hands on a piece of greasy white towel.

"I thought this job had been shut down," Harry said, pushing open the door and stepping out of the Rover.

"Central office says it is. Hawkins says it ain't. Things are in a helluva mess. Some of this is your doing. Leastwise, you're getting blamed for it."

"Sounds right. Are you getting ready to haul the Caterpillar away?"

"Not today. Hawkins told me to put it in working order and leave it where it is."

"Have you heard from the district attorney's office?"

Clampett lost his smile. "I've been summoned to testify before a grand jury, if that's what you mean."

"What do you think about that?"

"I can tell you I don't look forward to it."

Harry nodded. "Can I make a suggestion?"

"Make away. I need all the help I can get."

"Lying to a grand jury, Wetherell, is a serious offense. So is refusing to answer their questions. Tell them the truth every minute you're being questioned. If you lie, they'll find out. To hell with your job, Wetherell, tell them what you know."

"You're the second one to warn me about that," Clampett said unhappily.

"Who's the other person?" Harry was afraid that Hawkins or Roberts or possibly Fontaine Bevel had been working on him.

"My father."

"Good," Harry said, relieved.

They spoke briefly about the auditors working on Bevel's books and the district attorney's presence in the company offices and on the work site.

"They're talking to everybody," Clampett complained.

"Doing their job," Harry said.

"I wish I knew where it was all going," Clampett said.

"So do I," Harry said and meant it.

He went home and called Helen, having finally admitted that his tough love stance was bogus. Red-eyed jealousy was at the root of his refusal to intervene.

"Is this a charity call?" she demanded.

"No. I'm working for my Eagle Scout badge, and I need you to help me complete a project."

It was the right answer. She laughed.

"Seven o'clock," she said, "and you better have something nice planned."

Harry put down the phone feeling better than he had for a while and went to his office with some bounce in his walk. Now, if he could just think of way to get Martha to a doctor and Esther out of the mess he had led her into, the world would begin to look less like a tar pit.

31

Dinner with Helen had gone well until he tried to approach the issue of her drinking. At that point Helen had put down her fork, looked at him across the linen tablecloth, the gleaming dishes, and the candles and said quietly, "It's your call, Harry. Either you drop the subject right now or I'm leaving in a taxi."

They were about twenty miles north of Avola, but Harry knew that, being Helen, she would do what she had threatened. Angry, disappointed, rejected, he turned away to watch the boat lights winking on the water. Their table was next to the railing on a wide hotel veranda looking out at the inner passage between the mainland and Sanibel Island. A light breeze whispered in the palms, and a harpist was playing an adaptation of Ralph Vaughn Williams's *Fantasia on Greensleeves*.

He quickly squelched several sharp responses. Once past the initial shock of her ultimatum, he saw with a sinking sense of helplessness, which quickly overwhelmed his anger, that it would be pointless to argue.

"I think you're making a mistake," he said evenly, "but I'll let it go."

"Good," Helen said cheerfully and picked up her fork.

To Harry's surprise, she drank very little. Apparently untroubled by the brief confrontation, she went on talking and joking in her usual, sardonic fashion, and Harry was soon enjoying himself. The rest of the evening went very pleasantly. After dinner they walked on the hotel beach and watched the moon rise.

When he took her home, she asked him in. He stayed. And although he was still troubled about Riga Kraftmeier's role in her life, he managed to keep it from intruding on their night together. Driving home the next morning, he told himself that she was in control of her life again.

Everything on the Hammock seemed in order, and Harry settled down to a morning of case-report writing. A little after eleven, there was a woof at his lanai door. He recognized the voice. Sanchez was standing with his front paws on the step, wagging his tail and grinning. A note was pinned to his bandanna.

"Come in," Harry said, holding open the door. "I'll get you a drink, and I'm pretty sure there are still some sugar cookies left."

While Sanchez was eating and drinking, Harry read the note. Tucker had invited him to lunch. He wrote his thanks and said he'd be there at noon. He spent a few more minutes telling Sanchez about a doe and her fawn he had seen on the Hammock road while he was driving home that morning. Then he pinned the note back onto his collar, let him out, and returned to his desk. Before sitting down, he remembered that he had been talking with a dog. He shook his head and went back to work.

"You may think Bevel's repairing that tractor and leaving it sitting where it is doesn't have any significance beyond indicating the company's disarray," Tucker said as they cleared the table, "but I read it differently. I think somebody plans to use it."

"Well, sure," Harry answered. "That seems reasonable. What I don't agree with is your idea that it's going to be used to damage the Atalas. By the way, have you been in there to look at them lately?"

Tucker passed him a blue and white striped dish towel. "To answer your question, yes, I have. Things seem to be in good order. A lot of the grubs we saw have spun cocoons, and the adults have laid a lot more eggs. So that side of things looks good. What you don't have a grasp of is the lengths some people will go to in order to get their own way. I'm saying there's somebody in Bevel's management team who wants that road pushed through there. Come court orders, grand juries, or hell itself, he'll see it happen."

They argued over that until the dishes were put away.

"I've got a lot more report writing to get through," Harry said, hanging the towel on its hook beside the sink. "Thanks for lunch. I'd like the recipe for that meat loaf if you get around to writing it down. And I've got another request. Those two young deputies have been leaving us alone for a while now. Don't do anything to stir them up."

Tucker laughed and walked Harry to the door, his hand on the younger man's shoulder. "Don't worry about it. I'm reasonably responsible. Wait a minute. Oh, Brother!, Sanchez, and I will walk you out to the road."

Harry worked steadily for an hour and was thinking about taking a break when the phone rang.

It was Esther Roberts. "Harry, we've got a situation with Martha I can't handle. Come out here as quick as you can."

Before he could ask what was wrong, she hung up.

He ran up the stairs and came down strapping on his shoulder holster.

Harry pulled off the road while still out of sight of the Robertses' house and pushed his way through the bushes screening the slash pine and saw palmetto woods that flanked Panther Trace. Five minutes later he was studying the Roberts house through a thin place in the ficus fence.

Martha's car was the only vehicle in the driveway. The house was closed and still. All Harry could hear were the wind in the pines and the chattering of an annoyed squirrel behind him. Moving carefully, he followed the fence until he had gone three-quarters of the way around the house without seeing any movement inside.

He sat on his heels for a while and thought about what he should do. It occurred to him that he should have called Jim Snyder for some backup, but his next thought was that Snyder, quite rightly, would have told him to bark and chase cars. In fact, he might have said something even more graphic.

Harry decided to wait and watch for a while, but at the end of ten minutes, his legs were cramped from crouching in the saw palmettos, ants were crawling up his pants legs, and his face and neck were burning from mosquito bites. He shifted uncomfortably and decided that if he was going to find out what was going on inside the house, he would have to go in. He was reasonably sure that if anyone was trying to lure him into the house, it was probably Matthew, still trying to make it all go away. And if that was so, he might as well go in the front door.

Holding his pistol behind him, he walked up the path and knocked on the door. Esther opened it and, without speaking, stood back to let him in. He stepped past her with the Luger in his hand, held down beside his right leg. Stepping from the glare of the sun into the shadowed room left him momentarily blind. Before his eyes adjusted, a harsh voice said, "Drop the gun, Brock, or I'll kill her."

Harry hesitated long enough to make out a woman with an arm across her throat and a man towering behind her, holding a pistol to her temple. Harry thumbed on the safety and dropped the pistol.

He did not recognize the voice and couldn't yet see the

speaker's features.

"What's going on?" he asked.

"Get over here and shut up," the man said.

Harry walked slowly forward, thinking Katherine may have been right in saying he was in the wrong line of work.

"Stop right there," the man said. "Sit down. Put your hands behind your back. Old woman, pick up that piece of rope and tie his wrists together. If the knot's not tight when I check it, I'll belt you hard."

Harry eased himself onto the floor. The man with the gun was Freeman Todd, and it was his arm crushing Martha's throat. To his left Ruth Roberts was getting slowly out of her chair.

"Hurry up," Freeman told her.

Ruth did not move any faster, but she knelt behind Harry and said, "Cross your wrists."

He did and she tied him with what felt like a piece of clothes line. As soon as she was finished and had stood up, Todd flung Martha away from him. She struck an armchair and fell across it.

"Sit down," he said to her.

She began to cry. Todd took a step toward her. "Shut that whining, or I'll give you something you won't get over in a hurry."

Martha crawled into the chair and clamped a hand over her mouth. Then Todd pointed his gun at Ruth and motioned her back to her chair. "You," he said to Esther, "get on the couch."

Harry played the only card he had. "What's this all about, Todd?" he asked calmly.

Todd strode forward and drove his foot at Harry's head. Harry twisted away and caught the blow on his shoulder. The force of the kick knocked him onto the floor. His head banged against the thin rug. For a moment he was aware only of the blazing pain in his shoulder and a black roaring in his ears.

Todd reached down and, grasping Harry by his shirt collar, yanked him back into a sitting position. He had raised his gun to strike Harry when Martha began screaming. The sound cleared Harry's head. The screams were pouring out of Martha as if they were being produced by a mechanical pump. Esther leaped up and ran toward the young woman, but Todd got to her first and slapped her so hard that Martha's head spun away from the blow, and her head bounced off the back of the chair like a ball. The screams stopped.

"You pig!" Esther shouted and flew at Todd, who reached out a long, powerful arm, grasped her by the hair and flung her back onto the couch.

"Stay there," Todd said, "or I'll break your fucking neck."

Esther dragged herself into a sitting position. Martha held her face in her hands and stared with wide, empty eyes at nothing.

"I'll tell you what this is about, Brock," the big man said, leering down at Harry. "It's about making it impossible for that fucking Dillard to make a case. You following me?"

He appeared to Harry to be smiling with only half of his face. Then Harry realized that the livid scar running from the corner of Todd's left eye to his chin had immobilized that side of his face. It was like looking at two frightening aspects of the towering man.

"I'm not sure I am," Harry lied, hoping to keep Todd talking. It might only be delaying the final moment, but he was still capable of hoping something would turn up.

Todd gave a growling laugh. "Maybe that crack on your head rattled your brain. I made a mistake not killing you that first time, Brock. I should of stopped to make sure you were finished."

He glanced at the three women and brought his attention back to Harry. Only Mrs. Roberts appeared to be listening to

Todd, but her eyes told Harry nothing. He thought she was probably lost in that gray, unfeeling world Esther said she had sunk into.

"I just about was finished," Harry said.

"Hawkins and Roberts are going to let me take the fall," Todd said, ignoring Harry's comment.

"That would be Mark Roberts," Harry said, shifting into another position, trying to ease the throbbing in his shoulder.

"Mark Roberts doesn't know shit. It's Matthew, stupid."

"Ruth," came a frail, quavering call from another room.

Feeble as it was, Harry recognized James's voice. Esther started to push herself off the couch. Todd pointed his gun at her and said, "Sit." She did. Ruth went on staring at Todd as if she had heard nothing.

"They were hot enough back when I did the retard," Todd continued.

Harry saw that airing his grievances was making Todd angry, and he tried to deflect his attention. "Who's the retard?"

"John, Bunny, whatever the hell they called him." He pointed the pistol at Martha, who was sitting with her hands still pressed to her face, rocking slowly backward and forward. "But when she began stirring up that old crap, they began to whine like sick puppies. If they'd left her to me, I would have shut her mouth permanently, the way I did the old nigger's. And the way I'm going to shut yours."

The voice rose again, calling for Ruth. This time Ruth stood up and stayed up, despite Todd's warning. "Shoot me," she said. "My husband's dying. I'm going to him."

She walked toward the hall door, and Todd followed her with the gun, then lowered it.

"You're all dying," he said with a harsh sound that might have been a laugh. Ruth turned toward the kitchen. Todd seemed to lose interest in her.

"We might be worth more to you alive than dead," Harry said.

Todd turned back to Harry and shook his head. "With the four of you dead, the DA's got no case. All he's got is that fucking gun that killed the retard, and nothing to tie me to any of it."

Harry was going to say that Wetherell Clampett could still testify when he saw Ruth step back into the room holding a double-barreled shotgun, its stock pressed against her right shoulder.

"Mr. Todd," she said in a calm voice.

Todd turned, swore, and jerked up his pistol. Ruth fired. The blast from the first barrel slammed him backward. He tripped over Harry and crashed to the floor in a welter of blood. Terribly wounded, Todd tried to struggle to his feet, but Ruth strode forward and, standing over Harry, fired the second barrel into Todd's chest, almost tearing him in half.

The shotgun's roar left Harry's head ringing. Martha sat as she had been sitting, holding her face and rocking back and forth. Esther was slowly getting to her feet. Ruth broke open the shotgun, ejecting the spent shells, and reaching into her apron pocket, took out two shells, slid them into the still-smoking barrels, and snapped the breech shut. She slid on the safety and stood looking down at Todd.

"Now Bunny can rest in peace," she said.

"Ma," Esther said in an unsteady voice.

"It's all right," Ruth answered calmly. "I'll go back to your father. Untie Mr. Brock. He'll know what to do about Martha."

Turning away from what was left of Todd, she rested her hand briefly on Martha's head as she passed her, and, moving without haste, the shotgun in her right hand, she walked out of the room. Harry got painfully onto his feet, and Esther untied the rope. He stood for a moment rubbing his wrists, staring at Martha.

"Where did she get the gun?" Esther asked.

"The first time I came here, she told me your father had kept a loaded shotgun under their bed for as long as they'd been married," he said, his head still ringing from the blasts of the shotgun and feeling as if his voice was borrowed.

Coiling the rope, Esther stepped up beside Harry and said, "She's going to need a lot of help."

For a moment they stared in silence at the young woman rocking back and forth in her chair. Then Harry, astounded that any of them were still alive, forced himself to move.

"I'll make the call," he said.

32

James Roberts died that night with Ruth holding his hand.

Later, Esther told Harry that when her father was gone, her mother had folded his hands across his chest and said, " 'There.' And that was all she said. Go figure. She had every reason to hate him. I hated him."

Harry had stayed at the Robertses' house until Snyder and his team arrived. When the photographing and the rest of the crime scene work were completed, he and Harry went outside and talked. Harry told him what had happened and what Todd had said before he was killed. Snyder listened, made some notes, and occasionally shook his head.

"You came out here alone, didn't call me, and walked into the house through the front door," Snyder said when Harry was finished.

"That's about it."

"It's no wonder Katherine left you. You scare me just about to death, and I'm a long way from being married to you."

"Should I look forward to a proposal?"

Snyder's ears got very red. "This is not a joking matter."

"Thanks for telling me. Have you got enough evidence yet to arrest the Roberts brothers and Ralph Hawkins?"

Snyder ran a hand over his face. He looked as wasted as Harry. "Dillard will want formal statements from all of you," he said. "But I doubt Martha will be talking to anyone for a while. If your statements are generally in agreement, it should only be a short step to the grand jury's giving Dillard the revised warrants he'll be asking for."

"What about the Bevel audit?"

"It's not official, but my information is that Mark Roberts and Hawkins have been stealing from the company for a long time."

"Add that to what you've got here, the grand jury should have no trouble issuing indictments."

"We'll see, but this stays between us until they're under lock and key."

Harry nodded. "Todd said Matthew is tied into this, probably through the gun, but I'm not sure how."

"It's possible Mark Roberts and Hawkins can shed some light," Snyder answered.

The two men were quiet for a moment. Then Snyder said, "Did Mrs. Roberts really say that about Bunny resting in peace?"

"Yes."

Snyder sighed. "How do you suppose she found the strength to shoot Todd?"

"Todd called her youngest son a retard and told us he'd killed him. He threw Esther around and slapped Martha hard enough to bounce her head like a basketball. I think she decided it was payback time, not only for what Todd had done, but what her husband and possibly her oldest son had dished out all those years. I know from what she told me that she blamed James for Adam and John's deaths."

Snyder looked troubled. "I wonder if she's . . ."

"No," Harry said flatly. "She's saner than either one of us."

"That may not be a helpful comparison, at least where you're concerned."

"Thanks. She came in with the shotgun just as I was about to tell Todd that Wetherell Clampett knew what had been going on at Bevel's and that maybe he should rethink killing us."

"Wouldn't have done any good," Snyder said grimly.

"Why not?"

"He thought he'd killed Clampett, but the doctors say he's got a slim chance of pulling through."

"Shot?"

"No. Knifed in the back as he was getting into his truck this morning on his way to work. He's still not out of the woods, but the blade missed his heart. His father heard Wetherell holler and shouted back. That scared Todd off. He probably thought the old man kept a gun in the house and decided to clear out. Mr. Clampett caught a glimpse of Todd as he was driving off."

"I wish I'd known about Wetherell being stabbed before I got Esther's call," Harry said. "I might have been a little more careful."

"Why don't I believe you?"

Harry drove back to the Hammock feeling older than the man in the moon. His head ached, his shoulder hurt, and he took little satisfaction in knowing Freeman Todd was dead. How different had Todd been from a dangerous dog, kept by some apparently respectable, law abiding people to act out their aggression? Perhaps he would have some sense of closure when the men behind Todd were sentenced.

Driving past the butterfly woods, he noted that the tractor was still standing in the parking lot, its treads remounted and most of the damage to the paintwork repaired. He wondered for a moment or two why the tractor was being left where it was. Then his mind slid away to Esther and what might happen between her and her mother. As for Martha, he felt profound sorrow, eased somewhat by the that fact she was still alive.

He found a note on his door from Tucker, asking him to stop by. As usual, the old farmer had not bothered to say why. Harry cleaned himself up a little, put an ice pack on his shoulder, and, despite his weariness, decided to walk to Tucker's farm, to ease his mind. As always, the partly shaded road with its soft earth and the encompassing tranquility of the Hammock delivered him to Tucker's place feeling at least partially restored.

Sanchez and Oh, Brother! met him partway along the road. After they had greeted one another, he walked between them with his left hand resting on the big mule's shoulder in a healing companionship.

Tucker was in the garden bracing one of the bean poles.

"The vines got too heavy on the southeast side and pulled it over," he explained, dusting off his hands on the sides of his overalls before shaking Harry's hand.

Harry flinched at the pain that went through his right shoulder as Tucker gripped his hand.

"What happened to you?" Tucker demanded, studying Harry more closely. "You look as if you've been run through a wringer."

"I got kicked," Harry said, and on their way to the house, he told Tucker what had happened at the Robertses' house.

"Well, I'd like to congratulate you on the outcome," Tucker said wryly when Harry was settled in the rocking chair and the kettle had begun to sing, "but I think you must have left your thinking cap somewhere when you decided to walk straight into that house."

"Yours is the majority opinion," Harry replied. "It even has my vote."

"Look on the bright side," Tucker said, bringing Harry a mug of tea and a plate of molasses cookies. "If you hadn't made that very dumb mistake, all those women might be dead."

"I've heard that nothing is an unmitigated evil," Harry said with a straight face as he looked at the tea and the cookies.

"Speaking of evil, it's likely that Freeman Todd stabbed Wetherell Clampett early this morning."

"Snyder told me," Harry said with his mouth full of cookie.

"He was planning to kill everyone who could testify against him. If Ruth Roberts hadn't stopped him, he might have made a clean sweep."

"It's too bad Hubbard hadn't been a little quicker this morning. He forgot for a moment where the rifle was and didn't get outside soon enough to pop Todd. He blames himself for that, but I suspect it's just as well. A man as big as Todd takes a lot of killing. And Hubbard's eyes aren't all that they were."

"Snyder said Wetherell's condition is pretty bad."

"A little while before you got here, Hubbard called to say they're giving Wetherell a better than even chance of pulling through."

They talked for a few minutes about the Roberts case, but Tucker seemed to have only a part of his mind on the subject. Finally he said in an obvious effort to sound unconcerned, "Bevel's hasn't hauled that tractor away."

"You're worried about that."

"Well, yes, I am. Why is that valuable piece of machinery sitting there unused?"

Harry's first impulse was to quote Wetherell Clampett at Tucker and tell him that the threat of indictment had disorganized the company and that the tractor's being there had no sinister meaning. But a second thought persuaded him to change his approach. Justified or not, Tucker felt the butterflies were threatened. And although Tucker would have denied it, Harry knew the old man considered those butterflies to be his personal responsibility.

"Do you think Fontaine Bevel has something nasty in mind?"

"Almost nothing he and that outfit did would surprise me." He poured himself more tea as if underlining the risks.

"Bevel did what he could to keep himself out of the DA's clutches. It would be a poor time for him to get across the law by bulldozing the Atalas' breeding ground."

"That's true, but he's not the only snake in that rock pile."

"I think you're letting your imagination get away from you."

"You could be right, but it doesn't feel that way."

Harry went home, iced his shoulder again, and then forced himself to go out on the lanai and stretch out on a lounge chair. It was a struggle because between the events at the Roberts house and Tucker's tea, he felt too wound up to rest. But within a couple of minutes he was sound asleep with the Hammock humming and buzzing around him. He woke up with a start. The sun was setting, and what passed in Southwest Florida for a cool breeze was rustling the leaves in the oaks and carrying onto the lanai the fragrant smell of evening.

Harry threw his legs off the lounge and gave a grunt of pain. His head was hurting again, and his shoulder exploded every time he moved his arm. Carefully, he levered himself onto his feet and went into the kitchen. The prospect of making his own supper was so unattractive, he had no trouble persuading himself that what he really wanted was a toasted ham and cheese sandwich. Leaving the cleanup for the morning, he made a slow progress up the stairs and put himself to bed with a couple of aspirins for a nightcap.

He woke expecting to see the sun. Instead, he saw the moon and lay for a moment wondering what had wakened him. Muffled but distinct, he heard the unmistakable crack of a rifle. For an instant, he forgot that Freeman Todd was dead and flung himself out of bed. The insult to his shoulder cleared away the dregs of sleep, and his memory kicked in while he was rubbing is shoulder and swearing.

There was a second shot, followed by several more banging away in rapid succession. Harry pulled on his clothes, grabbed his Luger from the bedside table, and got himself out to the Rover. He drove to Tucker's and found the place in darkness with Sanchez and Oh, Brother! standing guard in the driveway. Harry stopped long enough to speak to the two animals and put the Rover through a U-turn that made the sand fly.

If Tucker had been home, Sanchez would have been in the house and Oh, Brother! in the barn. That meant Tucker was on foot and probably in the butterfly woods. Harry sent the Rover flying down the Hammock road, hoping the old farmer was not playing vigilante again. Once on the county road, Harry switched off his lights and parked a hundred yards short of Bevel's parking area. The moon was past its zenith, and Harry trotted along the shadowed side of the road, making good time without being conspicuous.

There was a car in the parking lot, and even in the moonlight Harry could see that it was sitting at an odd angle. At the same time he saw that the tractor was gone. Keeping to the trees, Harry began circling the parking lot. Halfway around the area he came to a place where the brush and small pines had been crushed under the treads of the tractor and a hole punched through the forest wall at the edge of the parking lot. Harry swore silently and followed the path of the tractor, moving parallel to the track.

Within fifteen yards the track swerved to the left, and there was the yellow Caterpillar, resting with one tread on a stump and no sign of whoever had been driving. Harry waited motionless, straining to see or hear someone moving, but there was only the quiet pinging of the tractor's engine cooling and the flicker of light and shadow from the movement of the pines in the gentle wind.

Several minutes passed, and Harry was preparing to make a circle of the tractor when a voice behind him said in a whisper, "You're pretty good, Harry. I almost missed you, but you'd do better with a matte finish on that cannon you're carrying."

Harry blew out his breath in relief. "You put a lot of faith in me," he muttered.

"That's right, I do. Somebody's loose in the woods. Whether he's armed or not, I can't say. Let's move a bit just in case he is and saw you coming in."

When they had worked themselves into denser cover, Harry asked, "Were you responsible for that cannonade I heard?"

"I'm sorry I woke you up, but I had some trouble convincing the son of a bitch driving that tractor to do something else with the remainder of the night. I didn't want to shoot him."

"Are you sure you didn't?"

"Oh, yes. No wounded man could have run the way he did."

"Who is it?"

"I don't know, but he's on foot. I let the air out of a couple of his tires."

"What do you want to do?"

"I want to go to bed, but I'm afraid he'll come back and finish what he started."

Harry didn't have to ask what that was. "If you can cover me, I'll take care of that."

"I can try."

They moved slowly closer to the tractor.

"This should only take a minute," Harry said.

"Be as quick as you can."

Harry holstered his gun and crept up to the tractor. Working with his jackknife, he got in amongst the wires, and making very little noise quickly crippled the engine.

"You're sure it can't be started?" Tucker asked when Harry returned.

"Not without a lot of new wiring."

"Then let's go. The dampness is making every joint I've got ache. Oh, Brother! could be right. I may be too old for this night work."

33

Coming out of the woods onto the road, Tucker told Harry that he had tried to check the registration, but the car was locked.

"But unless it's a stolen car, he's caught, whoever it is," Tucker added with satisfaction. "It will have to be towed and there's the tag number."

"It looks like something Todd might have done, but he's dead. Who's left?"

"Bevel, Mark and Matthew Roberts, and Ralph Hawkins," Tucker replied.

"It's hard to believe any of them would be that stupid," Harry responded.

"We're going to find out," Tucker said.

Harry wasn't as confident. The car could have been a company car or, as Tucker had mentioned, stolen. But he let it go, and they drifted from that subject to the Roberts family. Harry found he wanted to talk about them.

"The family's shredded," he said with a mixture of regret and anger. "Adam and John are dead, both victims of their parents and their older brothers. Luke has broken away completely. Esther is likely to go back to Angel Wing and Heather, and who can blame her? Martha's mind has collapsed under the stress of trying to buck the family, and God knows what it's done to Ruth—not even counting her shooting Freeman Todd."

"It would be tempting to blame that narrow and primitive fundamentalism they're involved in," Tucker responded. "But if

I'm honest, I'd have to say I think that the root of their trouble lies with James and Matthew. Those two seem to have turned their faith into a justification for personal tyranny."

"How about Mark?" Harry asked. "It doesn't look as if he was driven into theft by anything his family did to him."

Tucker nodded. "It's tempting to blame it on bad seed, but I'm not too happy with that answer."

Harry agreed, and the conversation came to an end when they reached Tucker's driveway and Sanchez and Oh, Brother! hurried out to greet them.

"The moon's gone and there's first light over the marsh," Tucker said. "Come in and have breakfast. It's too late to go back to bed."

Once inside, Harry called the sheriff's department and reported on the car and the tractor without mentioning Tucker or the shooting. He gave the duty officer the tag numbers and said whoever had driven the tractor into the woods was probably breaking the law.

"You're turning into an accomplished liar," Tucker said when Harry hung up the phone.

"And you're turning into a desperado," Harry replied.

When Harry left Tucker, the sun was well up, the last of the mist was burning off Puc Puggy Creek, and flights of waders were making their way to their feeding grounds. Harry went home and spent a couple of hours working at his desk. Then he called Esther.

"How are you?" he asked.

"Better than I was yesterday," she said. "Last night when I came home from the hospital, Ma and I sat down and had a long talk."

"And?"

"I'm not sure, but I feel a lot better. Coming home like this has been tough, Harry. And even if none of the trouble involving Freeman Todd, Martha, and Bunny had been here waiting for me, it would still have been tough."

"I believe you. How is your mother?"

"She's coping with everything much better than I am. I thought for a while she was totally shut down, but I was wrong. She talked about all of it with me, and I feel wretched about the way that I've neglected her."

"From what I've heard, the separation wasn't all your fault."

"No, it wasn't, but I badly misjudged Ma. She told me she was too ashamed of having failed to protect me to try to stay in touch with me. Harry, she hated what my father and Matthew did to me. Then she was angry with herself for not putting up more of a fight when they turned against Adam and me and finally Bunny. I tried to tell her she couldn't have changed anything that happened, but she's not ready to believe it, and maybe she could have done something. But I've come to think that she's a brave and honest woman."

"There's no doubting her physical courage," Harry agreed, the picture of Ruth standing over Todd still vividly present in his mind. "What about Martha?"

"I called the hospital an hour ago. She'd had breakfast and was out of bed. I didn't ask to speak with her because I thought it might upset her."

When he'd finished talking with Esther, Harry called the hospital. The nurse who took his call told him he could visit Martha, if she wanted to see him. He gave her his name.

"It's okay," she said. "But don't try to make her remember anything about her assailant or the shooting. Don't ask her to make any decisions, and don't tire her."

Martha got up when Harry came into her room and took a few steps to meet him. When he put out his hands, she took them. Her grip was firm.

"You are looking good," Harry said.

Her hair was carefully brushed, and she was dressed in a rose dress that, despite her being very pale, was a becoming color. But she looked fragile to Harry and very vulnerable.

"Thank you," she said without smiling, drawing him toward the chairs. "Come and sit down. I've been feeling lonesome."

"That's good," Harry said. "You must be feeling better."

She managed a watery smile. "Aside from lonesome, I don't feel much of anything."

"That will pass. You'll be ordering me around and finding fault in no time."

"Harry," she said, a frown darkening her face, "I can't remember anything from the time Felicity left until I woke up in here. I don't know why I'm here, and they won't tell me."

Harry thought that over for a moment and made a decision.

"There's plenty of time for you to remember things. Don't worry about it." He leaned forward in his chair and caught her hands. "You're in here," he continued, looking straight into her dark eyes and speaking softly, "because you were in a lot of pain. You needed some help in dealing with it."

"I must have had an accident of some sort." She turned the right side of her face toward him. "My jaw aches, and I've got a terrible bruise."

"You certainly have, but cheer up. It might have been a black eye."

She didn't respond to his joking comment. "What happened to me, Harry? Did Matthew hit me?"

"No."

"I probably shouldn't be talking to you at all," she said, as if indifferent to his answer. "I've done a terrible thing in getting you involved in my troubles. Felicity made me see how wrong it was."

Harry stood up. "It's all right, Martha. It's all over, and you're going to be just fine."

"I don't want you to go, Harry," she said defiantly.

"I'm glad to hear that. I'll be back very soon."

She stood up, her eyes brimming. It was too much for Harry. He put his arms around her and said, "Remember, no worrying. Believe me; everything's going to be all right."

"Maybe," she replied, clinging to him, "but it doesn't feel that way."

For the next three days Harry worked on an insurance surveillance he had been neglecting and some research for a local law firm that handled a lot of insurance fraud cases. They were the routine tasks that kept him in business, but they did not make his heart beat faster. He also spent some time with Jennifer Fortunato discussing his testimony regarding the deaths of John Roberts and Jefferson Toomey.

"Mark Roberts came in," she told Harry when the formal part of their meeting was over.

"I'm glad to hear it," Harry said. "How did it go?"

"You know better than to ask," she protested, but relented enough to say, "He's cooperating. Now forget I said it."

"Forget what?" he asked.

Harry's next stop was the sheriff's office, having delayed responding to Snyder's phone call demanding his presence. Snyder was not happy about the tractor incident, and Dan Springer and Berker Szalay's report on the affair had only increased his concern.

"I'm not hearing the whole story here, am I?" Snyder demanded in his mountain twang that broke through whenever he was agitated. "For instance, who let the air out of those tires?"

"First, tell me whose car it was," Harry demanded.

"It was one of Bevel's company cars," Hodges said, "and it

had more prints on it than a barroom door."

"Frank," Snyder said, "don't go on." He turned back to Harry. "Now you know as much as we do about the car. Who was doing all the shooting out there?"

"What shooting?"

"The shooting that put the bullet holes in that tractor. I'm thinking whoever was driving that tractor may look like a sieve."

"I didn't see any blood on the tractor or hear any shooting while I was there."

"Why were you out there in the first place?"

Harry decided to stop playing games. Both Tucker and Jim Snyder deserved better. "I was wakened up by what I thought might have been shooting."

Snyder rocked back in his chair. "I'll spare you some pain by telling you instead of asking you who was doing the shooting. It was Tucker. He let the air out of the tires. Then he went into the woods and used whoever was driving that tractor for target practice."

Harry shook his head. "If Tucker had intended to kill somebody, that person would be dead." Curious to learn just how much Snyder knew, he tried probing a little. "What makes you think it was Tucker?"

"Who! Not what," Hodges said in a loud voice. "The who is Springer and Sally."

"Szalay, Frank, Szalay," Snyder said, his ears turning red. "It's not Sally!"

"Whatever," Hodges said. "Those two are dumb but not that dumb. They figured it out from the start. It was LaBeau who blew up the tractor and it's LaBeau who was doing the shooting."

"We know why he did it," Snyder said. "Is anybody dead?"

"No," Harry said. "Somebody might be winged. But I didn't see any blood. Did Springer and Szalay?"

"No. Who should we be looking for?"

"You've checked the emergency room records at ACH?"

"Yes. There was nothing helpful. Try again," Snyder said.

"It's a guess, but I'd start with Ralph Hawkins."

Snyder got to his feet. "We'll do what we can, but I don't have a lot of hope."

"What about Tucker?" Harry demanded.

Hodges opened his mouth and shut it again when he saw the look on the captain's face.

"At this point we're not filing charges."

"Good," Harry said with relief and left.

Two days later, Martha was released from the hospital.

Esther called Harry from her mother's house. "She's at her trailer. The doctor said she should not come back here. Can you get out there today sometime?"

"Yes. Is she going to be staying there alone?"

"As far as I know," Esther answered stiffly. "I'll tell her you're coming." She hesitated, started to speak, and stopped. "Never mind," she said and hung up.

More complications, Harry thought sourly. That afternoon, he drove to Pecan Grove, trying not to worry about what he was going to find.

"Come in, Harry," Martha said without enthusiasm.

Harry attributed her behavior to medication. He had expected to find someone dragging around in a robe, looking extremely ill, and was pleasantly surprised. Martha was dressed in beige slacks and a pale orange blouse. She looked rested and calm. Her black hair shone from a recent brushing, but something stiff, even stony, about her expression troubled him.

"I hope you feel half as good as you look," he said. "How do you like being home?"

"All right."

"When are you going back to work?" Harry asked into the silence.

"What day is this?"

"Thursday."

"Maybe next Monday, depending on what Dr. Pensall says."

"Are you ready for that?"

"God, Harry," she replied in a burst of irritation. "You sound like Pensall. I tell him something, and he asks me how I feel about it." She furrowed her brow, whether in thought or pain, Harry couldn't tell. Then she said, "I have something to tell you."

"I'm listening."

"You're not working for me anymore, and I don't want anything you've learned about Bunny's death to be revealed to anyone."

Harry leaned forward in his chair. "Isn't it early to be making that kind of decision?"

She shook her head vehemently. "No, it's not. It's very late. I should never have hired you." She winced as if she was in pain and pulled her eyes away from his.

"Martha," he asked, "what is it?"

"How did you know I was here?"

"Esther told me you were home," he said quietly.

"Esther," she said harshly, "is living in sin with another woman."

"She's living with Angel Wing and their daughter, Heather. I don't think there's much sin involved."

"No, you wouldn't. Neither would Dr. Pensall. But Matthew and Felicity have helped me to see the truth. I went against God when I hired you. God took Bunny home because Bunny couldn't care properly for himself. I was wrong to interfere. It was going against His will, but Matthew says God has already forgiven me. Now I must make sure I don't do any more harm."

Harry groaned inwardly. Pensall had a battle on his hands. He gave a moment to asking himself what to do next. As calmly as he could, he asked her if she remembered the last time he came to her parents' house.

"Esther fainted," she said angrily. "And it served her right. She had said terrible things to Matthew and Felicity."

"And that was the only time you saw me there?"

"It's the only time you were there."

"You're right," he said quickly. "My memory failed me for a minute."

He gave up on his plan to tell her what the district attorney was doing with John's case. Instead, he pushed himself out of his chair. He felt more heartsick than angry, and he would like to have wrung Matthew's neck. Although there were a lot of things he wanted to say to her, he knew saying them would only cause her pain. It would take more than his arguments to turn her head around.

He said goodbye and told her he would talk with her later, but she didn't answer him or indicate in any way that she had heard him or was aware that he was leaving. As he let himself out the door, she remained rooted to the couch, her hands clenched in her lap, staring blankly at the chair in which he had been sitting.

34

Harry found Tucker pulling his buggy out of the barn.

"You're just in time," the old farmer said with a broad grin. He passed Harry a putty knife and a sheet of sandpaper. "Wherever the paint is peeling, scrape it off. Where it's thin, sand it."

Under the critical supervision of Sanchez and Oh, Brother!, Harry went around to the other side of the wagon from Tucker and started working. As he sanded and scraped, he told Tucker about his conversation with Martha Roberts.

"The poor thing," Tucker said, stepping back to study his side of the buggy. "Being forced back into the house with Felicity, Esther, and her mother regressed her. If you add in the fact her father was dying, it's easy to see how it happened. Does she know he's dead?"

"I don't think so."

Harry hated sanding almost as much as painting a ceiling, but he found talking with Tucker made any task easier.

"That means she didn't go to his funeral."

"No. She was still in the hospital. I doubt that she was told anything about it. She doesn't remember Freeman Todd's being in the house. And looking ahead to the trial, unless her condition improves, Harley Dillard won't be able to question her."

"Even if he could, I doubt she'll give him any help," Tucker said. "By the way, it's all right to sand and talk at the same time."

Harry sanded some more.

"Am I showing ignorance or unjustified pessimism to say that even with her testimony the case against Hawkins and the Roberts brothers is shaky?"

"I think Dillard will nail Mark Roberts and Hawkins for embezzlement," Harry replied, "but hanging John Roberts's murder on Matthew and Hawkins is going to be difficult. All Dillard's got is the gun, the fact it came from the Evidence Section, and the testimony of Esther, Ruth, and me that Todd said Matthew and Hawkins hired him to kill John Roberts, Toomey, and me. The testimony of a dead felon who can't be interrogated."

"He may have a case."

"Not a strong one."

"No, but without you, Esther, and Ruth there's none at all. That suggest anything to you?"

"I don't think I'm in much danger. They all know indictments are going to be handed down. That puts them under some degree of police scrutiny. And I don't see any danger to the butterfly woods now that you've run off Hawkins—if that's who it was you were shooting at."

Tucker lifted his hat and ran his hand over his head. "If I were Matthew, I'd gamble that Ruth could be persuaded not to testify against him, but that leaves you and Esther."

"I'm not worried," Harry said. "With Todd dead, I think their teeth are drawn."

"I hope you're right. By the way, I've had visitors," he said.

"Let me guess, Dan Springer and Berker Szalay." Harry leaned his elbows on the side of the buggy and tried not to laugh.

"Well, yes." Tucker made a show of knocking some of the paint dust off his sandpaper.

"I'm still listening."

"They more or less let it be known that they know who dynamited the tractor and then used it and whoever was driving it for target practice." Tucker blew out his breath. "I don't see how they can know."

"Tucker, the whole county knows. I expect it's the talk of Tallahassee."

"Well, make a joke of it if you want to, but I have to admit that I'm a little annoyed."

Harry couldn't let it go. "You're going to be more annoyed when they send you to jail."

Tucker finally laughed. "Why did they come out here to tell me that?" he demanded.

"Pride. They want you to know they know. The two tall trees are feeling a little discomforted that they can't arrest you."

"Because they haven't any evidence?"

"No, because Jim Snyder won't let them. I think your night rider activities have turned you into a local hero. But, for God's sake, stop where you are."

Tucker grinned. "I plan to."

Harry walked home through the late afternoon, finally beginning to believe the case was winding down. Freeman Todd was dead, and Harley Dillard would probably issue indictments against Mark Roberts for embezzlement, Ralph Hawkins for embezzlement and possibly for murder, and Matthew possibly for murder also—if the grand jury gave Dillard the go-ahead to issue murder charges.

Harry was surprised he didn't feel worse than he did about not laying John Roberts's murderers by their heels. Perhaps it had something to do with John's having been dead so long and something more, possibly, with what had happened to Ruth, Martha, Esther, and Adam. Hadn't there already been enough anguish?

When he reached the house, he found the phone message light blinking. A woman, speaking very softly, gave him a number and asked him to call. He didn't recognize the voice, but as he dialed, he felt he should have known who the caller was.

"Perkins House, Althea Watson speaking." The voice was polite but cool.

Harry experienced an unpleasant jolt of recollection. "Hello, Mrs. Watson. This is Harry Brock speaking."

"Hello, Mr. Brock. What can I do for you?"

The response was still polite but colder. Well, Harry thought, trying to make some space for her, I suppose she's only trying to protect Theresa. "I'm returning Theresa Allgood's call."

"Why did Theresa call you?" Watson demanded, her anger sharpening her voice.

"I don't know. May I speak to her?"

There was a long pause. Then Watson said, "Please wait."

Theresa answered. "Hello, Mr. Brock," she said quietly. "Thank you for returning my call."

"It's been a while. How are you?"

"I'm all right. Have you learned anything about . . ." She paused and Harry could hear her struggling with her breath. Crying? God, he thought with a twist of shame, I'd forgotten all about her. "Bunny?"

For an instant, Harry considered lying to her. She obviously didn't know that his suicide had been officially redefined as murder. But just as quickly, he quashed the impulse. She deserved to be told the truth.

"You were right, Theresa, Bunny didn't commit suicide. He was killed by a man named Freeman Todd."

"Why did he want to hurt Bunny?" Her voice was stronger, and Harry decided anger accounted for it. Good. She had a right to be angry.

"I think someone paid him to do it." He made another decision. "He won't hurt anyone else, Theresa. He's dead."

"Harvey Bosco wouldn't want me to say I'm glad. So I won't. But I am."

"So am I, Theresa."

"Will whoever paid Mr. Todd to kill Bunny go to jail?"

"I hope so. The district attorney is doing his best to make that happen."

"There's more than one person?"

"The police think so."

"Why would these people want to hurt Bunny?"

"I think they had done something wrong and Bunny found out about it. They didn't want him to tell what it was."

"Mrs. Watson wants me to stop talking. We're not supposed to use this phone for very long. Others might want to use it. Thank you for telling me the truth. Goodbye, Mr. Brock."

Harry put down the phone, glad he had been able to say that Bunny had not abandoned her. He would have felt a lot better if he had remembered to call her with the news.

Talking with Theresa Allgood and being reminded that forgetting was a feeble excuse for not doing what should be done led Harry to the somewhat unwelcome recollection that he had not talked to Helen for a while. But even before he could reach for the phone, the impulse died.

Calling her would probably lead to seeing her, and then either they would quarrel over Riga or not talk about her at all and spend the night together. But for Harry there would be three people in the bed, which was one too many. The events of the past week had shaken him in ways he did not yet fully understand. But they had left him more aware of his feelings, and he found that sharing Helen with another sexual partner was no longer acceptable.

With almost no appetite, he turned to the task of making his supper. After he had eaten, he took a walk, worked at his desk, and climbed the stairs to his bedroom with a barred owl's soft hooting for company.

He came awake to a silent house and a quiet wind whispering through the screens. But he had no interest in the wind or the moon in the trees. He was certain someone was in the house. Very slowly he slid his hand out from under the covers and carefully lifted the Luger from the bedside stand without raising his head. He pulled the gun under the covers and a moment later saw the dim rectangle of the partially open bedroom door fill with a darker shadow. Then the door swung in with a faint creak.

Harry stirred slightly, just enough to get the remaining weight off his right arm, and gave a short, quiet sigh, and hoped it sounded as if he was sinking back into sleep. He heard a slithering sound beside the door, and the overhead light came on.

"Sleeping Beauty," a heavy voice said.

Harry rolled up onto his left elbow, pretending confusion. At the foot of the bed stood Matthew Roberts and Ralph Hawkins. Hawkins was pointing a gun at him, and Matthew was gripping in a big hand what looked to Harry like a piece of iron pipe.

"End of the road, Brock," Hawkins said with a stiff grin.

"Shut up," Roberts said. "Kill him."

Firing from under the blanket, Harry shot Hawkins in the chest. Swearing, Roberts raised the pipe over his head and threw himself at the bed. Harry fired at Roberts, missed, and rolled away from the blow. The pipe grazed his back and thudded into the bed as he crashed to the floor.

"Shit!" Roberts shouted and scrambled across the bed in pursuit.

Harry rolled onto his back and raised his gun.

"Hold it!" Harry shouted as Roberts's head and shoulders

loomed over him.

"Fuck you," Roberts snarled and raised the pipe. Harry shot him. The big man pitched forward and hung waist down from the bed, blood streaming from his head.

35

"They're both alive," Snyder said, coming into the kitchen.

Behind him men were shepherding a pair of gurneys toward the front door. Harry looked up from the report he had begun writing.

"For how long?" he asked. The adrenaline that had been pumping through him was nearly dissipated, leaving him feeling wrung out.

"The medics say they're stabilized," Hodges responded, coming into the kitchen as the second gurney went out the lanai door.

"Good," Harry said and meant it.

Snyder sat down opposite Harry and propped his elbows on the table. "I owe you an apology," he said.

"The whole department owes you one," Hodges added. "We sure as hell didn't see this coming."

"I guess we weren't looking hard enough," Harry said, remembering Tucker's asking if Hawkins and the Roberts brothers posed any threat to anyone. "Tucker tried to warn me, but I wasn't listening, so why should I blame you?"

"I'm pissed that Mark Roberts didn't tell Dillard what Matthew and Hawkins were up to," Hodges said.

He had been roaming around the kitchen looking for something to eat.

"There are blueberry muffins in the green cake tin," Harry said.

Hodges broke into a smile as he reached for the tin. "I've been running on empty," he said with relief.

Snyder stood up, frowning. "I don't think Mark Roberts knew his brother and Hawkins had anything to do with John Roberts's disappearance, the death of Jefferson Toomey, or the attack on Harry."

"Maybe not," Hodges mumbled, his mouth full of muffin. He paused a moment to swallow, then pointed at Harry. "But sure as hell, if you hadn't stopped them, you'd be dead and Esther Roberts and her mother would have been next."

"Probably," Harry said and passed the report to Snyder.

"Thanks," Snyder said. "We should be done with the bedroom by noon, not that you're likely to be in any hurry to go back in there." He waved the sheets of paper Harry had given him. "I'll have this run into the computer. You can sign it later. Come on, Hodges. Let's let the man get some rest."

They left, but Harry did not get any rest. He could not use his bedroom. It was a blood-soaked mess. And trying the bed in the spare room, he found his back was too sore to let him rest, and his mind kept rerunning the shootings. As the first light was breaking, he left the house and took a long walk into the Hammock. It quieted his mind and eased his back, but he couldn't walk forever.

He came home to find Esther Roberts sitting on his lanai.

When he reached the door, he said, "Esther, I've got some bad news for you."

"The police called," she said. "Are you all right?"

"Yes. Does your mother know?"

"She knows. Mark and Rebecca are with her. Things are pretty bad. Felicity showed up with the children last night and tried to take Ruth out of the house, but Mark put an end to that. It was ugly."

"What about Martha?"

"That's really why I came. Someone in the sheriff's department got their signals crossed and called her and told her Matthew had been shot and was in the hospital in critical condition. She started screaming, and whoever was on the phone with her had the wits to send an EMS vehicle out there. She's back in the hospital."

"Now what?" he asked.

"Just as soon as Dillard is finished with Ma and me, I'm taking her back to Arizona. She wants to go, and I want to take her. If we have to, we'll come back for the trial. I'll stay in touch with Martha's doctor, and when she's well enough to leave the hospital, I'll come back and get her. I've already talked with him and told him Felicity must be kept away from her. He agrees, and Ma and I will have a restraining order served on Felicity before I leave."

"Then your coming has probably saved two people," he said.

"And you made it possible," she said. "For that, I thank you for all of us."

"From here it looks as if I destroyed a family."

She shook her head. "Somebody else did that."

She drove away, leaving Harry feeling a little less like Rasputin.

As he went into the house, the phone rang.

The woman's voice was both apologetic and strident. "Mr. Brock. I'm terribly sorry. There's been the most awful muddle."

Then she stopped speaking.

"Who are you?" Harry asked into the breathy silence.

"I'm Nona Ashcroft, director of patient services at the Avola Community Hospital. You should have been called hours ago."

Harry assumed it was about Martha Roberts and was about to ask what was wrong, but the explaining voice suddenly gathered speed and volume. "Dr. Spengler left instructions that you were to be called and asked to come to the emergency wing as soon as you could. I don't know how . . ."

"Who's been hurt?"

"What? Oh. Let me see. It's a Ms. Helen Bradley. She was admitted at about three this morning in a very unstable condition."

Harry felt as if he had been punched in the stomach. "Is she still alive?"

"Oh, yes, I think so."

"What happened to her?"

"I think she attempted to take her own life. I believe it was a very close thing."

Harry slammed down the phone and raced out of the house. Guilt and regret were pouring through him like ice water.

He reached the hospital to find that Helen had been moved out of emergency to a private room. The duty nurse said she was still unconscious but no longer in danger and that someone was with her. Checking his name against a list, she said he could go in.

He found Riga Kraftmeier sitting beside the bed. Helen lay with her eyes closed and a drip attached to her right arm. Although she was very pale, she looked to Harry as if she was free of pain and, for the moment at least, perfectly at peace. Her thick, honey-colored hair lay spread on the pillow. With a swelling heart he offered up a prayer of thanks that she was alive.

He picked up a chair and put it down beside Riga, startling her. She jumped up and, to his surprise, grasped his hand and led him a few steps away from the bed. It had been nearly two years since he last saw Riga, and despite the strain she was obviously under, Harry thought that she was even more beautiful than he remembered. Her pale face, vivid blue eyes, and light golden hair seemed to endow her with an unearthly perfection.

To Harry's astonishment, she dropped his hand and threw her arms around his neck, her eyes brimming with tears.

"God, Harry," she said in a hoarse whisper, "what have we done to her?"

Recovering from his surprise, he put his arms around her. She was trembling, and she clung to him as if he was the last stick floating. He held her, his scrambled emotions preventing him from answering her question.

"I think it's my fault, Riga," he said finally.

Before Riga could respond, a hoarse, shaky, but familiar voice said, "If this is heaven, I've been misled."

Harry and Riga sprang apart like guilty lovers.

"Don't stop on my account," Helen continued, managing to imbue her croak with sarcasm. "Did either of you want to ask how I'm feeling?"

"We already know," Harry said as they sat down by the bed.

Now that she was talking, Harry found his relief was salted with anger at what she had tried to do. Riga laughed. Harry looked at her in surprise and saw that she was beaming at Helen through her tears.

Helen reached out her left hand toward Riga, who took it in both of hers. "Christ, Riga, don't cry," Helen said. "You'll make me start and I'm too weak to cry."

Riga said, "Welcome back, my love."

As he watched them holding hands, Harry braced himself for the wave of jealousy he expected to crash over him, but it didn't happen. Instead, he felt only a gentle upwelling of love for Helen and happiness that she was alive and that the person she belonged with wanted her.

When Helen slipped back into sleep, he rose and so did Riga. He put out his hand but she embraced him.

"Take care of her, Riga," he said quietly. "She's not half as tough as she pretends."

"I know." She leaned back in his arms. "This makes three times you've saved my life, Harry. Thank you. If you ever . . ."

"Need a reference," he said, "I'll call." Then he did something he had thought he would never do—he kissed her. And, to his astonishment, she kissed him back, and it felt right. An old wound began to heal.

"Good luck, Riga," he said when they separated.

"Take care of yourself, Harry," she replied.

As he drove home, the good feeling of closure stayed with him, but increasingly it was shaded with a sense of something left undone and an eagerness to make amends. The closer he came to the Hammock, the stronger the impulse grew. He shot under the oak tree and yanked the Rover to a stop. By the time he was halfway across the lawn, he was running. Once in the house, he picked up the phone and dialed. A young girl's voice answered.

"Hello, Minna," he said.

"Harry!" she cried with delight. "Harry! Wait! Wait! Katherine is right here. Momma, it's Harry!"

ABOUT THE AUTHOR

Kinley Roby lives with his wife Mary Linn Roby in Southwest Florida.